Beyond Borders

©2006 by Don Glander

Published by American Imaging
Cover Design: Jim Grich
Format and Packaging: Peggy Grich

Printed in the United States of America

First Edition 2006

ISBN 978-1-4243-1020-3

Beyond Borders

Murder and High Crime on the Waterway

DON GLANDER

For Nydia

*Hope and fear are inseparable: You cannot have fear
without hope, and you cannot have hope without fear.*
                          Francois, Duc De La Rochefoucauld

If it were not for hope, the heart would break.
                                              Proverb

Acknowlegements

At the very beginning there were confident visions of sitting before my PC in the evening, a glass of wine within easy reach and as the nights rolled by, I'd in short order knock out a work of substantial literary merit. This would happen in, oh, a five to six month time frame, if not sooner. Hey, I was an English major for Pete's sake! I even understand Faulkner! Well, sorta'.

Within a night or two, with only a few rough paragraphs written, the rude realities set in. By the end, I hesitate to admit, it took two or so years for the book to finally come together. Granted, there were weeks and even months when little to nothing was written, but as any writer will tell you, the work is never far from the mind.

The other fallacy I encountered along the way is that writing is considered, basically, a lonely art form. Yes, when it comes to divining the right words and committing them to the blank sheet, or more accurately in my case, the blank screen, it is lonely, but also very exhilarating. However, well before the last sentence has been written, more often than not, the writer had to emerge from his or her cocoon to ask some questions, to display some ignorance, to bounce an idea off someone, to read a chapter or paragraph to a relative or friend, and in general, to get advice from those he or she trusts. At the start I thought I could do it all myself. In the end, this book would never have seen completion were it not for the encouragement and assistance of several magnificent and caring individuals.

To new-found friends who share the love of writing, I'll be forever grateful. I only wish I had met each of you incredibly talented people many years ago. The support and keen wit of Pat Gambarelli and Mark Smith, the cheer leading and superb edit of Deloris Gausch and Ralph and the tough but honest advice and edit by Jack DeGroot played a major role in this work. To each member of Writer's Bloc, a sincere thanks. Jim Lowell's early reading and that of Linda "The Voice of Literacy" Patton are greatly appreciated. Chief Wally Layne's advice, which kept me within the straight and narrow, was a critical contribution. Thanks to Tom and Myrna McSwain for their observations on several technical matters. And then there was Jesse Hayes, who left us much too soon. Standing on a shrimp boat's deck, docked along side Captain Pete's, he patiently explained the workings of the old vessel. Thanks, Jesse; you're missed by many on both sides of the bridge. Rob and Lindy Collinson, many thanks for your early read, your constant encouragement and for Rob's terrific cover shot of the Intracoastal Waterway. And thanks John Lytvinenko for your wonderful back cover shot of the perfect martini. Bill and Sue Schwartz, your positive comments, suggestions and edit gave my confidence a needed boost, thanks dear friends. And to my daughter Nina Wheeling, who has a strong aversion to four letter expletives, thanks for letting your Dad slide with those he thought necessary. Lastly, to my room mate of close to fifty years, Nydia, who frequently referred to the writing of this book as something akin to a two year pregnancy, my unbounded love and appreciation. Your understanding, patience, support and assistance were paramount in the writing of *Beyond Borders*. As with all significant things in my life, it never would have happened without you.

Beyond Borders

Prologue

Miguel Delgado pushed back from his elegant inlaid-teakwood desk and walked over to his well stocked liquor cabinet. He lifted a bottle of *Recuerdo Tequila* from a sparkling glass shelf and poured a portion of its amber contents into a crystal brandy snifter. Taking a small sip, he gave a quiet sigh of satisfaction. A cynical smirk crossed his face. *Recuerdo* cost two hundred and eighty dollars a fifth. The piss ant peasants he arranged to be smuggled into this country certainly could not afford *Recuerdo*. *What the hell,* he thought; *chances were good that none of those little cockroaches had ever even heard of the stuff.*

With the smirk still etched on his face, he walked across his office. Looking out the large picture window, his gaze took in the pool and its adjacent white cabana, the expanse of the lush garden and back lawn, his clay tennis court and then, a little beyond, the Poseidon Golf and Yacht Club marina. Just past the marina lay the deep blue of the Atlantic. His gaze returned to the marina where his yacht, *TO LIFE*, rested in her slip. Even in a marina full of luxury yachts, *TO LIFE* stood out.

Not bad, not bad at all, in fact it's incredible, he confessed to himself. And it was. For a guy who didn't know the identity of his father and who'd been raised in the slums of L.A. by his immigrant Mexican mother, his *illegal* immigrant mother, he'd done, by most yardsticks of success, extraordinarily well. It had been one hell of a ride, but the ride had taken him exactly where he'd fought his entire life to be: rich, powerful, and accepted. Delgado had won the trifecta he had fantasized about since those horrible times in the slums.

He took another sip of *Recuerdo* then massaged his right shoulder, where, underneath his shirt, the letter *M* had been painfully tattooed those many years ago. His left shoulder sported a tattooed number *13*. The recollection of having the tattoos crudely needled into his body by a fellow inmate while he was incarcerated for attempted murder still made him grimace. He had only been a teenager at the time; yet, to this day he was fiercely proud of both tattoos and what they represented.

For the most part the only ones who'd ever paid attention to the tattoos were the several women, mostly of the professional variety, he had bedded over the years. When asked what the tattoos stood for he'd laugh and say that he'd made a mistake when he was thirteen, gotten drunk, and had the tattoos done. Then he'd say, with another laugh, that the *M* stood, naturally enough, for *Mother*.

This little story, not surprisingly, was willingly accepted by his paid female companions but was, of course, a big lie. In truth, the 13 stood for the 13th letter of the alphabet, *M*, which in turn stood for Mexico and further, and more significantly to Delgado, the Mexican Mafia, of which he was now a Chief. Most often those within the organization simply referred to it as *la Eme*.

Just how unaware the *gringos* in the United States were of *la Eme*, the Mexican Mafia, was something that truly amazed Delgado. Not only was *la Eme* operating in every state, but it was now seriously challenging the Italian Mafia in all aspects of illicit activities from drug running, extortion, murder, prostitution and smuggling to money laundering and white slavery. How they'd been able to remain beneath the radar of the American public, the *gringos*, for so long was a mystery to Delgado.

Having been sentenced to prison as a teenager for attempted murder turned out to be a stroke of luck for Delgado, for it automatically qualified him for *la Eme* membership. He'd joined without hesitation and shortly thereafter, by successfully carrying out the assassination of an imprisoned rival gang member of *la Eme's*, caught the attention of the honchos on the other side of the prison walls. His star rose rapidly in the organization, even as he served time.

And his luck continued. Crowded conditions, along with, ironically enough, good behavior, led to Delgado's release after serving only three of his ten-year sentence. Once out, it was time for this son of an illegal immigrant to show *la Eme* bosses just how good he really was. It was time to get going and make his mark.

And make it he did. Initially assigned "gopher" tasks by the organization, within a brief period of time the jobs increased in importance. Sucessfully carrying out every assignment thrown his way, from the most menial or risky to the more brutal and dangerous, he proved exceptionally capable and advanced rapidly through the ranks.

After four years, his loyalty, talent and tenacity paid off when he was promoted to the number one position in the southeast; he was in total command of *la Eme's* operations for North and South Carolina and Georgia. This move elevated Delgado into the top ranks of the organization and, significantly, meant that he would now be making serious money. Rather than simply a paid employee, with an occasional bonus tossed his way, he now received a percentage of the take from the many illicit and legitimate activities throughout his area of responsibility. He had arrived.

Looking back out to the Atlantic, he recalled how he'd initially agonized over where to locate. Having no familiarity with the southeast, he at first was tempted to select Atlanta, as had his predecessor, as it was the largest city in the territory. But wisely, he thought, he chose to locate in an exclusive development along the Atlantic coast in the Cape Fear area of North Carolina. It gave him the luxury and privacy he desired, and with today's communications technology, he could keep a close eye on every aspect of the operation, even from this remote area.

A small formation of pelicans flew over the marina. He'd once counted thirty-three of those prehistoric-looking creatures flying in a single line. *Amazing*, he'd thought at the time. Raising his glass to the pelicans and smiling, he congratulated himself on his initial excellent decision. Yes, he'd definitely found his place here, yes, he was doing just fine, and yes, he was unquestionably on his way to becoming wealthier than he'd ever imagined possible.

Not to say there wasn't the occasional glitch. A glitch like the one he was confronting today; a glitch that pissed him off and was the reason for the *Recuerdo* in early afternoon. Delgado snapped out of his revelry and looked over at the papers on his desk. He sighed, walked back to the liquor cabinet, refilled the snifter and returned to his desk.

Picking up the piece of paper that was the source of his irritation, and reading it for the third time, he already knew what must be done. The paper was a printout of an e-mail received earlier from Cárdenas. The organization relied heavily on e-mail and employed an anonymous server who received and sent messages, thereby concealing original addresses and making it difficult, if not impossible, to perform a trace.

This particular e-mail had been sent by Señor Don Orencio Nuñez of Cárdenas, Mexico. Delgado had never met Don Orencio Nuñez, had never even spoken with him on the phone, but the two men, over the past four years, had successfully coordinated the smuggling of hundreds of illegals from Mexico into the southeastern United States. The message from Don Orencio was quite simple, as were all messages sent by the organization. It read: *We have not received payment for the last shipment from Cárdenas.* It was signed, *D.O.*

Damn it, Delgado muttered aloud. He shouldn't have let it go this far. He should have sent the money to Nuñez and *then* pressured Collinson's *gringo* ass to collect it.

The *shipment* Don Orencio referenced was the four piss ants from Cárdenas who hadn't yet paid the back end of the smuggling fee they owed since arriving in North Carolina. Delgado not only had his honor and reputation to maintain within *la Eme*, and that was critical, but there was also the matter of the twenty percent cut he received for collecting the illegal's payments at this end.

The previous month they'd smuggled dozens of illegals into Delgado's territory, and although one couple, Carlos and María

4

Martinez, had paid a token amount, it was too small for Delgado to mess with. Another couple, Pablo and Gina Rodriguez, had paid nothing. *Nothing!* He'd told his man, Dean Collinson, an officer he'd planted on the local police force, to collect the damn payments. Collinson came back with the half-assed excuse that both men were painters, and that with all the rain recently, the two men weren't getting any work.

Delgado, becoming more irritated, finished his drink. *I don't give a rat's ass about the rain. If they can't paint, there's a shit load of other work out there the gringos won't touch. I'll wire the money to Don Orencio now, what the hell, it's chump change anyway, and get it back from the cockroaches one way or another.*

Well, perhaps not all of it. It had been almost three years since he'd last found it necessary to provide an example to the illegals, but apparently, with so many new arrivals, it was time for another reminder. The list of piss ants who were behind in their trailer rent was growing, as was the list of those cockroaches with over extended credit at the stores owned by the organization. Now there was this new problem with the four from Cárdenas. No question about it, it was time for a lesson.

He picked up his gold plated Mont Blanc pen and listed two names on a piece of blank paper.

Carlos Martinez

Pablo Rodriguez

He then looked around his desk for the list of names of those who were behind in their rent, found it, and added another name to his list:

José Díaz

The last time this was needed he'd brought someone in, but this time around, in addition to the illegals needing a lesson, Collinson could use one as well.

Three years earlier Delgado had learned the local police chief was looking to hire an additional officer. He contacted Collinson in L.A., where Collinson, still employed by the L.A.P.D., had once worked on the inside for him. The local police chief interviewed Collinson and was so impressed he hired him within twenty-four hours of the interview. As in L.A., it was an excellent arrangement having a cop on board, but of late, Collinson was getting lazy and even arrogant. Yes, this was definitely the opportunity to straighten Collinson out, and have him earn his pay for a change.

Delgado lifted his drink and staring into it, swirled the remaining tequila around the glass. He took a sip, set the glass back down, and looked at the short list he'd prepared. He again picked up his pen, hesitated for a moment, and circled a name.

Chapter 1

María and Carlos Martinez sat slumped in the bed of the filthy black '67 Ford pick-up as it rambled through the scorching hot afternoon desert. There was another couple traveling with them, their close friends, Pablo and Gina Rodriguez. Both couples were braced against the back of the cab where there was occasional shade. But the shade was infrequent, of little consequence, and all four sweated profusely.

Each had paid a great deal of money, fifteen hundred American dollars, to Señor Don Orencio Nuñez, who had made the arrangements. The money had been saved, begged and borrowed from friends and family with promises, on their lives and to the Virgin Mary, to repay. Each of the four was to pay Señor Nuñez an additional thousand dollars from their earnings in *Los Estados Unidos*. Although they could have attempted this on their own, they had heard the many horror stories regarding those who had tried and failed. They'd been convinced that by arranging it with Señor Nuñez, it would guarantee their safe arrival to the other side of the border.

None of the four knew where they were, how far they had traveled, or precisely where they were going, but each was aware of being far from the harsh lives they had led in Cárdenas, Mexico, where their flight had begun. They had traveled, now in a second truck, for several days and nights, with stops only for gas and to relieve themselves.

The coyotes, the middlemen responsible for getting them to the border, and then across, took great delight in refusing to stop when one of the passengers banged on the side panel indicating a need to relieve themselves. They heard the coyotes laughing in the cab of the truck; it apparently was great sport for them. The four from Cárdenas realized too late that at this point they were simply cargo to the coyotes, human cargo that must be delivered, but with no concern for the cargo's condition upon arrival. They also realized there was nothing they could do about it.

Eventually reaching the border, they were kept hidden until the night they were told it was time to cross the river into *Los Estados Unidos.*

The crossing had been dangerous. The river was rapid and at one point Carlos slipped, lost his grip on María and she was swept downstream. Even in her panic she knew not to scream for fear of revealing their location, and in a flash she saw her dreams of a new life vanish. Pablo, their closest friend from Cárdenas, grabbed her by her hair at the last moment, then by her arm, and pulled her the rest of the way across.

After the border crossing and entry into the United States, the four were immediately whisked into a pick-up truck and driven to a drop house; a dilapidated, aged, brick apartment building located near the border.

There were many illegals temporarily housed in the building. Most of the single bed, single bath "apartments" had ten to twenty people packed into them. Many of the illegals, like them, stank, as the showers were broken and without exception, all occupants were in the same clothes they wore when they left Mexico. The toilets in most of the "apartments" did not work. Some illegals were waiting for transportation to their final destination, while others were being held until relatives, or friends, paid the balance of the up-front portion of the smuggling fee. If, after two weeks, the balance of the fee had not been forthcoming, the illegals were taken back into Mexico with no reimbursement of what had already been paid, and with no regard to their place of origin. Some were dropped off in the desert without food or water. Many died.

Although most of the temporary residents of this building

were young married couples, there were also a number of men by themselves who hoped to find work, send money back home and eventually have their wives and families join them in the states.

Days passed as the four from Cárdenas were forced to remain inside the stinking building being fed only red beans, rice and water. Twice Carlos came close to a fight as one of the single men continuously made passes and obscene gestures at María, who was by far the most attractive woman in the drop house.

The fifth day found them, mercifully, leaving their squalid conditions and back on the road, this time sequestered in a van. At this point, none of the four could have told you how long it had been since they'd left Cárdenas. They were weary. Time had become meaningless. It ceased to matter. They were going to *Carolina del Norte en Los Estados Unidos*, a place where they would find work, have food every day and a decent place to live. And most importantly, it was the place where Carlos and María's baby would be born.

None of the four had ever seen a map of Mexico, let alone of the United States. If they had been told they were going to a place called Minnesota, they would not have known the difference. María didn't care. She was filthy, tired and . . .excited. She and Carlos were to join her cousin Rosa when they arrived in *Carolina del Norte*. She looked over at Carlos and whispered in his ear for what must have been the hundredth time; *"Nuestro bebé nacerá en Los Estados Unidos. Nuestro bebé será ciudadano Americano.* Our baby will be born in the United States. Our baby, yours and mine, will be an American citizen."

Carlos again felt her tears of joy upon his neck. He shared in her happiness, in her hopes, in her excitement, but he was frightened. It was a fear Carlos felt to his very bones, and he dare not speak of this fear to María.

As the van sped through the dark southeastern night, Carlos sensed that, at the end of their journey, in this place they call *Carolina del Norte*, there would be trouble, much, much trouble.

Chapter 2

It snuck up on me out of nowhere. What for many years had given me so much pleasure, and at times had even been exciting, was now becoming more like work, something to which I'd grown keenly adverse.

Pulling the traps from the water, shaking the crabs out into the cooler, then steaming and cleaning the ill tempered little beasts, not to mention the actual picking of the meat, well . . .it had lost a good deal of its enjoyment. From water to table, there just can't be a more labor-intensive delicacy consumed by man.

Yup, granted, it's an age thing, but I really didn't care to dwell on that at the moment. At the moment what I wanted was to get the traps out to the waterway, drop them in my usual spots, and get back in. The downsides of the aging process could be reflected upon later, best accompanied by a glass or two of wine and a cigar.

My name's Matt. Lindy and I live along the southeastern North Carolina coast, not far from the South Carolina border. We'd built the beach house as a weekend retreat some twenty years ago when we were both stressed out, gainfully-employed contributors to the industrialized world's economy. Our excuse at the time was our need for a secret little corner of the world where we could run and hide on weekends, away from the pressures of our respective jobs; Lindy's in the International Division of a major bank in Raleigh, and mine as a sales VP for a national hardware chain. The irony of my position being that if my, or anyone else's life depended on it, I couldn't build or repair a thing. We both retired at age 62 and knew there was only one place we wanted to head for—the beach house.

Water access attracted us to this location. It was an easy five-minute walk to the surf and offered a perfect set-up for crabbing and fishing. The front of our cozy little bungalow was on the Intracoastal Waterway and the back, on a deep canal. A couple of hundred yards down the canal was the inlet to the Intracoastal Waterway. I could load three or four traps on *Ol'Crab*, my antique Boston Whaler, scoot out to the waterway, drop the traps in front of our house and be back at my dock in fifteen minutes or less. Within twenty-four hours I'd normally catch 30 to 40 crabs. It couldn't get much better than that, not if you were a crab lover.

I'd just finished baiting the traps with a combination of fish heads and chicken backs, and was loading the last trap onto *Ol'Crab* when I heard my neighbor, Tommy Lee, call over from his deck.

"Matt, y'all goin' crabbin' again?" Tommy Lee had, amazingly, made again a three-syllable word; "a-gay-in." T. L. was deep, deep South, and I also was originally deep South . . . as in Jersey. But we'd hit it off from the git-go several years back when he and Lizzie bought the place next door. He was my choice Redneck and I was his absolute favorite, numero uno, Damn Yankee.

"One more time TL," I hollered back, placing the last trap on board. "Ya know, I figure I've caught, cooked, cleaned, picked and prepared more crabs this summer than all the restaurants in Calabash and Myrtle Beach combined. This is it 'til next spring."

"Bullshit," he replied, "y'all love 'em too much."

He was right about that. In spite of all the work involved, we did "love 'em," and that's why I kept going back to the Intracoastal. There wasn't a way you could prepare blue-clawed crabs that Lindy and I hadn't tried over the years: crab cakes, she-crab soup, crab salad, crab newberg, crab bisque, crab chowder, deviled crabs, crab imperial, crab fritters, crab puffs, crab dip, you name it —we'd made it. But for all the fancy recipes, our favorite remained to simply steam 'em, clean 'em up, pile them on some old newspapers on the table on the back deck, make certain there was a sufficient quantity of chilled beer on hand, then invite some friends over and pick crab, drink beer and gab away until the wee small hours. As we constantly reminded each other–"Nothin' could be finer . . ."

I gave Tommy Lee a wave and shoved off.

It was an incredibly gorgeous Carolina morning with a bright sun, a slight ocean breeze and an endless, blue sky. We'd had a lot of rain over the last month, and it was forecast again for the afternoon. I wanted to take full advantage of this pleasant break and was in no hurry to leave the water. In fact, it was the kind of day a man could be tempted into enjoying a cigar as he cruised about in his personal watercraft. I had however, promised myself, and more importantly, Lindy, only one per day; it was still morning, and I knew I'd crave one even worse come the cocktail hour. There was also the consideration that if Lindy should detect I'd already indulged, the balance of the day would be something less than Carolina beautiful.

I slowly motored towards the inlet, sans cigar, checking the other boats tied to their docks and looking to spot any waterfowl that might be hanging around.

For the past several days, I'd noticed an adult blue heron habitually stationing itself on the sea wall of the corner lot, just where the turn is made into the Intracoastal. The first couple of times I'd passed by, it had flown off. But for the last two days it remained fixed in place; apparently we were bonding.

The blue heron is a stunningly attractive creature that's been blessed with a majesty and grace to compliment its regal beauty. As if to balance things however, the creator, in his wisdom, chose to give the blue heron the ugliest, god-awful screech imaginable. It is truly a hideous thing to hear, and I can't help but feel this particular creature would be considerably better off, and more appreciated, if it only opened its mouth to feed.

It was quiet on the water, which was unusual for October, as many of the Yankee yacht owners chose to navigate the Intracoastal at this time for their annual sojourn south. They come by the hundreds; million and multi million-dollar vessels, one after the other, all day long, day after day. The fact that so many folks have so much money boggles my mind. Go figure. In addition to the basic cost of the yacht, which is astronomical, there's a captain to pay, a crew, the upkeep and gas and . . .okay, sorry, it's becoming evident, I'm envious as all hell.

Envy aside, I was grateful for the quiet morning. Many captains of these fine crafts do not choose to back off for us small fry, creating large wakes and making it difficult to stand and throw our traps without being washed overboard.

I placed one trap on the far side of the waterway in a spot that had been a good producer for the last three years, then dropped two more on the near side, in front of our house.

Having accomplished the task at hand, and deciding it was much too nice to head back in, I turned leisurely towards the Lockwood Folly Inlet. A cigar, at this very moment, would have been pure ecstasy.

My pleasant waterway cruise was just underway when, from the corner of my eye, I noticed something unusually large along the bank. There, partially hidden by marsh grass, was, good God, an alligator, and it was in front of our house! In twenty years I'd never seen one remotely close to our place. There were gators farther north along the rivers leading into the waterway, but never here. My first impulse was to rush back for my camera. But, fearing the gator might slip away in the meantime, I gave *Ol'Crab* a slow turn and headed quietly towards the bank for a closer look.

This was exciting stuff and my heart was racing. Drawing closer, I realized nothing had changed. In twenty years I still hadn't seen a gator in our area. What I was looking at was a body, a human body. And there were no two ways about it, it was a dead one.

Chapter 3

The van driver told his four fatigued passengers from Cárdenas that their next stop would be the last. They would soon be arriving at their final destination in *Carolina del Norte*. Nervous smiles passed amongst the four. Fear, joy and apprehension created a conflict of emotions that raced through the body of each. They would know shortly if they had been told the truth; that a good life, *la vida buena*, was waiting for them at journey's end, or, as Carlos believed, there would be much trouble. The answer was not far off.

After what felt to be an eternity, the van slowed, and they realized it had turned off the highway. It traveled a bit farther, continued along a bumpy road for a short distance, and came to a stop. Everything was quiet. The four passengers sat silently in the dark on the floor of the van, each heart pounding. . . each of the four's nerves ready to explode in anticipation of the unknown world that was moments away on the other side of the van's doors.

Abruptly, the silence was broken and they overheard both English and Spanish being spoken. Shortly thereafter, the van's back doors were flung open and the four looked out into a dark, cool night. They were in a wooded area and the unfamiliar scent of pine came to them. The coolness of the evening took each by surprise. They had expected it to be much warmer.

"*Bueno, ya pueden salir,*" said the driver. "Okay, you can

come out now."

Carlos was the first to rise. With some hesitation, he walked, crouched, toward the opening, looked around, and jumped out. He turned and helped María down. She was then followed by Pablo and his wife, Gina.

They huddled together, eyes nervously searching the night to see who was there to meet them.

"I don't see Rosa," María whispered to Carlos. "Señor Nuñez told us it would be arranged for my cousin to meet us when we arrived. She is not here." There was panic in her voice. Pablo also had a worried look. "My sister and her husband were to meet us. I don't see them. I don't like this," he said to Carlos. "This is not good."

"*Si*," Carlos replied. "Something is wrong. Maybe we should not have come. Don Orencio lied to us. He took our money and lied to us."

The van driver, who had been speaking with an *Americano*, joined the group.

"The *gringo* says there are a couple of problems. María, your cousin Rosa could not come now, but she's sending someone to get you and Carlos. He will be here soon. Pablo, your sister will not be meeting you. She and her husband are gone. They left this area several days ago. You will have to find some place else to stay."

"What do you mean, 'they left?'" asked Pablo, now clearly agitated and throwing his arms in the air.. "*¿Qué pasó?* What happened?"

"I don't know, I was just told they left quickly."

Pablo put an arm tightly around his wife's shoulders. "What are we going to do?" he asked, looking first at the van driver, then Carlos.

María spoke to the frightened couple. "You must come with us to my cousin Rosa's. She will know what to do. We have to leave this place soon, I'm freezing! Where's our ride?"

As she spoke, a car, its shocks squeaking loudly in the quiet night and with one bright beam on and the other headlight out, slowly bumped its way toward the group and came to a stop.

The young driver, a Mexican, got out, walked over and said he had been asked by Rosa to come for them. María, now noticeably shivering, hurriedly explained the situation with Pablo and Gina to the driver. The driver shrugged his shoulders, said it was okay with him and told the four of them to get in the car, and they drove off.

It was a short drive to the trailer park. Although late at night and quite dark, they could see that there were many trailers, all parked close to one another. Most trailers were very small. The car came to a stop along side of one of the smallest.

"This is it," the driver told them.

As they were getting out of the car, María's cousin, Rosa, opened the front door and stood in the doorway of her trailer holding a baby. "*Hola María, como estás? Al fin llegaron*! Hi María, how are you? You made it!"

"Yes, we're finally here! And look at what you have! I didn't know you had another baby!"

"My third," Rosa laughed. "But come in, come in. It's a little warmer inside."

They nodded thanks to the driver and the four bone weary travelers from Cárdenas entered Rosa's trailer. They had finally made it to their destination in *Los Estados Unidos*.

Once inside María hugged Rosa and apologized for how dirty they were. She quickly introduced Pablo and Gina and explained their situation.

As María was speaking, it became immediately apparent to her, and to the others, that they had a problem.

There was hardly room for Rosa and her family, let alone anyone else, in the trailer. An ancient white refrigerator, producing a noticeable humming noise, stood in one corner. There was a dented avocado color stove with a burner missing, two large maroon velour chairs, a light blue plastic couch with torn cushions, and in another corner, a large TV with rabbit ears sitting on top. One of Rosa's children was in a circular play pen with plastic netting around it; another child was sleeping in a scratched and marred wooden crib. At the other end was a tiny enclosed area which contained both a miniature bedroom and bathroom.

With the five of them standing in the twenty-five foot trailer, there was barely room for anyone to move.

There was no heater. The mixed odors of fried tortillas, boiled beans, musty furniture and soiled diapers permeated the trailer.

"We have no heater yet, that is our next big purchase. But it is still much better here than outside, yes?" said Rosa, smiling. She looked around. "We will make room for everyone tonight, at this hour nothing else is possible. Tomorrow, we'll look for a place for Pablo and Gina. María, you and Carlos will stay with us. My husband has a job arranged for you, Carlos; it's where he works. You and María will be able to get your own trailer very soon."

"Where is José?" asked María.

"He works in a restaurant most nights," Rosa explained. "Then he comes home to sleep for a few hours before he goes to work in the morning painting houses." She paused, "María, are you okay?"

"Yes, I'm fine Rosa. I haven't told you, but I am pregnant and every once in a while I get a little queasy."

"Pregnant! How wonderful! How far along are you?"

"I think about three months."

"Ah! That's why you don't show yet! Your child will be an American citizen like my three! That's why you came! It is so wonderful!"

"There are several reasons why we came, but yes, that is definitely one of them."

Perhaps it was the result of the cool night air, or perhaps it was the fatigue. Then again, it could have been the nauseating odors combined with the extreme anxiety she was experiencing at the moment. After all, this was certainly not how she had envisioned their arrival in *Carolina del Norte*. She had expected something much grander. In all likelihood, it was the consequence of all these things. For, just as she was about to continue her reply to Rosa, she felt a sharp pain in her abdomen, followed swiftly by a second.

"Dios mio, no ahora! Dios mio, por favor, es muy temprano," María sobbed. "My God, not yet! My dear God, please, it is too soon!"

Chapter 4

"**S**on ofa bitch!" I heard T.L. scream as I quickly tied down *Ol'Crab.*

His tirade continued as I scooted up the back steps to get to the kitchen phone.

"Damn it, just look at what the hell you're doing!"

I didn't take the time to look, but clearly heard my neighbors' boats banging against their docks as a result of the wake I'd created. I should have been more considerate.

"Every damn boat in the canal is getting the crap beat out of it! You probably busted some hulls, you probably broke some docks, hell you probably broke the 'NO WAKE ZONE' sign, you probably...."

I didn't hear the rest of his outburst as I was already in the kitchen dialing 911.

They answered quickly and I'd just finished giving the details as Tommy Lee came flying through the back door.

"Damn boy, what in the Sam Hill's going on?"

I excitedly told him about the body.

He hurried through the house to the front porch, with me following close behind.

We live on a narrow, barrier island. Each house is built on pilings, with most homes being ten to fourteen feet off the ground. From the front porch we look out across a street and have a clear view of the marsh, the Intracoastal Waterway, and its banks. I could see the hot pink buoys of the three crab traps I had just dropped in the Intracoastal.

"Where the hell is it," he asked looking out to the waterway.

I pointed in the vicinity of the body.

At first he didn't spot it. Then he uttered a low: "Holy shit, there it is!"

"Wait," I said, and went inside for the binoculars.

Back out, I handed them to Tommy Lee.

Another low "Holy shit, when did you spot it?"

"Just after I dropped the traps and just before I convincingly established the outboard speed record for our back canal," I replied.

"Smart ass; how close did you get?"

"Pretty close."

"And?"

"And... it looks like some poor sucker floating in sea grass."

"What else?"

"T.L., once I realized it was a human body I didn't think it best hang around, ya know?"

"You must have noticed something else. What's he wearing? I can't tell."

"I don't see how that's important, but if you have to know, I think he's wearing a tee shirt and jeans.

"And?"

"And that's it . . . hey, you with Homeland Security or something? You've never mentioned that to me T.L."

"You get a look at his face?"

"Damn, when do you break out the rubber hose? Yeah, I got a look at his face, well, sort of. I'd say he's a fairly young guy, black hair and if I had to venture a guess, I'd say he's Hispanic."

"Whoa...now we're getting somewhere; Hispanic?"

"Whoa... yeah, like Mexican, maybe."

"Well now, see, that's good."

"Huh?"

"That's good," he repeated.

"I'll bite, how's that good?"

"Ah, come on boy, use your head."

"I'm trying T. L., but I'm just a smart-ass, or is it 'dumb-ass,' Yankee."

"Okay, listen Matt, if he's Mexican, or Guatemalan, or whatever in the hell, and he's decked out like you said, then chances are he isn't one of us–he's not from around here. In other words, it's not someone who belongs here. And that's good, right? It's probably one of those illegal crop pickers, you know, an immigrant, one of those illegal aliens, or whatever they call 'em, that're running around all over the place. That's it and I'll betcha' five pounds of jumbo shrimp I'm right."

"Tommy Lee, I . . ."

Just then we heard the siren.

"Terrific response time," I said.

"For sure," said Tommy Lee, looking at his watch.

We saw the squad car make the turn onto our street and I leaned over the railing so the officer could spot me.

He pulled into the drive and our local police chief, Curt Everhart, stepped out.

"That was quick," I said, looking down to the driveway.

"Emergency Operations radioed me as soon as they hung up with you. What's this about a body in the waterway?" he said, looking up.

I pointed to the waterway and he turned and started toward it.

"You can't see it from there Chief," I called down. "And you can't walk out there now 'cause of the tide, come on up."

He took the steps two at a time. Tommy Lee and I knew the chief from a few social outings, and the three of us had done some off-shore fishing together.

When he reached the top, I handed him the binoculars and pointed. As he adjusted them, I explained how I'd come across my find.

"An alligator, huh?" he said, focusing in on the body.

"T.L. thinks it's an illegal alien," I replied, attempting to shift gears.

"Well now, you're pretty quick there Tommy Lee. If it turns out you're right, we sure as hell could use you on the force."

"Ah, come off it, Chief. From what Matt said, it looks like a Mexican or something, and the only Mexicans, or whatever, we got here are pickers, painters, and grass cutters and we know none of 'em are here legally, right?"

"Whatever," the chief replied.

Once he'd analyzed the situation, events moved quickly. He radioed for the police boat and crew. They arrived in short order and retrieved the body while the three of us watched from the porch. He radioed for an ambulance to meet him and the police boat at the dock under the bridge to the mainland. He told us the body would be taken to the county hospital, ID'd and the next of kin notified–all the usual stuff. He thanked me for being a model citizen, told me to keep my eye out for any more alligators, smiled, winked at Tommy Lee and headed down the steps to his squad car.

"Ya know," I said to Tommy Lee as the chief pulled away, "I have a feeling I'm going to be hearing about this alligator thing for a long time to come."

"Hey, and why not? . . . we're proud of you my boy! . . .got us our own regular Crocodile Dundee here on the island! But not to worry, if I'm right, which I am; it'll be over soon. If it's an illegal, the chief just passes it off to the county to handle. He and we, my great reptile hunter from the wilds of New Jersey, are done with it."

He couldn't contain himself. As he headed down the steps, I suggested what he could do with his reptile-hunter comments, which got him chuckling even harder.

"Glad I provided some amusement to the lowest class of redneck society on the island," I said, heading back into the house.

So there it was, from an alligator, to a dead body, to a joke. I wouldn't be a bit surprised if by tomorrow folks on the island were addressing me as "Gator."

But the truth of the matter was, the humor of the situation was lost on me.

Chapter 5

María resisted Rosa's attempts to get her to the hospital—the pain had subsided, and she feared she and Carlos would be discovered and returned to Mexico. She didn't yet know how the system worked, and Rosa couldn't convince her that there would be no problems.

"You are in the United States now," she pleaded. "You need help! The doctor will see you! They will not send you back! They will care for you!"

But María refused to have any part of it.

"I'm okay now," she persisted. "The pain has left, I just need to rest."

The others, concerned for María, but fearful of being discovered and sent back to Mexico, agreed that if María said she was okay, they would not take any chances on being noticed.

That night, María, her cousin Rosa, and the three children slept in the only bed. Pablo's wife, Gina, slept on the couch. The two men made themselves as comfortable as possible on the two maroon chairs.

After they had settled in, Pablo looked over at Carlos. "Have we done the right thing Carlos? I think not. We should go back home."

"I don't know Pablo, I don't know. What would we do back home even if we could get there? Don Orencio said he would get us here, that was all he promised, and he has. Perhaps things will be better tomorrow. *Quizás*. Perhaps."

It was very early in the morning when José, Rosa's husband, quietly opened the door to his trailer and stepped in.

Carlos heard José enter and rose to meet him.

"*Hola*," he said quietly. "I'm Carlos, María's husband. We arrived a few hours ago."

"*Sí*, we've been expecting you. *¿Como estás?* How was the trip?"

"There were problems, but we made it."

José suggested they go outside so as not to disturb the others.

The night had become even colder. José offered Carlos a cigarette.

"I haven't smoked since we left Cárdenas. This really tastes good!"

"I'm trying to quit," replied José. "This shit is very expensive here."

Carlos took a deep drag and told José the story of their flight from Cárdenas. He told José of the problem with Pablo and Gina, how Pablo saved María when they crossed the river, how terrible things were at the drop house and how they still owed a lot of money to Don Orencio Nuñez. He told José of María's pregnancy and how worried they were of being caught and sent back.

"*Eso no es problema, Carlos.* That's no problem. You and María, and the other two will not be sent back, I promise you. The *gringos* need us here. We are cheap workers. We do all the shit work for the *gringos*. Carlos, listen, I have a friend who crashed into a *gringo's* car and it was a big accident. This same friend had been caught by the police two times before for driving very fast, many miles over the limit. He's an illegal like us. You know what they did to him each time? Nothing! All he had to do was pay some fines. That's all. *Nada más!* Nothing more! And listen to this; he does not even have a driver's license! And Carlos, you will not believe this, he is still driving! I have another friend who was arrested by the police for driving when he was very drunk. You know what they did to him? *Nada!* Nothing! He too just paid the fine. He also has no license. It is crazy Carlos, but I swear to you, unless you murder someone, you will not be sent back!"

"*Es increible*! That's hard to believe José!"

"*Es verdad.* It's true."

He offered Carlos another cigarette. "We'll have one more then go back in. I need to sleep. Tomorrow, if it does not rain, you will go to work with me painting houses. You know how to do that?"

"*Sí,* I painted in Cárdenas. But there was little work and when we did work we were paid shit. Sometimes we weren't paid anything."

"Okay. I don't know if we will work tomorrow or not, we have had much rain, but I have told my boss you are a hard worker. He will pay you six dollars an hour. If you are good, he will keep you and pay you more. You and María will stay with us for one month. You will pay me one hundred dollars for the month and save the rest so you can rent your own trailer."

"How much will I make?"

"We don't work every day because of rain and other problems, but if we have a good month you will make seven to nine hundred dollars."

"José, that is a lot of money! It's a fortune!"

José flipped his cigarette to the ground and stepped on it. "It is shit Carlos. Things are very expensive here. Why do you think I have two jobs? It sounds like much money, but it is not. You have much to learn. But I need to sleep. We will talk tomorrow."

"Is there work for Pablo?" asked Carlos.

"I don't know. We weren't expecting him. We will see tomorrow, but I doubt it."

"What happened to Pablo's sister and her husband? We were told they left quickly."

José started to answer, then thought better of it. "Let's go in. It's cold and I am about to fall over. I have much to tell you, but it must wait until another time."

The two men re-entered the trailer. Less than a minute later, José went back out, got in the back seat of his car and laid down, exhausted. There was no room for him to sleep in his own trailer.

Inside the trailer, Carlos felt bad that José had insisted he sleep in the chair. But sleep was impossible. What had happened to Pablo's sister and her husband? How could it be that seven hundred dollars was not much money? In Cárdenas, they would be rich! And what more did José have to tell him?

Perhaps Pablo was right. They should not have come.

Unable to sleep, Carlos went back outside. He looked inside the car and saw José sleeping soundly in the rear seat. He wanted another cigarette, but knew he shouldn't bother José.

He turned, walked back towards the trailer, stopped, and kneeled to the ground. In the chill of the night air, by the light of the moon, he crawled on all fours until he had found three of the butts they had earlier discarded. He'd smoke the butts, then go back in the trailer and wait for tomorrow to come.

Chapter 6

Lindy normally would call during her lunch break. I'd decided not to tell her of my morning's adventure over the phone, but rather, save it for the cocktail hour. Let's face it, I seldom had anything of consequence to tell regarding my daily activities, so I had to play this for all it was worth.

With our retirement to the beach, Lindy had volunteered to help, part time, interpreting for the county. She's one of those extraordinarily decent souls the world so desperately needs. Finding herself with little to do, she determined it was time to "make a contribution," to "repay society," and all that other rationale of high and noble purpose.

Born in Havana, Spanish was her native language. She was also fluent in French, Italian and could even handle conversational Portuguese. Various county departments would call requesting her expertise and she'd hurriedly put on her professional attire and enthusiastically head out the door, ready to face whatever challenges the day might bring.

North Carolina, with somewhere in the area of 400,000 illegal immigrants of Hispanic origin, needed her principally for her Spanish. Invariably, whether it was the health department, legal services, the sheriff's department or social services, when she received a call, it was to assist with Mexican laborers and their families, and you could, with a great degree of certainty, bet they were illegals.

26

I, on the other hand, was a bit selfish regarding my time, wanting, after forty years of toiling in the market place, to pretty much do as I pleased. And in the spirit of full disclosure, what pleased me was to fish, crab, listen to my jazz and classical music collection, read, walk the beach, develop my culinary skills and then each evening enjoy a glass of wine or two, accompanied by a cigar. Although no one had ever asked, I considered it one of life's perfect plans.

Speaking of plans, I didn't have one for the balance of the day. The crab traps were out, one of the more exciting mornings of my life was over and it wasn't even quite noon; I decided to hit the beach for my daily jaunt.

In late October, except for those obsessed golfers who were convinced that with a slight adjustment of the wrists, or knees, or back, or neck, or eyes, or hip, or tee height, or stance, or club choice, or back swing, or shoes, or glove, know they will positively master the game and go on tour, the tourists had basically fled our beautiful beach. There were a few fishermen with their dual 350 horse power vessels, but they'd head out early each morning and weren't heard from again 'til after sunset.

The beach was barren of bodies baking, boom boxes blaring, discarded cigarette butts and empty Budweiser cans. The point being that we permanent residents could now reclaim our little island paradise. In season, the population swells to 10,000 or more fun loving souls frolicking in sand and sol and yes, we are grateful for their significant financial support, via tax dollars, to our economy and the critical beach renourishment programs. How else to keep this narrow hunk of sand, this fragile barrier island, from being washed over and slipping into the depths of the Atlantic? Their support is indispensable to our very existence. But now we 1,000 or so fine, upstanding citizens, well, for the most part, were the island's sole inhabitants and for many of us, this was our preferred time of year. The weather was ideal, we had the beach to ourselves and, most importantly, we could cross Ocean Boulevard without fearing for life or limb.

There was no one on the beach as I picked up the pace, wanting to get my five miles in under an hour. Fortunately, it was low tide.

If it had been high tide I'd have done my bit on Ocean Blvd. as a high tide made it difficult to walk, let alone jog.

Years ago I'd ceased collecting shark's teeth, sand dollars, "unusual" shells and "attractive" driftwood. We already had an excess of sea "treasures" scattered throughout the house and yard. Occasionally, during tourist season, I'd stop if I happened upon an interesting piece, pick it up and subsequently present it to a treasure-hunting tourist. Treasure hunting tourists are not difficult to identify as their *derrieres* are, generally, the first thing one encounters. Some *derrieres*, admittedly, could not be passed by quickly enough. On the other hand, if the treasure hunter turned out to be an attractive member of the female sect, well now, so much the better. The magnanimous gesture of my offering a treasure of the sea was normally reciprocated with a smile, which was what I had hoped for in the first place. My quite prim and proper, aged aunt, with a devilish look on her face, referred to these folks, regardless of *derriere* size, as members of the AIAC, *Ass In the Air Club.* She counted herself a proud member of the AIAC for most of her eight decades, and could still be found occasionally walking the beach, looking for yet one additional treasure offered up from the briny depths.

✒✑

The phone was ringing as I entered the house. Glancing at my watch I hurried to pick up the receiver in the kitchen and said, "Hi Hon, how ya doing?"

"Fine Sweetie, nice of you to ask," answered Chief Everhart.

"Oh good God, this really isn't my day. I thought you were . . . ah . . ."

"I know what a disappointment it must be for you."

"Okay Chief, you can let it go."

"Hey, it was too easy to pass up, but you're right, I'll get off it. We got some serious stuff to go over."

"How's that?"

"Your body, you know, the one you found, had no ID, so we're running his prints now. If we don't turn up anything with that, we'll run an international search. If nothing happens with that then all we can do is sit back and hope for a missing person call."

"I understand, but you said something about some 'serious stuff?'"

"Matt, I hate to admit it, but it looks like Tommy Lee was right. The coroner's certain he's Hispanic, and running with the odds, we're assuming Mexican. His clothing had a couple of paint splotches, but no ID. Hispanic, house painter–for the moment we're regarding the corpse as that of the body of an illegal, Mexican immigrant."

"Damn. So what you're telling me is that I owe my red neck neighbor, and it's gonna kill me, a mess of jumbo shrimp and that you, and it's gonna kill you, have to put him on your payroll. Chief, you're right, that is 'serious stuff.'"

"Listen Matt, we gotta stop the kidding around now, there's more, and I'm only telling you this because you found the body."

"Okay."

"There were three bullet holes in his chest."

"Oh, my God."

"'Oh, my God' is right. The best anyone can remember, we've never had a homicide on the island–never, this is a first."

"Never? That's incredible."

"Matt, there's more."

"What's that?"

"The entry wounds form a distinctive pattern. So distinctive that we don't think this was an amateur or random killing. Matt, we're pretty certain it was a professional hit."

"Good grief," I said. "But Chief, in the first place, why would there be a professional hit around here, and secondly, on an illegal Mexican house painter of all things? That just doesn't make any sense."

The chief hesitated a moment. "We can't be certain at this point, but we're going under the assumption it was mob related."

"Mob related? Here? You mean 'mob' as in 'Mafia?'"

"Yes and no, but it isn't what you're thinking. Most folks around here aren't even aware of it, but there's also a south of the border mob."

"You mean, like a Mexican kind of Mafia?"

"I mean exactly that–*the* Mexican Mafia. It's very real Matt . . . and it's here."

Chapter 7

Lindy looked forward to Wednesdays at the clinic. Normally, she'd be given a desk in the reception area, which meant that on Wednesdays, Pediatrics Day, she got to see and play with most of the kids who came in with their mothers. Although often chaotic and noisy throughout the day, that was fine with her; she enjoyed her time with the children.

At the moment it was abnormally quiet, and not being needed by any of the doctors or nurses, she was translating a recently-issued state bulletin into Spanish. Hearing a commotion at the entrance and looking up, she saw Rosa Díaz hustling towards her. She had known Rosa and her husband, José, for three years and knew each of their three children, two of which were now clinging to Rosa's skirt, while the baby was cradled in her right arm.

Lindy stood up as they continued toward her desk. Along side Rosa was an attractive young girl Lindy had not previously seen.

"*¿Hola Rosa, como estás?*"

"*Bien, Señora Lindy.* We are all fine, and hope that you are.

"*Sí Rosa,* I am well. And who is this with you?"

"I have brought you someone new for the clinic. She needs your help. This is my cousin María. She is from Cárdenas, like me, and she is four months pregnant."

"*Hola María,*" said Lindy, turning to the pretty, young girl.

María lowered her head, not responding to the greeting.

"How long have you been here?" Lindy asked.

Once again, there was no reply.

"She didn't want to come," Rosa explained. "She is still afraid she'll be sent back to Mexico, and doesn't believe you will help her."

Lindy turned to María. She continued to be struck by the young girl's beauty, and there was certainly no evidence of her pregnancy.

"María, I am here to help you."

"*Gracias Señora*," María replied quietly.

"You see all these children running around here? I am like a grandmother to them, and a mother to their mothers!"

"That's right María," Rosa broke in, "I told you before. Lindy was here when I was pregnant with each of my children and she has been like a mother to me!"

"María, we will help you. That's what we are here for. And we will not send you back to Mexico. Please, believe me."

"*Sí Señora*."

"And my name is Lindy, no more '*Señora*,' okay?"

"*Sí Señora*."

"Now, how long have you been here?"

"*Un mes*."

"A month!" cried Lindy. "You should have come when you first arrived!"

"I tried to tell her, but she and her husband would not believe me," Rosa broke in.

"Okay, María, now listen to me, the first step is for you to trust me. Will you do that?"

María hesitated, then nodded her head.

"*Bueno*, now the next step is for you to have one of our nurses examine you, and don't look so worried, I'll stay with you the entire time. Everything will be fine. When you're finished with the nurse, we'll sit down and sign you up for a special program that helps pregnant women like you, other mothers and their children. The program will help make sure that you and your baby remain healthy. Do you understand?"

María nodded her head.

"I tried to tell her, but she wouldn't listen," interrupted Rosa.

"Well, Rosa, now she knows. María, it's a very good program for you and your baby. You'll be given coupons, and you'll take these coupons to the grocery store and get things like milk, eggs, fruit juice, cereal and vitamins with them. And after your baby is born, you'll continue to get these coupons until your baby is five years old. We want to be sure you and your baby stay healthy!"

"See, I told you María! And it won't cost you and Carlos anything. I get them for all my children," Rosa emphasized to María.

"Rosa is right María; now let's get you to a nurse."

By the time María was finished with her check-up and Lindy had qualified her for the Women, Infants, Children program, the workday was over. Except for Lindy, the reception area was empty as María, Rosa, and her children left the building.

Sue, one of the nurses, came by Lindy's desk and slumped into a chair.

"Wow, what a day," she sighed. "Lindy, how do you say 'it was a bitch of a day' in Spanish?"

Lindy laughed. "I don't think I can give you a literal translation. Let's see, how about, *"Fué un dia muy malo."*

"What's that mean?"

"It was a bad day."

"Well, it was a lot worse than that, but it was indeed a *'dia muy malo,'"* said Sue

Lindy couldn't help but laugh at hearing Spanish spoken with Sue's southern drawl.

"It really was non stop, I didn't even get a chance to call Matt."

"Do you think they appreciate it?" Sue asked.

"What do you mean?"

"The illegals, do you think they appreciate everything we do for them?"

"I guess some of them do, but certainly not all of them. I just had a new one today, a beautiful young girl. After her exam I made arrangements with her for WIC, but I doubt if she's given it any thought. I'm sure it is still a bit overwhelming for her."

"And when and if she does understand," said Sue, "she'll

probably just take it for granted. The thing is, this isn't even the half of it! When I first told my husband that these women come to the United States illegally to have their babies because the baby will automatically be a United States citizen, I thought he'd blow a gasket! Then, when I told him the baby automatically gets a Social Security card and is entitled to Medicaid, I really thought he was going to go through the roof! I don't dare tell him that he's also paying for prenatal care, maternal care, all the actual birth costs and then food stamps for each kid once it's born. He'd, excuse my French, shit a brick, if he knew about all that."

"I know what you mean, but Matt and I haven't really talked about it much. I can't say I even know how he feels about this whole illegal immigrant thing. To be honest, I've given it some thought, but probably not as much as I should."

"I don't want to," said Sue, "It might make me not want to help so much."

"Well, there's that," replied Lindy.

❧

Of course Lindy thought the right thing was being done, and she was glad to help, but every once in a while she'd run across or hear about an abuse to the system that would get under her skin.

On the drive home, she decided she and Matt needed to talk about this entire illegal immigrant situation.

As she turned onto Highway 17, a smile crossed her face. She could picture Matt at this very moment. He'd be sitting on the front porch with a martini in one hand and one of his damn cigars in the other. He was probably reading, or listening to some jazz on the portable CD player, or both. Of course she'd be obligated to give him the proper amount of static about the cigar; that was expected by both of them.

His days were all the same, and as far as she could see, rather monotonous. He had his routine which he obviously enjoyed and she was happy for him, but nothing much ever happened. She couldn't understand why he was never bored.

Chapter 8

After placing the second of two anchovy stuffed olives into a perfectly dry martini, grabbing a cigar and the most recent *New York Times Book Review*, I headed for the porch. It was all part of the perfect plan.

No sooner had I settled in when Lindy's car pulled into the drive and I heard the garage door rise.

The immediate crisis I faced was whether to light up before she hit the steps, or wait until she had settled in and then dutifully receive my obligatory reprimand.

"I can smell it from down here," she said from the bottom of the steps.

"Just lit up," I replied, realizing my timing, as usual, had been lousy. "You ready for a drink?"

"Make it tawny port; I'll change while you get it. No wait, make it a screwdriver."

Within a few minutes we were enjoying cheese and crackers, along with our drinks, on the porch. I had ditched the stogie.

An old shrimp boat passed by. Come to think of it, I've never seen a *new* shrimp boat. I was sure they'd stopped building them years ago, but these old boats were well kept and a pretty sight as they slowly cruised the waterway. We stood and waved, as we normally do, and the Captain sounded his horn.

"So Hon," I said, sitting back down, "I assume it was another day of fun and frolic while making everyone happy and healthy?"

I asked, reveling in the knowledge that mine was the scoop of the day.

"It was long, but good," she replied. "Lots of noisy kids, and several expectant mothers."

"I don't know how you do it. That would drive me berserk."

"How well I know. Oh, and we had a new girl come in. She's a recent arrival, Mexican, eighteen years old, pregnant and quite pretty.

"Illegal?" I asked.

"Hon, that's basically all we're getting now, but this one is the prettiest I've seen since I started working there. She's really quite gorgeous with long black hair, beautiful black eyes, a cute figure and she's very, very shy. Her cousin had to force her to come in."

"How's that?"

"She was afraid she and her husband would be sent back to Mexico if they were found out."

"That doesn't happen often, does it?"

"No, I'm not aware of it ever happening. But when they first get here they're frightened, and it usually takes a while for them to learn the ropes. Anyway, her name's María. I think she'll be okay, but she was like a timid little kitten at first. By the time we finished, I think I'd gained her trust."

Lindy took a sip of her screwdriver and looked over at me.

"Okay, that's my report from the real world, what happened with the island beach bum today?"

I sipped my martini, stabbed, secured, and ate an olive, then looked back out to the waterway.

"Well, let's see . . .I dropped three traps out front and . . ."

"I can see the buoys," she interrupted. "Since the state made you use hot pink, they're impossible to miss."

"I put out the three traps," I resumed, "had a couple of chats with Tommy Lee, took a nice, long walk on the beach, read a little of *Jazz Times* and in the midst of all this tumultuous activity, prepared for your dining delight, my love, a shrimp dinner fit for the most fastidious of gourmands."

Yesterday afternoon we had purchased five pounds of beautiful, jumbo shrimp which had just been off-loaded from the shrimp boat docked at Capt'n Pete's Seafood. They hadn't been frozen or dipped in a preservative, so we knew they'd be about as fresh as you could hope to get.

"Thanks, sounds yummy... so, that's it?"

"*Yummy?*" I asked.

"Okay, it sounds delectable and I simply can't wait! Is that better? Now, why do I have the feeling you're toying with me?"

I sipped the martini, savoring both the taste and the moment.

"Well, actually, I'm not . . . Oh wait . . . Gee-will-a-kers, I almost forgot, there's that small matter of the body I found in the waterway . . . the dead one that is . . . and calling 911 and having the police arrive and observing as they recovered the poor stiff, and then having Chief Everhart later tell me that the corpus delecti I'd found was in fact the result of a murder, an apparent professional hit at that . . . but really, all told, it was pretty much the usual same 'ol, same 'ol around here."

The incredulous expression on Lindy's face surpassed any I'd seen in our many years together.

"You're pulling my leg, of course," she said.

"Not in the least," I said, my beam quite possibly out-shining the Cape Hatteras Lighthouse.

I filled her in, with as much dramatic flair as my limited story telling talents could muster, on the events of the morning. After becoming convinced I hadn't spent the afternoon drinking and conjuring up this story, and that I was giving her the truth and nothing but the truth, we headed back in for dinner.

The shrimp were every bit as delicious as anticipated. Given a blindfold test, it would have been difficult to tell the difference between these shrimp and lobster.

Over dinner, we chatted more about my crazy morning. Finished, I got up and started clearing the table when Lindy said, "Some of them do okay you know, but a lot of them are having it really tough."

"Who are we talking about Hon?" I asked.

"The illegals" she answered. "Matt, you and I haven't really talked about this, but what's going on is absolutely insane. You know I love my work, I really do, and I've become fond of the people I assist and work with. I go out of my way to do everything I can to help them all, and it's because I want to—but sometimes it gets so *darn* frustrating!"

Hearing such an emphatic *darn* from Lindy, I knew she needed to talk, so I suggested we sit on the front porch and enjoy the imminent sunset, and chat.

The weather had remained simply magnificent, and we once again were witnessing the beginning of a fabulous, flaming, orange sunset over the Intracoastal Waterway. This spectacular show that nature magnanimously provides us happens with some frequency. But no matter how often we witness this glorious event, it never fails to inspire and humble. Allow the world leaders, for one early evening, to sit on *this* porch and watch *this* sunset and they would, quite possibly, with the assistance of some fine wine, resolve most problems regarding the injustices of today's world. Hey, it's possible. Highly unlikely mind you, but we'll hold the invitation open.

Settled once again in the rockers, I asked Lindy, "Okay, from whence comes all this sudden frustration?"

"Oh, I don't even know if 'frustration' is the right word Matt. Sometimes I just get plain mad. I told you about the new girl who came in today with her cousin. I certainly understand why she and the others want to get here, it's really such a squalid life, not to mention the mere act of surviving down there. Who wouldn't want to get out if they could? My God, everybody would! And I understand their wanting to get here so their kids can be born citizens of the United States. Again, who wouldn't? But sometimes, well, sometimes I feel like we're being taken advantage of."

"We?" I asked.

"Yes, 'we' . . . you and me, and the rest of us good 'ol American tax payers."

"Listen Hon, you've told me more than once that if these people are to have any chance at all, they need help. I don't even know what all that help is, and honestly, I don't even care to know, but if you say they need it, they need it. I've gotta think that without it, they'd be just as bad off as they were in Mexico . . .we agree on this. So what's the problem all of a sudden?"

"I just told you about this new girl, María, who showed up today with her cousin. Well, this cousin, Rosa, has three kids, each one of them has been born here, which means each of her kids is automatically a citizen and each is given a Social Security card. Since her husband hasn't been able to earn enough for them to get by on, each child receives Medicaid, health care, and each one gets food stamps. Since they're so young, the food stamps are issued in Rosa's name. That's over three hundred dollars a month just in food stamps, plus all the other stuff! Now, I don't know how many, but there are a bunch more "Rosas," out there and some with a lot more kids than three."

"Oops, stop–I don't think I want to hear anymore about this."

"Well, no, listen, you should know this, and here's the thing that really bugs me, we've counseled Rosa several times about not having more kids! We *gave* her the choice of using the pill, getting the shots or using an I.U.D. She chose the pill–and has never taken one! We gave them to her, and she never took the first one! When we talk to her about it, she just giggles and says she wants more kids. It's so frustrating!"

"Hon let me ask you a question; do you still like what you're doing?"

"Absolutely! I've gotten to know the mothers, and I love all the kids! They're mostly wonderful people who have had an incredibly brutal life just trying to survive! It's just that, like I said, sometimes I feel we're being taken advantage of."

"Well, we most likely are, at least in some cases. But if we hold to the premise that if we'd been in their shoes, and had found a way out, we would've done exactly the same thing. And what's more, we'd take advantage of every bit of help we could get, just as they are. You can't let the extreme cases get under your skin. Hey, you only work at this part-time because you want to, so keep enjoying it and stay cool."

"I know," she sighed. "I really don't think about it that often. One of the nurses remarked today that she was afraid that if she thought about it too much, it might affect her enthusiasm. She's probably right."

"Could be, just don't let it get to *you*. And if it does Lindy, and I'm as serious as I can be, you walk away. We didn't retire for you to get yourself wrapped up in more frustrating situations. We both had enough of those while we were working. I can tell you right now, *I'm* not, and if I see this stuff affecting you, you're going to give it up. We both understand why these people leave Mexico, and what's happening at this end as far as what you do to help them…but we can't become personally involved, not if it's going to get to you and affect *our* lives. That isn't why we retired."

Considering the conversation finished, I headed upstairs to listen to some music and finish *The New York Times' Book Review*. We have a small room upstairs containing an audio system, our computer, a small library, a TV and a work table for whatever project one of us happens to be involved with at the time.

Selecting a Dave Brubeck CD, one of his solo sets containing several sentimental, old standards, I sat back and tuned into his marvelous playing. Well, almost. Our dinner conversation kept bouncing around in my mind. Tonight I'd learned more than I cared to know, and one situation was becoming apparent to me–cheap Mexican labor may not be quite so cheap after-all. I wondered what the real cost would be if the many benefits and social services the illegals received were tossed into the financial equation. Interesting. Somehow, in the end, it would, as it usually does, work out. Our country would get what we needed from them, and the illegals, hopefully, would get what many of them risked their lives coming here for.

Refocusing on Brubeck, I realized it was towards the end of the CD. I couldn't help but smile at the appropriateness of the last cut, a melancholy song of hope from *The Wizard of Oz*, it was Dave's hauntingly beautiful rendition of *Over The Rainbow*.

Chapter 10

Earlier in the week, as of Tuesday afternoon, Pablo had found only a few hours of work since he and Gina and Carlos and María had arrived, a little over a month ago. The rain had brought new construction work to a halt, along with a stop to the farm jobs. He left on foot each morning, or bummed a ride from someone in the trailer park, looking for any kind of work available, anything at all, only to return each evening empty handed and more despondent than when he had left.

He and Gina were living in a small, cramped trailer with four other illegal couples. Between the five couples they barely earned enough to cover the rent and a minimal amount of food. Pablo was becoming desperate. He and Gina had contributed nothing and were a drain on all the others. He had never known such hopelessness.

To make the situation worse was the matter of not having paid *el hombre* the money he still owed. He knew it was simply a matter of time before he was threatened, before some kind of force would be applied. Unfortunately, there was no way for him to realize just how soon that would be.

Pablo walked the drenched road toward the trailer park late Tuesday afternoon, the torrential rain pounding down upon him, his worn work boots slouching through the mud. He was soaked clear through and with the noise of the battering rain, didn't hear Collinson's car as it slowly approached, not until it had pulled directly along side him. He then heard a quick, almost inaudible, honk of the horn. Pablo stopped, looked, and watched as the window of the car was lowered. He couldn't quite make out the face of the driver through the rain, but whoever it was looked out at Pablo, and he heard the man offer him a ride.

かんか

On Tuesday evening, Miguel Delgado was in excellent spirits. During the course of the day, each of *los hombres* had reported in, and there were no problems of consequence. With his man in Atlanta he'd even discussed the possibility of a trip to do some up-scale shopping within the next couple of weeks.

The exception to this perfect day was the local situation with those Cárdenas peasants, and that other piss ant with the rent situation. He'd been assured that the instructions he'd issued would be carried out today.

Carmen, his housekeeper, at his request, had prepared his favorite chicken dish, *pollo poblano* for dinner. Finishing, he topped off the meal with freshly ground Mexican coffee and a small glass of Kahlua. Although born in L. A., he very much enjoyed the food and drink of his heritage. Retiring to the den with a larger snifter of Kahlua, and having selected a Cuban cigar from the humidor, he turned on the plasma HDTV and settled into the recliner, prepared for an evening of relaxation. The Latino cable channel from Miami carried his favorite shows, particularly those with the older, slapstick comedians and the good looking babes with the huge tits; some of them were simply incredible.

The cell phone rang as he was lighting up.

"*Hola*," he answered.

"*¿Hola*? What happened to 'Hello?'" said the voice on the other end.

"Sorry, it's an old habit from our Los Angeles days, *mi amigo*."

"Whatever. Okay, listen, I told you up front that this wasn't my cup of tea, if you know what *that* means, and this kind of shit wasn't part of our original arrangement."

"I'm familiar with the expression thank you, but remember, you got yourself into this jam, *mi amigo*. If you had collected the money, as you are reimbursed quite handsomely by me to do, it would not have come to this."

"Well, anyway, it's handled."

"*Bien hecho,* well done."

"Listen, Delgado, I'd appreciate it if you didn't give me any more of that '*Bien hecho*' and '*mi amigo*' crap. Just speak to me in good 'ol American if you don't mind."

"I'll speak to you in any goddamn language I choose!" screamed Delgado. "And I'm telling you this for the last time you stupid shit, don't ever . . .let me repeat in clear, 'good 'ol American' so that even that *gringo* pea brain of yours gets it . . .don't *ever* use names over the phone again!"

Enraged, he held up short of throwing the phone against the wall. Everyone knew not to use names. This jerk was the only *gringo* in his entire operation and he'd been useful, but now Delgado was having serious doubts.

An hour following the call Delgado had finally settled down after resolving that he'd do something about Collinson soon, very soon. The man was becoming a liability and his usefulness definitely compromised by, among other things, his crappy attitude.

But for tonight, he'd relax, have a couple more drinks, and watch the babes from Miami with the big tits.

Chapter 11

Crab (krab) -n. 1. *any decapod crustacean of the suborder Brachyura, having the eyes on short stalks and a short, broad, more or less flattened body, the abdomen being small and folded under the thorax.*

Well, that's the definition in my humongous Webster's New Universal Unabridged Dictionary. I think my definition of the little beasts is considerably more definitive:

crab (krab) -n. 1. *a mean-tempered, ferocious, salt water scavenger, which, if given the slightest opportunity, will sever a finger from your hand, and then, just for spite, spit in your eye.*

My love for all things crab-related goes back to when I was a kid and my Dad would take me crabbing along the Jersey Shore, usually around the Beach Haven, or Ocean City area. Those marvelous memories I hold near and dear. Now, here I am, years later, an ingrate with the perfect set-up for crabbing, complaining; must be the weather.

We'd invited T. L. and Lizzie, along with Karl and Evie Vogelsang, friends from our Indianapolis days, over for a little dinner party Saturday evening. Lindy and I planned to serve an incomparable crab cake recipe we had recently invented. Because of lousy weather during the week, I had to pull the traps, cook, clean, pick and prepare the crab cakes all on Saturday. Not fun, not fun at all. I doubted if our guests would even begin to appreciate the lengthy labors I had gone to in order to satisfy their fickle palates.

They were to arrive at six, but at about a quarter 'til, as I was checking the wine situation, I heard footsteps coming up the front steps. It was the Vogelsangs.

"Sorry, we're a bit early," said Karl, handing me a bottle of Merlot.

"No problem, this bottle of Merlot gains you early access to the evening's festivities. There's wine already open on the kitchen counter, along with your spirit of choice and beer in the fridge. Grab whatever you want and we'll go out to the front porch."

When we had company, I could usually get away with two cigars, one before and then another after dinner.

Karl and I went out while Evie stayed behind to help Lindy.

T. L. and Lizzie arrived as Karl and I were discussing his tomato garden which, as a result of the incessant rain, had produced hardly any tomatoes.

"Last year it was the damn birds that got them, this year it's the rain," he bemoaned.

"I gave up a couple of years ago and just run over to Ludlum's produce stand during the season. It's a lot easier," I told him.

I directed T. L. and Lizzie inside to the libations, and T. L. returned shortly with a gin and tonic.

"First today, here's to y'all." T.L. raised his glass, the three of us clicked, and our little dinner party was officially off and running.

"So, what's on the menu tonight, Chef?" asked T.L.

"T. L., I'm simply aghast that you weren't taught any better. You never ask your hosts what they've prepared for dinner. It just isn't done in proper circles."

"We're in a proper circle?" he asked.

"Well, two of us are," said Karl, smiling.

"Okay T. L., even though your incredibly poor manners and red neck attitude are much in evidence, I'll tell you that this evening you'll be enjoying one of the truly all-time, great American, classic, gourmet dishes which I personally prepared for my dear next door neighbor . . .a simple but elegant, old fashioned . . .*Yankee* Pot Roast."

Karl chuckled.

T. L. moaned, "You're shitting me"

"I am indeed. To be honest, and being acutely aware of your sensitive southern palate, I actually created a new dish in your honor; I've named it 'T. L.'s Southern Sensation.' It's a casserole consisting of cheese grits, okra, black-eyed peas, fat back and collard greens all soaking in red eye gravy…T. L., you'll think you've died and gone to red-neck heaven."

T. L. stared at me, and then looked at Karl.

"He's pulling your leg, T. L.," said Karl, "at least I hope to God he is!"

෴

The crab cakes were an enormous success. "The best ever," "I've got to have this recipe," "They're to die for," etc., were all praises bestowed on the cakes. The nicest compliment though, surprisingly, came from Tommy Lee. In the slowest, sincerest drawl he could muster, he said, "I haven't tasted anything this good since back when my knees were under my Mama's kitchen table." Truly, I was flattered.

Unfortunately, towards the end of the meal, I became concerned; T. L. had been hitting the gin and tonics heavy prior to dinner, and had continued at an alarming rate during the course of the meal. I knew from past experience that once he got into the sauce, particularly gin, he could become belligerent.

Surprisingly, the incident of last Wednesday hadn't surfaced. It wasn't until the dishes were being cleared that Karl asked if there was anything new.

"Nope," I replied. "I spoke with the chief yesterday morning and they still hadn't ID'd the body."

"What difference does it make?" asked T.L.

"Well," said Karl, "I'd assume the police would like to find the killer if possible; an I.D. would help in that regard, and I'd also think the dead man's family should be notified."

"Who gives a shit about that?" said T.L.

"Tommy Lee!" snapped Lizzie, "watch your language!"

"Well, really, who does? The family, if he has one, is probably in Mexico somewhere, or if they're here, they're illegals and ought to get their butts back where they came from anyway."

I didn't like the tone of T.L.'s voice, or the direction of the conversation. Either Lizzie or I would have to pull the reins in on Tommy Lee.

"Okay, listen, no need to get into any serious stuff tonight," I said. "Let's sit on the back deck and enjoy another gorgeous Carolina evening."

Karl, unfortunately, missed my cue.

"I don't understand why you feel that way Tommy Lee. These people are trying to give their families a better life, just like immigrants here have always done. They paint our houses, mow our yards, break their backs picking crops, and perform a lot of really dirty work that no one else is willing to do. You know that, or you should."

"My God Karl, what are you talking about? They're coming across the border by the hundreds of thousands. We've lost total *control* of our own damn borders! Don't you watch the news? They're destroying the school system, they're absolutely killing the health care system and law enforcement can't begin to keep up with what's going on. This whole thing is costing us tax payers out the ass! "

"Tommy Lee!" Lizzie broke in again. "That's it. One more remark like that and I'm marching you back next door!"

"Well, just ask Lindy," continued T.L., "she can tell you all the free stuff we give 'em. My God, we pay for them to have babies, and then make their babies citizens! And you think they just make six or seven bucks an hour and that they're cheap labor? Oh no, no, no! You toss in all the other goodies they get and it's costing us out the...," he paused, caught himself about to use a word that would lead to the path home, and said, "a fortune!"

"Well," replied Karl, "if you were in their shoes what would you do?"

"Probably the same da...," he looked frustratingly over at Lizzie pleadingly. "Just one more?"

"Okay, one more 'damn' but nothing worse than that. I'll even give you an extra 'hell' if you behave. But that's it for the rest of the evening buster, and I mean it."

"Okay, where was I? Oh, I'd probably do the same *damn* thing, but we gotta get control of the situation, Karl. We haven't even mentioned the security problems! Jesus, do you realize how easy it'd be for terrorists to sneak in and bring chemical weapons along with them! Man, talk about easy. And did you see where they're singing the National Anthem in *Spanish* for God's sake? *Our* National Anthem . . .in *Spanish*! How do ya like that? Oh, oh, and how do you like having to press "one" for English on the phone, or when you're checking out at the store. Isn't that just great? In your own country you gotta press "one" for your own da..., uh, language."

Tommy Lee had really gotten himself worked up and I was about to repeat my suggestion of heading outside, when the phone rang. It was too late in the evening for friends or family to be calling, unless it was an emergency.

Lindy excused herself and took the call in our bedroom.

As we got up from the table I took after-dinner drink orders and Lindy returned to the dining room. I caught her glance as she gave me an almost imperceptible shake of the head.

Everyone had settled on White Russians. I made certain to prepare T. L.'s on the light side, mixing in an excessive amount of half and half.

The night was gorgeous with a slight breeze, sparkling stars and one of those abnormally huge moons. The conversation, thankfully, turned light, with a few mangled jokes told, several large lies concerning fishing and golf retold for the zillionth time, and Karl and Evie filling us in on their recent Alaskan cruise.

The two couples left at the same time, with T.L. grinning from ear to ear. He thanked us for one *hell* of a fine evening, thus, with obvious delight, spending the last four letter word he had been allotted by Lizzie.

Lindy and I returned to the kitchen to clean up.

"Matt, I know it's late, but I'd like another White Russian."

"Sure Hon, does this have something to do with the phone call?

It did. The call concerned the body I'd found. But more significantly, as we were soon to learn, it was a call that would lead to an inconceivable turn in our lives.

Chapter 12

I mixed the White Russians and began loading the dishwasher.

"Matt, I think I know whose body that is."

I caught the plate as it slipped from my hand.

Lindy gave me a quizzical look. "The body you found, I think I know who it is."

"I heard what you said . . .was that the call during dinner?"

"Yes. Well, no. They didn't tell me whose body it was, but from what I was told, I'm certain I know, but I didn't want to say anything while we had company."

I leaned against the kitchen counter. "I don't know how you managed to contain yourself, so . . ."

"So . . ., the call was from Rosa Diaz. I've told you about her. She's the one with three kids who lives in a trailer park and treats me as though I were her mother. She's also the one who brought that new girl in, her cousin María. You know who I mean now?"

"I know exactly who you mean, but before you go any further, I'd like to get something straight, how did she know to call you here? You told me these people aren't supposed to call you at home, and don't even have our phone number."

"They aren't supposed to, and I don't give out our number."

I waited. The prospect of our phone number being in the hands of a group of illegal immigrants had me more concerned at the moment than learning the identity of the body.

"Matt, I may have given it to Rosa when I first started at the clinic. I didn't know any better, she was one of the first patients I worked with, she was pregnant and having problems and I felt sorry for her. That was three years ago. We sort of bonded at the beginning. She must have kept my number all this time. I know I've never given it to anyone else. I'm certain I haven't."

"Okay, I was just concerned, but it should be all right. Now, about the call . . ."

"Rosa was very upset and I had to keep telling her to slow down. She was speaking so fast I couldn't catch much of what she was saying, but I got the gist of it."

"Which was?"

"Well, bear with me for a minute, I need to back up. I told you that her cousin, María, and María's husband, Carlos, are living with Rosa and her family. All seven of them are in this really tiny trailer. But, what I didn't know until tonight was that when María and Carlos left Mexico, they left with another couple, some close friends of theirs. Pablo and Gina are the names, I think she said. The thing is, since the four of them arrived they haven't been able to work, at least not much, because of the weather. Apparently both couples still owe a lot of money to someone Rosa calls *el hombre*; I think it's the guy who got them out of Mexico. Pablo has earned so little that he hasn't been able to pay anything to this *hombre* guy. Rosa said both couples have been afraid something bad would happen if they didn't come up with the money they owe."

"Okay, it's a lousy situation, I can see that, but why'd they call you? Do they want money from us?"

"No, no such thing. Rosa said she didn't know who else she could talk to. She's afraid to call the police for obvious reasons, and no one has seen him since Tuesday morning."

"No one has seen *who* since Tuesday morning?"

"Pablo, Matt; he's been missing for five days."

Well, there it was. Lindy was right. With this Pablo guy not having been heard from for that many days, chances were good it was his body I'd found. The only question now was whether or not to call Chief Curt Everhart. My gut feeling was that a phone call, late on a Saturday night, wouldn't be appreciated by our number one law enforcement officer. Sunday was most likely out also.

"Okay, that's that, I'll call the chief Monday morning and he can go to work on it."

"Matt, I'm not so sure that 'that's that.'"

"What do you mean?"

"I think I'm right about this, and I know what's going to happen. You and Chief Everhart and everyone else will be satisfied to have the mystery of who it is, or was, resolved, but what about those poor people? What will they do? What will happen to them?"

"I'm sorry Hon, but I don't follow, what people, who . . ."

"Matt, someone murdered this man, Pablo. His wife and friends don't even know it yet, and when they find out, what will happen? Who will help them? Do you think our police department, or the county police, or anyone for that matter, is going to care about a murdered illegal . . . or the wife he left behind? You know some of the attitudes around here. They'll probably just consider it one less problem to deal with."

"Whoa, lady! I don't know where you're headed with this, but I'm calling Curt on Monday morning and that'll be the end of it for *us*. Mystery solved. I found a body, we now are pretty certain we know who in the heck it is and we're done. What happens from here on out is none of our concern. Hon, I know what kind of person you are, and how you feel, and how dedicated you are, but there's nothing more we can do. Come on now, it's been a long day, we had a pleasant evening with some good friends and it's time to wrap it up. Let's go to bed . . .I'm whipped."

"Okay, but I . . ."

"Don't say it. I don't want to hear any more about this. Now let's get to bed."

By three A. M. I still hadn't slept and knew that Lindy was also awake, but I didn't acknowledge it. This was not the time for further discussion. Quietly, I slipped out of bed and headed upstairs. Music was called for to soothe the nerves and calm the brain. George Shearing's *How Beautiful the Night*, certainly not his greatest recording, but a very pretty and wonderfully-arranged session, would fill the bill nicely in these wee small hours of the morning.

Listening to the gentle music flow from this great musician, I couldn't help but become more and more concerned about Lindy's comments. It was obvious she was planning to somehow become involved in whatever happened with these people come Monday. I hadn't forgotten what Curt had said about the possibility of the Mexican Mafia's connection with this death. I'd have to be firm on this. Once Lindy had set her mind to something, it was difficult getting her to change it. This had to be the exception. The more I thought about it, the more I was convinced that there was the real possibility of danger to her if she intervened in any way.

No . . . she, we, could not get any further involved.

Chapter 13

By late Saturday afternoon, the atmosphere in the trailer was one of total despair.

Everyone, with the exception of Pablo, was in the trailer. María and Carlos were beginning to fear they would never see him again. Gina was beside herself with grief. She wanted to move into Rosa's trailer, but there simply was no room. Even so, she had remained there most of each day since Tuesday and spent the better portion of that time in tears.

José, Rosa's husband, or possibly Carlos, had scraped sufficient money together for beer, and the two men had been drinking steadily since noon. They'd also obtained cigarettes and frequently stepped outside for a smoke. The two of them hovered by the doorway in order to stay within earshot of the women; cigarette in one hand, a can of beer in the other.

Rosa, who had three children to care for, plus her husband, now had the additional responsibility of preparing meals for the four from Cárdenas, and was kept constantly busy. She tried several times to reassure the others that all would be well.

"José and I have been here for three years and no one, not one of us, has ever been harmed, isn't that right José?" she asked looking towards the doorway.

Her husband took a drag on his cigarette, and replied from just outside, "Si, es verdad. Yes, that is true."

"*Puede ser verdad*. It may be true," said Carlos, as he stood smoking just behind José, "but each one before has been able to pay *el hombre* everything. I have not and Pablo has paid nothing, *nada, nada, nada!* Pablo would not leave his wife. I know him like a brother. He would not do that. Something has happened." He then poked his head through the door and leaned into the trailer and whispered,, "*Algo muy malo pasó.* Something *very bad* has happened."

Hearing this, even though she wasn't meant to, Gina let out an agonizing scream which, in turn, startled all three of Rosa's children, and each began to cry. It was cool in the trailer. Staleness and the odor of cooking grease hung in the air. To this was now added the piercing wails of the children and Gina's distressing sobs.

"Stop," hissed Rosa. "Can't you see what you are doing by such talk? There is no need for it! Everything will be fine, you will see. Everything will be fine."

Rosa was unaware that her own husband had received threats from *el hombre* as the result of his falling behind in the trailer rent. She really had never heard of anyone being harmed, and truly believed that, in spite of what Carlos had said, Pablo had given up and run off. The situation was not all bad and would be better once the weather improved. José would return to full time work, and they could buy a heater and maybe a new refrigerator. Carlos would also work full time and he and María would rent their own trailer as originally planned. In the meantime, they were receiving food stamps, some money, and María's pregnancy care, along with her own children's government aid. They would make it somehow.

Rosa's day had begun as it did every day, preparing tortillas. Tortillas were the staff of life and eaten at every meal. When she had started her preparations this day, she realized with growing alarm that the fifty pound sack of cornmeal leaning against the refrigerator was now only a quarter full.

Each morning Rosa would knead the dry corn meal with water and salt. She'd pinch off enough for a single tortilla, roll it into a ball between her palms, and place each ball into a bowl. When she had enough tortillas for each meal of the day, she would cover the bowl with a damp towel.

When it came time to cook the tortillas, Rosa would place one of the balls in a small wooden press and flatten the dough to its proper size and thickness. Each tortilla was then fried. When there was enough money, she would boil a chicken in spices, shred the meat, and fill the tortillas with chicken and vegetables. For the past two weeks, for every meal, the only filling had consisted of red beans and rice, and now they were running low of even these staples. But *somehow*, she thought, as she fried the tortillas for dinner, *somehow with the help of God, it will be okay.*

By evening the beer was gone, the cigarette pack empty, and the tortillas fried and eaten. Gina reluctantly returned alone to the trailer where she was staying.

María had been quiet most of the day. Seeing her husband drunk again and smoking to excess, discouraged her. She found it difficult to be upset with him as she understood what was happening, but his behavior only contributed to her feeling of hopelessness.

At this point in the evening, the men were sitting in the two big chairs, drowsy, and beginning to feel the effects of a hangover. María and Rosa were watching TV with the volume turned low. The children were each asleep in the small bedroom.

María turned to Rosa and said, "I know we can do nothing about the weather. We can do nothing about if the men work. But Rosa, we should do something about. Pablo."

"About Pablo?" Rosa asked. "What can we do about Pablo?"

"Find him."

Rosa turned off the TV. "Find him? What are you saying? How are we going to do that?"

"*No sé.* I don't know," answered María. "But we have to do something. Gina cannot go on like this. She is going to die of agony. You saw what she ate tonight, practically nothing. Carlos and I are worried that something bad has happened."

There was silence in the trailer.

Eventually Rosa spoke, "We should contact the police to see if they can find him."

Both José and Carlos, who had been half listening to this

conversation, leaned forward in their chairs and hissed loudly in unison, "No!"

"*No policía!*" repeated Carlos. "It is too dangerous; they will send us back, for God's sake, especially if they find that something is wrong!"

María had the fleeting thought that the way things were going, being sent back may not be the worst thing that could happen. But they needed to stay. They had to stay. She believed in her heart it would eventually turn out to be the right decision. And she wanted, more than anything, for her baby to be born a United States citizen.

"*Señora Lindy,*" she said softly, "Lindy."

"What do you mean '*Señora Lindy*'?" said Rosa.

"She will help us."

"*¿Porqué, María*? Why should she do that? She does enough for us! What can she possibly do about Pablo?" asked Rosa.

"I don't know, but she is a good woman. At least we can ask her. She can tell us what we need to do."

An intense discussion ensued. Of all the alternatives considered by this confused and frightened little group, María's suggestion of calling Lindy finally won out.

Rosa went back to her bedroom and found Lindy's phone number in the cardboard box she kept under the bed. The box contained what few important papers they possessed.

The men were instructed to remain awake and listen for the children.

María and Rosa left the trailer and walked the long block to *la tienda*. Rosa requested a credit to her account and was given the coins needed to place the call to Lindy.

They didn't know, of course, where Lindy lived. They didn't know that Lindy was having a dinner party at that very moment. They didn't know if she could, or even would consider helping. They just knew that they didn't know what else to do.

Holding the telephone to her ear, Rosa carefully unfolded the note Lindy had given her three years earlier and dialed the hand written number on it.

Chapter 14

For Miguel Delgado, Saturdays had acquired an importance of religious proportions. It was play day; no business, none whatsoever. Those who worked for Miguel knew that to disrupt his Saturdays, unless it concerned a matter of life or death, was to incur his unforgiving wrath, and no one had ever taken the chance.

The Saturday itinerary seldom varied: golf from mid-morning to mid-afternoon with a quick club house sandwich at the turn, followed by a couple hours of poker in the locker room, a dash home to freshen up, and then back to the club for a couple of drinks in the men's bar prior to dining in the club's renowned dining room.

His club membership, now in its third year, had not come easy. Well, actually, when all was said and done, it hadn't been all that difficult. It had just taken a little ground work, followed by a heart to heart chat with the club president, Louis Lusch IV, who also happened to be chairman of the club's board. Four generations of family residence in the area, combined with a large fortune and the finest of educations, entitled Louis Lusch IV to a privileged and prestigious position in the upper stratosphere of North Carolina's coastal society.

Delgado vividly recalled his initial and subsequent conversations (there were only two) with Lusch:

On his first visit he had been ushered into Lusch's posh office at the club by Lusch's attractive secretary, Myrna. Delgado pegged her age in the mid-thirties, and her bust line in the somewhat higher thirties. He took particular notice of such things. He also took note that Lusch enjoyed luxurious surroundings. Even for a prestigious country club, his office was regal. The furnishings were fashioned of heavy leather in dark greens and maroons with aged, polished wood; most likely all original pieces dating back to when the club had been built. On the walls, each with individual lighting, hung original oils of Jones, Hogan, Snead, Palmer and Nicholas. In the dimly lit room each beautifully executed portrait stood out.

Myrna introduced Miguel to Mr. Louis Lusch IV then left, leaving the door slightly ajar.

"Please sit down Mr. Garcia," offered Lusch.

"Delgado."

"I'm sorry?" replied Lusch.

"The name is Delgado, not Garcia."

"Oh, yes, well... have a seat."

Delgado's blood had already reached its boiling point, but he successfully struggled in maintaining his cool.

"Thanks," Delgado said. "If you don't mind, as I know you're a busy guy, I'll get straight to the point. I *intend* to join The Poseidon Golf and Yacht Club."

There was a pause. Lusch was trying to recall if he had ever previously been referred to as a *guy*. He didn't think so.

"You *intend* to join?" He eventually responded.

"Yes."

"Mr. . . ."

"Delgado."

"Yes, of course, Mr. . . . Delgado. You should be aware that The Poseidon is a closed club. By that I mean we have a limited membership of 150–no more, no less. This tenet, to which there has never been an exception, was written into the original charter of the club in 1918 by the founding members, one of whom was my great grandfather."

"I understand," replied Delgado. "But there's occasionally an opening if a member should leave the area or die, right?"

"It hasn't happened in many years. Memberships are willed to heirs or sold to family members. But even when that occurs, the prospective member must be approved by the board. However, I can't think of an instance where the board has not approved an heir, or the sale to a family member."

"Okay, but on the outside chance a membership was to open up, what's the financial arrangement?"

Lusch hesitated, and then decided there would be no harm in revealing the membership arrangement to this apparent wetback he'd never see again.

"It's quite simple," he responded. "The initial membership fee is one hundred thousand dollars." He hesitated again, waiting for the shocked expression to register on the wetback's face. Disappointed that there was not one, he continued. "There are no annual dues as such. Each member is simply assessed annually for his share of the club's annual operating expenses. To be frank, it's normally a rather considerable amount."

Delgado knew what Lusch must have been thinking; *Well, that should take care of this hot-shot wetback.*

"Yeah, I imagine it would be. But, like I said, I intend to become a member, and, *to be frank*, sooner, rather than later."

"I see," replied Lusch with a smirk that said it all . . . *Over my dead body.*

"If you would, please give Myrna your card as you leave. In the unlikely event there should happen to be an opening, we'll be sure to give you a call. However, I must say in all candidness, that I seriously doubt if that will happen in the foreseeable future."

"One never knows Louie, one never knows. Thanks for your time."

After Delgado left, Myrna poked her head into her boss's office. "That man gave me the creeps."

"I experienced some creepiness myself," said Lusch. "However, Myrna, I don't think we'll be seeing the likes of him again."

It took two weeks.

Two days after meeting with the crude Mexican, or whatever he was, Louis Lusch IV flew first class from Wilmington, North Carolina, to Charlotte. There he caught a connecting flight to Las Vegas to attend a convention of country club presidents which was being held at the luxurious Bellagio. Coincidently, it also seems that one Myrna Patton, the one with the high thirties bust line, traveled tourist class on those very same flights. Louis Lusch had a suite reserved at the Bellagio. Myrna had a nice enough room, but it was off the strip and a few blocks removed from the string of luxury hotels.

᠅

Two weeks to the day after they had first met, Delgado returned to The Poseidon Golf and Yacht Club for what would be his second and last chat with Louis Lusch IV. He appeared without an appointment, walked past Myrna's desk and headed straight into Lusch's office.

Lusch stood up as Delgado entered. "I don't recall your having an appoint . . ."

"Sit down," ordered Delgado.

Something in Delgado's voice made Lusch realize it would be best to do as requested.

"I'll make this quick and easy," said Delgado, placing a brief case on Lusch's desk.

He opened it, removed a portable DVD player and set the brief case on the floor.

"What's that?" inquired Lusch, looking at the DVD player.

"Oh, you haven't seen a Digital Video Disc player? It's the latest technology, Lou. It replaces that old VCR stuff. You can store a couple hours of video on one little disc like this." He showed Lusch the disc. "Amazing, simply amazing. The picture quality is terrific. You can even make copies very quickly, just in case you want to share with friends and family, or other club members. Hey, you're really gonna love this Louie."

Flipping open the screen, he slipped the disc in, hit play, and slowly, very slowly began to turn the DVD unit toward Lusch.

In a hushed, dramatic tone, Delgado spoke as the screen slowly came into Lusch's view. "And now ladies and gentlemen, for your viewing pleasure, direct from their recent scintillating appearance in Las Vegas, Nevada, The Poseidon Golf and Yacht Club proudly presents, the exciting, the absolutely sexsational, Louie and Myrna Show! Okay, let's give it up for this lovely couple! Come on now, let's hear a huge round of applause!"

Louis Lusch IV's eyes were riveted to the screen as it came to a stop directly in front of him.

Delgado's icy stare did not leave Lusch's face. He watched as the face turned from off white to ashen. He watched as beads of sweat broke out across the forehead. He watched as Lusch's lips began to quiver. He watched as Lusch's entire head began to twitch.

Still staring at Lusch, he reached into his jacket pocket, removed his check book, his gold Mont Blanc pen, and asked, "Now Louie, just how should I make out this membership check? Oh, and before I forget, how about if we commission a nice oil of Trevino for the wall? Tell you what Lou baby; I'll even spring for it."

❧❦❧

Following Delgado's visit, Lusch was not seen at the club for several days. Upon returning, he contacted the other board members, most of whom were family or life-long friends. He told each, in his well-rehearsed explanation, that he was receiving considerable pressure and advice from friends in D.C. and Raleigh, and that it would be advisable to accept a member or two of a minority persuasion into TPG&YC. He had a candidate in mind, he told them, one who "Wasn't that noticeably of a minority appearance, if you understand my meaning." They did. "Actually, he's a Latino of rather fair complexion, with not the slightest trace of an accent," he told them. Each board member, after exhibiting initial disgruntlement, told Lusch they'd reluctantly go along if he felt it absolutely necessary, and that they'd leave the selection up to him. The following week, TPG&YC's membership ranks totaled 151 for the first time since its founding in 1918.

❧

On this particular Saturday, Delgado was well into his routine and playing with three members he had befriended over the past couple of years. They seemed to accept him, and there was no question that they certainly enjoyed accepting his money upon his infrequent loss in a round. It was his regular Saturday morning foursome. These were younger members, ones who didn't appear to carry the burden of the historical prejudices of prior generations.

It had been five days since the body's discovery in the Intracoastal and the news coverage was minimal. The Wilmington Star-News ran a small article, buried well into the first section, a day after the body was discovered. To the best of Delgado's knowledge, not one of the Wilmington or Myrtle Beach TV or radio stations had even bothered to pick up the story. It was already a non-event. That alone, in spite of the rain, had him in a good frame of mind this Saturday. It looked as though Collinson had handled something right for a change.

They were playing in a constant drizzle. Even so, the foursome had foregone using carts as each golfer had his own caddy. The club, of course, had carts, but in a nod toward tradition, their use was frowned upon, even in the rain.

Delgado's regular caddy had not shown up, it was assumed, due to the weather.

The caddy master, Charlie, had stuck Delgado with a rookie at TPG&YC, and of all things he was a Mexican kid at that. Delgado felt certain it was Charlie's way of sending a message, *We really don't ever forget who and what you are.* He'd have to deal with Charlie later.

During the first few holes, Delgado spoke little to the caddy, only enough to find out he had some experience, and to ask for the club he wanted on each shot.

Towards the end of the first nine, something began to bug

Delgado, but he couldn't put his finger on it.

They had their usual quick sandwich at the turn and attempted to dry off.

Delgado was leaning over his putt on the 10th green when it struck him. He backed off the putt and stared over at the caddy. It had to be. He approached the ball again, stroked it and watched as it ran a good 15 feet past the hole. He missed his next putt and wound up taking a double bogey, a rarity for him.

On the eleventh hole he intentionally drove his tee shot into the woods. While under the pretense of looking for the ball, Delgado said to the caddy, "Back on seven or eight, you used my name, *Señor Delgado*. How do you know my name?"

If the kid had been a quick thinker, he would have told Delgado that the caddy master had told him, or that he had overheard one of the players in the foursome. But he didn't, and realized instantly that he had made a big mistake. He was at a loss for words, and stood there, his mouth open.

"Well?" insisted Delgado.

"Los Angeles, Señor," he replied.

"What about Los Angeles?"

"My brother Antonio, he worked for you."

Delgado was momentarily stunned. "Is your last name Domingo?"

"Si Señor."

Delgado couldn't believe it. Antonio Domingo had indeed worked for him in L.A., but still . . .

"So, how did you know it was me?" he asked, controlling his anger.

"You and my brother were playing golf. I was caddying in the foursome behind you. My brother, he pointed you out to me, Señor."

Of all the dumb fucking luck thought Delgado. This had been his worst fear since arriving in the southeast. Over the last three years he had taken every precaution to conceal his previous situation on the west coast.

"How did you wind up here?"

"Antonio wanted me out of L.A. He thought I might get in

some trouble there. He sent me here to live with our cousin."

"How'd you get this job?"

"It's what I do, Señor. I told the caddy master of the courses that I worked in California. He hired me two days ago when he needed another caddie. He called me."

The caddy didn't know it, but Delgado did. The call this kid had received from Charlie, the caddy master, was the unluckiest call the kid ever would receive.

"So, what's your first name?" he casually asked.

"Pipo."

"I see. Okay Pipo, I need to trust you. Don't ever, I repeat, don't ever mention that you know me. You don't mention this to your cousin when you get home, and you don't tell your brother. It's our secret. *¿Comprendes?*" asked Delgado in a friendly tone, giving the caddy a confidential wink.

"*Sí Señor Delgado.*"

Delgado knew he was simply buying time, a few hours at best–but that would be enough.

"Okay Pipo, get another ball out, and place it more towards the edge. Then holler over to me that you *found* it." He gave Pipo a bigger wink. "Then we'll get back on the fairway and whip those gringos' asses."

"*Sí Señor,*" said Pipo grinning from ear to ear. He couldn't believe his good fortune. He had met *the* Señor Delgado, the *hombre número uno*, and not only that, he was sharing an important secret with him! As he pulled out a new ball, one with the same number as the lost ball, Pipo still had a huge grin across his face... *How lucky can a guy get?*

ૠૡ

The crisis Delgado now faced was the biggest he'd confronted since moving to the southeast. On the last eight holes he played so poorly that he finished with his worst round since joining the club.

After the eighteenth, he paid off his bets then asked Pipo to "Stick around for a few minutes, maybe we can grab a bite and talk about the L. A. days. I'll pick you up at the caddy shack."

"That'd be great," said Pipo . . . and he meant it.

Pipo went to the shack only to find it closed. It was late afternoon and the rain had increased; no one else would be going out. He sat under the overhang of the caddy shack and waited excitedly for Señor Delgado.

Rather than going to the bar, the foursome had a drink out of the bottles each kept in his locker. After the ritual ribbing, and a couple of drinks, the others left the club. Delgado had told them he was going to clean up and grab a quick shower as he had some stops to make on his way home. He was buying time.

After checking to make certain no one else was in the locker room, he showered. In the few years he had been a member, he had not once showered when there were others around; there were the tattoos to consider. He could have had them removed, but wanted to keep them as reminders of his humble beginnings.

Once outside, he saw a couple of cars in the parking lot, most likely staff, as all the golfers had left and it was too early for the dinner crowd.

He got into his Town Car, continuing to check for signs of anyone about. When he saw no one, he drove to the caddy shack and spotted Pipo waiting for him underneath the overhang.

He pulled up beside the shack and Pipo got in.

"You hungry?" Delgado asked, taking another look around.

"You bet!" Pipo replied.

Because of his position, Delgado shouldn't have to do this. He'd rather have someone else do the dirty work, but there was no time, no alternative. He couldn't take the chance that the kid would talk.

They drove off, Pipo with a broad smile of anticipation. He was going to have dinner with el Señor Delgado!

They drove north. Delgado was familiar with this stretch of road, consisting mostly of pine trees and marshland, and knew where he wanted to stop. When they were in the vicinity, he told Pipo, that in spite of the rain, he needed to take a leak. He suggested to Pipo that he also go, as they had some distance to travel yet.

Pipo didn't have to, but if that's what Señor Delgado wanted, he would try. Delgado walked over to a pine tree, stopped, unzipped and started to pee. Pipo picked a tree close by; it turned out that he had to go after all.

With Pipo concentrating on the task at hand, with a couple of swift moves, Delgado was directly behind Pipo. He shot him three times in the back of the head, then put the boy's body in the trunk of the Town Car and took the short drive to the river.

After disposing of the body, he drove home and showered for the second time that day. He decided he'd clean the trunk of the Town Car in the morning.

Later that evening in the men's bar, Allan, his golf partner, came in for a quick drink and invited Delgado to join his table for dinner.

"Great, I'd love to Allan, but only on the condition that dinner's on me."

Allan laughed. "There are eight of us Miguel, nine with you. I can promise you it's going to be an incredibly outrageous and indecent tab."

"That's okay, after my embarrassing performance today I deserve nothing but all the cruel and unjust punishment you can give me. I can't believe how crappy I played!"

Throughout dinner, Delgado was in fine spirits, told several risqué stories appropriate for mixed company, and even ordered the club's finest champagne for the table.

Driving home he felt good. Without question it had been a close call, but he had handled it quickly, which was what the situation had required.

Everything was under control.

Chapter 15

"**O**kay, it's five bucks for the first keeper, five bucks for the most, and five for the biggest," explained T. L. as we made the turn into the waterway. We had just finished netting some live bait in the canal.

Tommy Lee, Karl Vogelsang and I had decided during last night's dinner to do some off-shore fishing today. We were taking Tommy Lee's boat, a Grady White with two 250 HP Johnson engines and every piece of navigational and fish locating equipment imaginable. The rig reflected T. L's insatiable passion for fishing and boating. The plan was to head out to the Gulf Stream, about forty miles, pick up some King and Spanish mackerel, and if we got lucky, maybe a Mahi-Mahi or two.

The bait fish had been plentiful, with several large schools skirting the water. Using a casting net, I'd quickly caught enough to last the day.

"You do pretty good with that thing," Karl observed.

"You want to give it a go?" I asked.

He did. After a few awkward attempts, each resulting in a mangle of net, line and lead weights, Karl handed it back to me in a twisted mess.

"I didn't realize this fishing stuff required so much skill," he laughed.

"I hope to hell you know how to bait your own hook," T. L. said from behind the wheel.

"I do if you have some worms on board."

"Worms? Ah shit, Karl, you've never been out before, have you?"

"Nope. Remember, I'm from Indiana; we catch bluegills and catfish on worms."

"Bluegills and catfish, now there's some real sport fishing for you," chuckled T.L.

"Good eating though," answered Karl.

"Boy, you'll find out what good eating's all about if the gods smile on us today," countered T.L. "We'll be going out about forty or fifty miles."

T.L. opened both throttles. "She's pretty slick today, should be at my first spot in a couple of hours."

Karl and I were seated on the starboard rail. "This is the part I hate," I hollered over to Karl, above the roar of the engines.

"How's that?" Karl shouted back.

"You'll see," I yelled.

Some guys become euphoric on the water, crashing through swell after swell at high speeds in search of fish. Not me. Having my guts turned upside down, walking like a Neanderthal and communicating by bellowed shouts just isn't my idea of fun. If it weren't for the possibility of picking up some great, fresh fish, I'd just as soon pass. On the other hand, there's the camaraderie. When you get down to it, that's what it's mostly about, at least for me.

"Who's buying?" shouted T.L., turning back to us.

"What did he say?" yelled Karl.

"Our captain desires a beer!" I shouted back.

Karl looked at his watch.

"We don't go by the time," I yelled. "We go by distance. We've determined that six feet from our dock is just about right for the first beer!"

Karl grinned and shook his head.

I lunged towards the Styrofoam cooler, desparately clutched it with both hands, steadied myself, lifted the lid, quickly stabbed around for three beers, stumbled forward, gave one to T.L., swaggered back to Karl, handed him his, grabbed the arm of a deck chair, swung myself around and successfully plopped my butt in the seat. *God, what fun!*

We had been underway less than an hour when Karl sprang up, grasped the side rail, and leaned over.

I shouted to T.L. He turned, saw Karl's condition and cut back the engines.

"You okay?" I asked, poking my head over the side. Karl was a shade of green I'd never seen."

He turned his head and shot me a look. "Now I know what you meant about this being the part you hate the most."

He pulled himself together slowly, and gingerly collapsed in the chair next to me.

"I can tell you one thing," he said. "This kind of thing never happened, not once, standing on the bank of the White River in Indianapolis."

"Listen y'all," said Tommy Lee, "we're only about seven miles out. As much as I hate to, let's change plans. I'd still like to get some fishing in, so let's just troll slowly for some Spanish and see how Karl holds up. If we have to go in, we go in."

That was fine with me. Karl gave a nod of approval.

T.L. rigged the lines, set them out and we started trolling.

"Sorry," said Karl, looking at T.L.

"Hey, it happens to the best of us. I've seen guys who've been doing this for twenty years run for the rail. With any luck, we'll pick up our limit of some nice Spanish and be in sooner than expected, no problem."

At least now, with the engines cut back, we could walk and talk. After a while Karl managed to get a few cheese crackers down and was feeling much improved.

"Hey," said T.L., "I forgot to thank you again for dinner. That was one hell of a spread you and Lindy laid on us last night."

"It was that," agreed Karl.

"Thanks, we enjoyed having you guys over." I hesitated, then decided I may as well fill them in. By the time we docked, it would be late Sunday afternoon and I'd be calling the chief first thing in the morning.

"Listen guys, Lindy and I are pretty sure we know who that

dead illegal guy is."

They both looked at me expectantly, neither saying a word.

I gave them the rundown, starting with the phone call we'd received the previous evening, and was finishing up, when suddenly, the line on the far left stern began to sing.

"Karl, grab that rod!" T. L. commanded.

Karl hurried back, pulled the rod from its holder and started working the reel. The line immediately went slack.

"Reel 'er in fast Karl, he might be makin' a run in towards us."

Karl rapidly did as T. L. instructed, and the line tightened.

"He's still on, and it sure as hell ain't no bluegill!" laughed T.L.

"Matt, take the wheel and bring her around real slow so I can gaff Karl's whale."

It took Karl some time to bring his catch close enough for us to get a decent look. It was a large King, still fighting.

"Don't give it any slack Karl," T. L. instructed, "he'll snap the line. Damn, look at that beauty! It's tournament size!" Karl eventually worked the King along side the boat, T.L. gaffed it, brought it up and threw it into the large cooler where it violently thrashed about.

"Welcome to the wonderful, wide, world of Atlantic sport fishing my man!" beamed T.L., giving Karl a high five.

"That was great," said Karl. "Really, it was terrific." He was all smiles. "What do you think it weighs?"

"My guess would be about thirty to thirty-five pounds, maybe more. They get a lot bigger, but that's a fine catch. Now, who's buying? We gotta celebrate the Hoosier's first genuine fish!"

"I'll pass for now," replied Karl. "Maybe I'll have one on the way in. I'd rather not put myself to the test yet."

T.L. reset the lines and we trolled for another half hour with no action.

"Tell you what," said T.L., "nothing's happening and I don't see anything showing on the screen. We'll troll back in, hate to do it though. To tell you the truth boys; I could stay out on the water forever."

I thought: *Not with me along, please, dear God.*

T. L. executed a slow turn, asked me to take the wheel, got a beer for both of us and sat down beside me. Karl stayed in the rear, declining the offer of another beer.

"Anyway, getting back to your story Matt, you and Lindy think it's this guy who's a friend of an illegal Lindy knows?"

"Right. I'm calling the chief in the morning. He can check it out."

"Well, if it is, that should pretty much wrap things up."

"You might think so, and I definitely think so, but my bleeding heart wife is concerned about the others."

"What others?"

"The dead guy's wife, the girl and her husband who were close friends with the dead guy, another couple with three kids. . ."

"Wait Matt, Jesus, what can Lindy do? Why should she do anything? I mean let's face it; these people bring it on themselves. They come up here not knowing where in the hell they're even going, what they're going to do once they get where ever in the hell it is, and on top of that, they don't even speak the friggin' language. They don't know diddly-squat about nothing, and yet they still come up, by the thousands, expecting us, mind you, *expecting us*, to take care of them. Gimme a break."

"I know," I said, now regretting I had brought the subject up.

"Matt, I'm not in the dark on this stuff . . . you want another beer?" T.L. asked.

"No thanks."

"Be right back."

"You okay?" T.L. asked Karl.

"I'm fine, thanks."

"No, I mean are you feeling okay?"

"Oh, yes, much better."

T. L. returned and handed me the un-requested beer.

"Do you know," he said, picking up where he had left off, "that in California the Latino vote, don't you just love it, repeat after me, the *Latino vote*, will soon be the largest voter block in the friggin' state? They'll run friggin' California! I'm telling y'all, da shit's gonna hit da fan! I read somewhere that there's something like 700,000 coming in each year, 700 friggin damn thousand! Do you know how many *illegals* there are in North Carolina?"

"Yes," I said.

"Take a guess."

"Somewhere over 350,000," I replied.

"Not even close Matt, somewhere around 450,000 is more like it, maybe even more than that, just here in friggin' North Carolina!"

T.L. was again working himself into a frenzy, and I decided my best bet was to remain quiet and let him get it out of his system.

"Let me ask you another question."

So much for that plan, I thought.

"Okay, there are people all over the world who want to get here, lots of good, fine, folks. Some of them have been waiting a hell of a long time . . . years. Why should these wetbacks be allowed to cut in line in front of them? Answer me that! You see those buoys at two o'clock?"

"Huh?"

"The red and green buoys," said T. L., head for them. That's the entrance to the Lockwood Folly Inlet. So, tell me why they should be able to cut in line."

"Come on T. L, you know I can't answer that question," I said.

"Tommy Lee," interrupted Karl.

"Yeah, Karl?"

"There are a couple of other things you need to consider."

"Such as . . . and I can't wait to hear this."

"Such as the fact that this country was formed by, and continues to be recreated by, immigrants. It's a national strength. It's *our* national strength. They, our ancestors, all those immigrants over the years, they shaped our country."

"But those guys came here legally, right? They didn't sneak in here like all these wetbacks."

"Most yes, some no. T. L., these people are doing jobs, tough jobs that no one else will do. That's a fact. And they're adding to the cultural diversity of our country, which is one of the things that makes this country what it is. Our national culture gets stronger.

Thank God. I think I'll have that beer now."

"Thank God for the culture or for the beer?" I asked

"Wait, hold it, back up," T. L. said, quickly thrusting his arm out like a traffic cop.

"*Cultural diversity*? What the hell," he continued looking at me. "Is your buddy Karl here a professor or something . . . *cultural diversity*?"

"As a matter of fact T. L., Karl has a doctorate in . . ."

"Whoa, there ya go, say no more, now I understand."

Karl smiled. "One last thing T. L., and then I'll shut the hell up. I asked you something last night, and you sloughed it off. But, let me ask you again. Suppose, for a minute, you're Mexican, you're living in absolute filth, and you've got starvin' kids and a hungry wife. You hear that if you can make it to the US there will be work, your family will have food and you'll have a place for you and your family to live. The question is, what would you do under those circumstances?"

"What would I do?" T.L. grinned, trying to lighten things up. "No question about it, I'd have another cool one."

"No, really," Karl asked, pressing the point.

"Really? Well Karl, I have to tell you, you can bet your sweet ass I'd get the hell out at first opportunity."

"Exactly, end of discussion," replied Karl.

"But that doesn't mean we shouldn't try to stop it, or at least put some kind of damn controls on it for Christ's sake. We've gotta get control." T.L. had made his final point.

They both turned to me.

"Hey, don't look this way for any profound words of wisdom. I ain't got the slightest damn clue as to the answer."

"It's a pretty day, let's just have a nice 'n easy cruise back in, okay?" said T.L wanting to stay on the water as long as possible.

We both nodded in agreement.

It had wound up being a friendly discussion with no hard feelings, each recognizing there were no simple solutions to what was a very complex problem.

We tied up at Tommy Lee's dock and off-loaded the coolers and tackle.

Karl hosed down the equipment while T.L. and I cleaned the boat.

T.L. got the King out. "Rather than filets, how about I just slice us some nice steaks?"

"Sounds great, Tommy Lee," I replied.

"Listen T.L.," said Karl, "I'm sorry about screwing things up, but thanks for a great day." He extended his hand to T.L. "Except for my little comeuppance, I enjoyed the hell out of it."

"No problem. Glad you caught the fish."

"Right, that reminds me . . ."

"Reminds you of what?"

Karl stood holding the plastic bag of King steaks high in the air, swinging it back and forth. He smiled at T.L., then turned and smiled at me.

"Ah shit, I don't believe it!" roared Tommy Lee.

"Ah man, I don't either," I said in mock disgust.

"Hey, I didn't set the rules," said Karl.

T.L. and I each pulled out our wallets and handed Karl fifteen bucks.

✶✷✶

Lindy was in the kitchen preparing a salad when I came through the back door.

"I saw the boat come in, you're back early."

"Karl got his first taste, literally, of offshore fishing."

"Oh my, he got sick?"

"Yup."

"Poor Karl; so other than that, how'd it go?"

"Well, it was slow, but we didn't get skunked. How about a couple of grilled King Mackerel steaks tonight?"

"That sounds terrific."

"Listen Hon, after dinner I'm probably going to crash, or go up and listen to a little music and then crash–these offshore trips are beginning to beat me up."

"Okay, so you want to tell me something now?"

"Yeah, here's the deal: we both know what's going to happen

75

tomorrow, right? My concern is that your friends are going to come running to you once the police make contact with them."

"I've been thinking about that," she said.

"So you're prepared to tell them that there's nothing you can do, right?"

There was an uneasy pause.

"Lindy," I turned my head to look directly at her. "We're talking about a murder here. We're talking about possible Mafia involvement, we're talking . . ."

"Oh Matt, for heaven's sake! You don't think I'd get involved in any of that stuff! How or why would *that* happen? But if they need me, if there is some way I can help them get through this terrible ordeal, well, I'll just have to see what's what."

"You're going to wing it?"

"Right, play it by ear."

"Lindy, promise me you won't do anything until after we talk tomorrow, after we see what's going on."

She paused, then said, "Okay."

"*Okay*" was apparently as good as I was going to get.

Chapter 16

"Lindy, *please report to the front desk. Lindy, to the front desk.*"

It had been the usual hectic Monday morning. Lindy was finishing lunch in the break room when she heard the page. Passing through the maze of corridors into the main hallway, she saw a sheriff's deputy standing by the entrance.

As she approached, she looked over to the receptionist who nodded her head toward the deputy, and Lindy went straight to him. "Yes?" she asked.

"You're Lindy, the interpreter?" he asked.

"Lindy Paskins, yes."

"Excuse me ma'am, but I need you come with me."

"Am I under arrest?" she asked, half jokingly.

"No ma'am."

"Well, could you tell me what this about, where it is you want to me to go, and how long it will take? I'm really needed here this afternoon."

"I've already cleared that ma'am, and I can fill you in on the way."

Lindy hesitated, and walked over to the receptionist.

"Do you know what this is about?" she asked.

"No idea," replied the receptionist. "But you've been cleared here for the rest of the day. I've got a couple of messages here for you."

"They'll have to wait. This guy looks like he's in a hurry. I'll get them when I come back for my car."

She went back her desk, picked up her purse, and left with the Officer.

⚮

Rather than call the chief, I decided to walk to the station. It was a two mile hike, but as I walk four to five miles a day anyway, it made sense to kill two birds with one stone.

"Why in the hell didn't you call me Saturday night?" roared Chief Curt Everhart, when I'd finished my story.

"Excuse me Chief, but it was late Saturday night and I thought I was doing you a favor by *not* calling, same with Sunday for that matter."

The chief was clearly pissed.

"And here it is Monday morning, 10 A. M., and you come waltzing into my office with this information just as though you were taking a delightful little stroll on the beach."

"Well, I got a late start, and as a matter of fact, I did walk."

"You walked." It was a statement.

"Yes."

"No urgency." Another statement.

"I didn't think so."

He remained behind his desk, glaring.

Finally he said, exasperation clearly in his voice, "Ah Matt, I wish to hell you had called me."

"I'm sorry Chief, but…"

"No, no, there's no way you could have known."

"Known what?"

"We have another one."

"Another what?" I asked.

"Floater."

"Floater?"

"Another body Matt. Another dead Mexican. Shot."

"Oh good God. Where? When?"

"Technically, it's not our case. I got a call early this morning

78

from the county sheriff's office. They pulled a body out of the Cape Fear River. So we're out of it . . . sorta."

"I don't understand."

"It was a kid Matt, or a very young man."

"Yeah?"

"He'd been shot three times, just like ours."

"Oh shit, same shooter?"

"Don't know yet. They'll run ballistics today to determine if there's a match. If I'd had your information first thing, I could have told them there's a lead on the ID of our body."

"Damn, I'm sorry Chief, I really am."

"I'll call the sheriff now."

"Okay." I got up to leave.

"Listen Matt, your information was late coming in, but thanks, it could be a big help. The county will probably send an officer out to pick up your wife and those people she knows and take them up to Jacksonville for a positive ID.

"Jacksonville?"

"That's where the morgue is. The state has possession of the body."

"Well, again, sorry I didn't notify you sooner."

"Matt, there's something nasty going on here, something we haven't seen around here before, and I don't like it one bit."

Walking home at a brisk pace I knew the first thing I had to do was to call Lindy and bring her up to date and warn her she might be asked to go to Jacksonville. I placed the call and was told she and a doctor were with a patient, but she'd be given the message shortly.

"Thanks," I said, and hung up.

I looked at the phone, considered calling back to tell the receptionist it was important that Lindy call me, but decided it wasn't all that necessary.

Chapter 17

"It was awful Matt, just awful. When we got in the officer's car and I asked him where we were going and he said Sand Dunes Harbor Park I knew, I just knew! The officer explained to me that they chose me because Chief Everhart told them I knew the people involved. Oh, God it was just awful!"

We were in our rockers on the front porch. I'd poured a screwdriver for myself and Lindy had opted for a gin and tonic. Her eyes were puffy, and she had tears again.

"I'm sorry, Hon. Did you call them on the way to their trailer?"

"No. They don't have a phone, and the Officer said it would be best if we just showed up. I did have him turn off the blue flashing light. That would've scared them to death."

"Did they tell you at the clinic that I'd called?"

"No, but I know there were some messages I didn't see. I didn't even go back in for them; I just wanted to come home."

"Well, it wouldn't have changed anything if you'd gotten mine, but it might have given you a heads up that you'd be needed to do the interpreting."

"When we got to the trailer, they all came piling out. Rosa with her three kids, María and poor Gina. Carlos and José were out looking for work."

"How'd you explain it to them?"

"Believe me, I thought about what to say the whole time it

took us to get there, but I still couldn't come up with the right words. I tried as gently as I could to explain to them that since Pablo had been missing for so long, that it was necessary for Gina to come with us to identify someone. Rosa asked, 'What do you mean identify, is the person alive?"

"When I said 'no,' it dawned on Gina what was happening, and she screamed. We got her into the car and then María said she'd go with us. I thought that was a good idea since they are such close friends.

"The trip to Jacksonville was just terrible, both of them cried almost all the way. When we got to the morgue and Gina looked at the body and saw that it was Pablo, she let out a heart-wrenching scream and passed out."

"I'm sorry, Hon. Was anything ever mentioned about why they thought he was killed?"

"María told me it's because Pablo hadn't paid any money yet for getting here. It cost them fifteen hundred dollars in Mexico, which they paid before they left, then another thousand is due at this end. Even working full-time, it would take forever to pay off what they owe. They're certain that the people, the ones who got them here, are behind this."

"The Mafia ?" I asked

"I don't know Matt, they never mentioned that, they referred to 'el hombre' several times, whoever that is."

"Probably the local guy who takes care of things around here for the mob."

"When we got back, Gina moved into Rosa's trailer, That means there are eight of them living in it. They're scared Matt, particularly now for María's husband, Carlos, who owes a lot of money to these very same people. I can't imagine what will happen with Gina, she'll have to start making some money, maybe as a cleaning lady or working with the pickers, who knows. But she's in no condition to do anything for a while."

"And if Carlos doesn't start paying . . ."

"Exactly, he could be next on the list."

"There's something else you should know; when I saw Curt this morning, he told me they'd found another body, this one in the

Cape Fear River."

"That's pretty far from us, is there a connection?"

"Well, they think the body is that of a Mexican, a kid actually, and they think it might have been another professional job."

"I don't understand, what's going on?"

"No one knows, Hon. But at least the police do know that it was Pablo who was killed, and have a pretty good idea why. This other thing may not be tied into it. They'll start an investigation and hopefully it'll lead to whoever is behind this mess."

"Matt, we're talking about illegals here, at least in Pablo's case. How much of an investigation do you think there will be?"

"Well, all we can do is hope the law gets a handle on what's happening and put an end to it. Anything's possible."

Lindy was staring at the sunset. It was turning out to be another beauty with multiple layers of long narrow streaks of orange across the sky and the waterway looking as though it were on fire once again.

It was several moments before she spoke.

When she did, I heard her speak softly, "It's those poor people who are important. That's what matters . . ."

I clearly heard her, but quite honestly, was hesitant to ask exactly what she meant by it.

Chapter 18

I checked in with Chief Everhart a couple of times over the course of the week. No progress had been made on finding Pablo's killer, but the body of the boy found in the Cape Fear River had been ID'd–a cousin had reported the kid missing. When the cousin was taken to the morgue in Jacksonville, his worst fears were confirmed.

The more I thought about it, the more I couldn't shake the feeling that somehow or other the two murders were related and I was curious to know if the chief had similar thoughts.

"Hell yes," he said from across his desk, or rather, from over the tip of his shoes.

It was late Friday afternoon and Chief Curt Everhart's size twelve's were propped on his desk, he was leaning back precariously in his chair and was clearly in the process of enjoying a cigar.

"Mind if I join you?" I asked.

"Nope."

We both sat and stared. It took a few awkward seconds before it dawned on the chief that I wasn't carrying.

"Oh, you need one?"

"Well . . ."

He handed me the box; I made a selection and lit up.

"Anyway, yes," he picked up on the conversation. "Two bodies, two Mexican bodies, both shot in a like manner, both found floating, both found within a week of each other and both recent arrivals to our area. So hell yes, there are similarities...I don't know if the two are related, but there are definite similarities."

"What have you learned about the boy?" I asked.

"His cousin said he'd only been here for a couple of days. The kid's brother sent him here from L.A., before he got into trouble out there. This cousin says he was a good kid and that he'd just started caddying the day he disappeared."

"Where'd he caddy?"

"Out at the Poseidon."

"Whoa. Talk about starting in high cotton!" I exclaimed.

"Yep, right at the top."

"So he caddied for the first time there and never went home, back to his cousin's?"

"You got it. He was supposed to call after he was finished. The call never came."

"What kind of trouble were they afraid he'd get into out in L.A.?"

"You sure ask a lot of questions," grumbled the chief.

"It's the cigar, puts me in an inquisitive frame of mind."

"Let's step outside, Matt; with the two of us smoking in here it looks like a foggy day in London Town."

"You ever heard Sinatra's *Foggy Day*? I asked.

"Yeah, but Torme's got him beat on that one."

We went outside. Although half a block from the ocean, we could hear the surf and see the gulls hovering above a small group of fisherman fishing off the pier.

"So what's next?" I asked.

"We try and find a connection. It's a little awkward to be honest, with two different agencies involved, but we get along good, so it should work."

"Chief, I got an idea. May I ramble for a minute?"

"You mean like a *stream of consciousness* kind of thing?" he asked sarcastically.

"Uh-huh," I said.

"Sure, shoot."

I paused, drew a puff, exhaled, not sure where I was headed

with this. "Let's assume that our earlier speculation is correct. Pablo was killed not just because he didn't come up with the money, but also because someone wanted to make an example to others about what could happen if *they* don't pay."

"Okay, that's reasonable, and that happens to be what I believe."

"So," I continued, "the question is: what is the possible connection between Pablo and the caddy?" I was about to continue when one of the officers, Collinson, came out.

"You got a call, Chief."

"Hold on a minute Dean, go on Matt, but make it quick"

"If there's a connection between the two, my guess would be that the caddy knew, or suspected, who killed Pablo. That's why he was murdered, so he wouldn't talk."

"Uh huh, brilliant, but you're forgetting something Sherlock. The caddy had just arrived here. This Pablo of yours was killed, what, a couple of weeks ago now? The caddy probably hadn't even heard about the murder. Hell, he may not have even been in the country back then."

"Damn, that's right–thought I was on to something."

The chief went in to take his call, leaving me with Officer Collinson.

"The chief's been on something of a short fuse lately," he said.

"Two murders don't help," I responded.

"Well, technically he's responsible for only that first one."

"But it's the first ever on the island. You working on it?"

"Yeah, a little, but come on, who really cares? It isn't like it was a local or something. If it was a resident, that'd be a different story, but why get all bent out of shape about some wetback? Why all the fuss?"

"I guess the chief considers murder, as well, murder, no matter who it is."

"Waste of time as far as I'm concerned."

The chief came back out.

"Looks like the county is gonna send someone over to the Poseidon to see what they can come up with on the caddy. They asked if I wanted to go along and I told 'em yeah."

"That's where he was last seen?" I asked.

"Right."

The chief turned to Collinson. "I'll be gone for a while Dean, hang in here in case there's an emergency."

"Right, Chief."

"Okay," I said, "I'm heading back to the house. Chief, I know you don't have to, but if you find out anything of interest, well, I'd appreciate a call."

"We'll see," he said and took off.

"What's your interest in all this?" Collinson asked, turning to me.

"My wife knows some of the people related to the dead guy I found."

"Ah."

"See you." I said.

"Yeah, see ya around," he said.

Chapter 19

Delgado was pleased.

On this Friday evening it was just shy of a week since he'd handled the caddy problem, and over two weeks since Collinson had taken care of that piss ant from Cárdenas. Certainly the other cockroaches would now think twice before trying to screw with the system. As far as the media were concerned, there was so little coverage it was difficult to tell either killing had taken place. But more importantly, there were no indications the police were even investigating the murders; either they didn't care, or the murder of two illegals was a very low priority.

He was in terrific spirits and regretted not having flown in one of his favorite hookers from Las Vegas. It would have made for a great weekend. But, it was now too late to make those kinds of arrangements. He'd definitely place a call and set it up it for next week. *What the hell*, he thought, *maybe I fly in two and double the pleasure, double the fun.*

At the club last Saturday, during dinner, one of the wives had ordered a *mojito*, a popular Cuban drink concocted of light rum, mint, lime, sugar and soda water.

He was now at his own bar, enjoying a Cuban cigar and experimenting. He too, had ordered a *mojito* after dinner last Saturday, liked it, liked it a lot as a matter of fact, had obtained the ingredients from the bartender and was now trying to improve on the bartender's recipe. He'd already determined that, and this was no surprise, it needed more rum than they used at the club, possibly less mint and definitely more lime.

Using a wooden pestle, he was in the process of crushing mint leaves in the bottom of a solid, cut glass pitcher when his cell phone rang.

Shit, Friday night and some ass hole's gotta call just as I'm at a critical stage in this extremely delicate operation. He grinned at his own seriousness.

He looked at the illuminated number on the cell phone and his mood swung 180 degrees. The grin vanished. It had been two weeks since he'd angrily hung up on his *gringo*.

"What is it?" he snarled.

"So why'd you snuff that kid, the caddy?" asked Collinson.

The phone nearly slipped from Delgado's hand. He squeezed it tighter, his hand shaking in rage. *How did . . . ?* He shouldn't have hesitated. Collinson had caught him completely off guard.

"What are you talking about?"

"You know what I'm talking about *amigo*."

"Careful, *gringo*. Wait. Are you accusing me of murder? I must tell you, listen carefully, you are walking on extremely dangerous ground here."

"Well, let me tell *you* something, what *I* think is not a problem for you Delgado. But what my chief and one of his buddies on the island think, well, that *is* definitely a problem for you."

"What the hell are you talking about and stop using my name!" screamed Delgado, coming unglued. "What do you mean what your chief thinks, and who is this buddy? You're not making any sense!"

"The chief and his pal, Matt-something-or-other, they're thinking there's a connection between the two murders."

"Well, we both know there isn't one, don't we? That is, unless *you* killed the caddy. Did you?"

"Come off it Delgado. We both know who did the kid."

There it was again, for the second time, the use of his name on the phone and another accusation. How in the hell could he know? There wasn't any way, not for sure. He was bluffing. There wasn't any doubt now in Delgado's mind as to what must be done, but for the moment, he needed to gain control of the situation.

"Who's this Matt guy?" he asked.

"Lives on the island, him and his wife. From what I hear, she does some kind of interpreting for the wetbacks, and knew ah, knows some friends of, you know, the first one."

Delgado was getting extremely irritated. He had been under the assumption that nothing was being done concerning the two murders, but was now learning differently. He poured a double shot of Bacardi Añejo into a tumbler and tossed it down.

"So, what are they doing?" he asked, feeling his muscles relax as the alcohol kicked in.

"Last I heard the chief was going out to the Poseidon with a couple county officers to see what they could sniff out about the caddy. Why, does that make you nervous?"

Delgado could sense the fun this bastard was having toying with him.

"Listen," Delgado hissed into the phone, "I pay you to work for me, not to be a smartass. You might have a day job, a job that I got you; in fact that day job is why you're worth something to me. But don't ever forget, and listen closely, don't ever forget who you work for. You understand?"

"Oh sure, I understand, but there's something you need to understand. Things have changed *amigo*. Actually, they've changed a quite a bit since that last assignment and I'm in need of a raise, a big one. That last job you had me do put me in a very, ah, vulnerable position."

So there it was, the squeeze was on. He should have seen it coming. Once again, he found himself needing to play for time.

"You're of value to me," Delgado replied. "But don't overestimate your position. I'll think about an increase, and you think about changing your fucking attitude, because right now it sucks."

"Uh huh," said Collinson.

"And in the meantime, find out what they learned at the Poseidon."

Delgado didn't wait for a response. He snapped his phone shut and poured another shot of Bacardi.

After a few moments, he popped the phone back open and dialed a Las Vegas number. It wasn't that of the hooker's he had earlier hoped to call. This call was indeed to make arrangements for a professional; however, unfortunately, not of the bedroom variety.

Chapter 20

They were all aware that they were in serious trouble. Rosa's optimism, which had previously been responsible for giving the group some degree of hope, had been crushed with Pablo's death.

Adding to Rosa's despair, José, no longer able to contain his own fear, revealed to Rosa that they were behind in the trailer rent. Additionally, the food supply was running low, and there were eight of them to feed.

María was in withdrawal. Since learning of Pablo's death, she had barely uttered a word. Back in Cárdenas, in the beginning, it had been her idea to leave Mexico. She knew there would be difficulties, but what could they be in comparison to a new start, a new life and having her baby born a citizen of the United States? She had convinced Carlos. Then the two of them convinced their best friends since childhood, Pablo and Gina, to join them. Many were the nights in Cárdenas when the two couples had sat huddled under the stars whispering of their dreams and how wonderful it would be when they lived in *Los Estados Unidos*. Now, Pablo was dead. And it was her fault. If only she had not been so persistent, so convincing about leaving Cárdenas, Pablo would be alive today.

Carlos's life was now in danger, and to a lesser degree, that of José. If they killed Pablo because of the money, Carlos must be on the same list.

Gina sobbed continually and they could not console her. "What am I going to do without my Pablo?" she would wail. "What am

I going to do? I am lost! I am lost! I have no Pablo! I have no *dinero*! I have no *casa*! What will happen with me? How will I survive."

No one had an answer.

As they sat on the front stoop of the trailer on Saturday morning, ignoring the slight drizzle and sharing damp cigarette butts that Carlos had found littered by the outdoor telephone booth at *la tienda*, Carlos and José discussed their situation.

"One of us will be next," said José.

"If so, it will be me," said Carlos.

"*¿Porqué*," why do you say that?"

"Because I owe more than you, José."

Carlos tried unsuccessfully to light another wet butt. "*Mierda*! Shit!" he said angrily, "we can not even smoke! With Pablo gone, I owe more than anybody . . . it is *mucho dinero*."

"I am not safe either," replied José, "and neither is Gina."

"Gina? Of course she's safe! Why would they harm that poor woman after killing her husband?"

"Because they are *hijos de putas*, Carlos. The bastards will do anything to get their money."

"But Gina has no *dinero* José. What good would it do to harm her?"

"Not harm her . . . they could force her to work,"

"But there is not enough work now," protested Carlos. "That is the *problema*, no work, no *dinero*!"

José paused, stared blankly ahead and murmured, "Not that kind of work *mi amigo*."

It took a moment for the implication of José's remark to sink in.

"No, no, *Dios Mio*, they would not do such a thing," Carlos exclaimed.

"*Es posible Carlos*."

"Gina would kill herself before letting such a thing happen!"

"Keep your voice down!" José paused. "We must find a way out of this *mi amigo*, we must find a way out soon. But now, *por seguro*, for sure, if we don't first find some dry cigarettes I will go *loco*!"

Chapter 21

You'd think that since I had more than a casual interest in the case that my good pal, the Chief of Police, would have the decency to call and give me an update. He didn't. Several days passed without a word.

It was a another spectacular fall morning with a blinding white sun blazing off the surface of our back canal, a temperature somewhere in the mid sixties, and a patented blue Carolina sky.

I'd baited the traps and was carrying the last one down to Ol'Crab, when I heard a familiar, gruff voice holler, "Shit, you doing that again? Thought you were finished for the year."

Looking back towards the house, I saw my foul-mouthed neighbor, T. L., headed towards my dock.

"I lied, foul-mouthed neighbor. As my dear departed pal, Count Basie, would've said, 'One more time.' And for God's sake don't ask me who Count Basie was!"

"I know who in the hell he was, played piano or trumpet or something."

"Right, 'or something.'"

"No, seriously, you dropping 'em again?"

"Yup, final shot before all those delectable crustaceans bury themselves in the muck."

"They bury themselves?"

"It's called hibernation."

"I'll be damned. I didn't know that."

"Your Yankee neighbor has a mind of encyclopedic proportions. Listen, it'll be about an hour before I go out, come on along for the ride. Better yet, we could take a couple of your traps with us."

"I haven't crabbed all year, no need to start now."

"Okay, fine, that's just great, but don't come asking about crab cakes in February, because I have to tell you right now, we ain't sharing."

"What the hell kind of neighbor is that?"

"The selfish kind."

"Most Yankees are."

"And *y'all* are lazy."

"Go to hell."

"And *y'all* cuss way too much."

Tommy Lee shook his head, turned towards his place, paused and called back, "Okay, damn it, I'll go. See you in an hour."

Crab cakes in February can be quite persuasive.

We'd already squirreled away our winter stash of seafood in the freezer. Each fall Lindy and I would pick up thirty or more pounds of shrimp, fresh off the boat. Along with the frozen crab meat, King Mackerel steaks, Spanish Mackerel, Black Bass and flounder fillets, our sea food cravings would be satisfied until spring, well, almost. We usually ran short of everything, but that was fine. The anticipation of the fresh spring catch made it even more delectable.

I headed inside to listen to a little music and knock out a couple of e-mails. Standing in front of the CD rack, I couldn't decide if it was a Brubeck, Bjoerling or Beethoven kind of morning. Being a jazz, opera and classical buff, it's an enjoyable, but often-faced high class dilemma.

On this particular morning, for whatever reason, Brubeck won out.

With his quartet gently swinging into its version of *Gone With The Wind*, I was cranking up the laptop when the phone rang.

It was the call I'd been hoping for.

"Hey Chief, been waiting to hear from you."

"Yeah, well, we've had…."

"You learn anything at The Poseidon?"

"Well shit, good morning to you too, Matthew."

"Sorry, it's just that I've been anxious to hear if…"

"Listen Matt, if you're not busy, why don't you just head over this way? I'll fill you in on the Poseidon when you get here."

"Sure."

"And Matt, drive this time."

"Be right there."

Something significant was going down; why else the urgency? The adrenalin kicked into high as I hurried out the door.

Wouldn't it be insane if I received a ticket driving to the police station? Would my good buddy Chief Curt Everhart take care of it for me? I backed off the gas. No need to put my pal to the test.

I passed Town Hall and turned into the small parking lot by the police station.

Our law enforcement staff consists of the chief and three officers. The building is a small, white, wooden structure located next to the recently renovated, very official looking, red brick Town Hall. Some referred to our police headquarters as the "Sheriff's Shack," but not within ear shot of Chief Everhart. Shack or not, it was the seat of law and order on our beloved island.

Entering the building it only took a second to realize something was amiss. Two officers were there, along with the mayor. Both officers were slumped against filing cabinets, hands in pockets, staring at their shoes. The mayor was sitting on the edge of a desk, arms folded, head down, looking grim. Each glanced up quickly as I entered, but returned to their former posture without venturing so much as a "Hi."

The urge struck me to perform an 'about face' just as I saw the chief emerge from his office.

He looked whipped. His face was haggard, his eyes blood shot and his normally crisply pressed uniform appeared as though he had slept in it, which, I had the feeling, just may have been the case.

He glanced over to the officers and said, "Listen fellas, there's nothing you two can do in here, so go back out on the job. I'll keep you posted."

The officers nodded in unison, grabbed their hats and ambled out.

Turning to the mayor, the chief said, "John, I appreciate your coming right over, but honestly, I don't know of anything you can do at this point. If I need something, I'll give you a holler."

"Don't hesitate Chief; just let me know if there's anything . . . anything."

"I will John, and I appreciate it."

The mayor turned to leave, finally acknowledged me with a soft "Hey, Matt" and went out the door.

The chief looked at me through bleary eyes.

"You haven't heard, have you?"

"Heard what?" I asked.

"Guess it's too early for word to have spread, Officer Collinson is dead. He was killed in a car crash."

"My God! I'm sorry Chief. What happened?"

"Don't know for sure. A motorist from Virginia, on his way to Myrtle Beach for a week of golf, came across the scene. He called 911 from his cell phone a little after four this morning."

"What scene?"

"Single car accident. It appears Officer Collinson was headed south towards Little River, veered off 17 just south of the Shallotte exit and ran his squad car into a goddamn tree at a speed fast enough to kill him on impact."

"Jesus. Was he chasing someone?"

"Don't think so. That location is way out of our jurisdiction. Second, on a high-speed chase on a four lane highway, he would've radioed for help. We checked. He never radioed in."

"I'm sorry Chief." I didn't know what else to say. "You see his wife?" was the best I could come up with.

"Dean wasn't married. That's about the only good part of this whole damn thing."

We were both silent, then the chief looked over at me.

"I didn't want to bring this up in front of the mayor or my men at this point. If I did, speculation would be running crazy all over the beach in a heart beat. Anyway, it'll eventually come out, but in the meantime I need to bounce something off you. You're a pain in the ass on occasion, but I like the way you think . . . most of the time."

"Well, I'll be sure to repay the compliment." As I gave a little laugh, I could sense the chief was snapping out of his deep funk.

"Here's the thing, well, two things. There were no skid marks . . . not a single damn one. It was like he aimed himself at that goddamn tree and went right for it, wide open. There should have been skid marks."

"You'd think," I said.

"But here's the kicker, it looked like he'd been drinking pretty heavy, there was an empty bottle of Jack Daniels on the floor board, and he reeked like hell of the stuff."

"Well Chief, he must have had too much and . . ."

"Wait Matt," the chief interrupted, "I said it *looked* like he'd been drinking. That's my point. Dean didn't drink. I've never seen him touch a drop."

"What? Never?" I asked, in disbelief. I didn't know anyone who *never* drank.

"Never. When we'd go out, or have a get together, he'd always bring along a six pack of Diet Pepsi. That was his beverage of choice. That's all he ever drank, that and iced tea if Pepsi wasn't available."

I considered telling him I never trusted a man who didn't drink, but thought better of it. It was clear that Chief Everhart suspected some kind of foul play.

"So, that's why you asked me over, to see what I think about the possibility of some funny business?"

"Hell, I *know* there's something funny going on, but I need a sounding board. Like I said, you're it."

"What're you going to do now that you suspect something's amiss?"

"They thought I was crazier than hell, but I asked the state special investigators to go over the squad car in fine detail, and I emphasized *fine*. And I asked the coroner not to assume anything –I want a detailed post mortem of Collinson's body. And I emphasized *detailed*."

"Sounds like you did the right thing."

"Yeah, I think so, but maybe I'm getting paranoid. I just don't get it. Not a serious damn incident around here for years and all of a sudden we've got dead bodies all over the damn place. What the hell's happening, Matt?"

I can recognize a rhetorical question as well as the next guy. I hesitated, then asked, "Anything out at The Poseidon?"

"Oh, almost forgot about that. Nah, nothing. We talked to every one. It was the kid's first day, he was given a foursome along with the other caddies, and after they finished, he wasn't seen again until his body was found."

"Weird, who'd you talk to?"

"The caddy master, name of Charlie, one of the caddies, and as luck would have it, two of the guys from the foursome that day were in the Pro shop when we were there. Seemed like pretty decent guys, rich, but decent."

"Nothing says rich guys can't be decent," I said. "What did these rich, but decent, guys have to say?"

"Nothing. Neither one of them even remembers talking to the caddy."

"They didn't talk to their caddy?"

"He wasn't their caddy. In fact, they thought it was ironical as all hell. One of the other guys in the foursome was a Mexican, a regular in the group, and they swore somehow or other, since the caddy and he spoke in Spanish, there was some cheating going on. Particularly on one hole when the Mexican, the golfer, drove his tee shot into the woods and the caddy found it, miraculously, near the edge of the fairway."

"Wait a minute Chief," I interrupted. "Are you telling me the Poseidon has a Mexican as a member? He must have been a guest."

"Nah, he's a member. I thought it sounded peculiar myself, but when I questioned it, they told me he'd been a member for about three years. They said, admittedly with wide smiles, that the club was 'broadening its ethnic base.'"

"Chief, you know as well as I do that no outsider gets into the Poseidon, ever. Even some insiders can't get in!"

"So, what're you saying?"

"Probably nothing. But for a Mexican to be a member of that

club is *extraordinaire*. Don't you think it looks kind of funny?"

"Well yeah, I guess. But no, it's not like in the old days; nothing is. Shit Matt, we've even got a broad, ah lady, in our poker group now. Would you believe it? It's been all guys for over twenty years. One of the wives insisted on sitting in one night when we were at their house and a regular didn't make it, and she's been showing up with hubby ever since. What's more, now some of the other wives want to play. To tell you the truth, it really pisses me off, changed the whole character of our getting together—we'll probably bust up soon. But the point is, 'we've come a long way baby,' and nothing surprises me anymore."

"You may be right. What else?"

"I guess that's it 'til I get some reports back."

Before leaving, I again expressed my condolences for Officer Collinson. In my few encounters with him we hadn't exactly hit it off, but the chief apparently held him in high regard.

During the brief ride home I attempted to rationalize a scenario for Collinson's accident, but couldn't develop one, not with missing skid marks and the situation regarding the booze. It also bothered me that the chief hadn't thought that the Poseidon having a Mexican member was worth pursuing a little further. I couldn't help but feel that Collinson's death had affected the chief's normally sharp wits and that he wasn't at the top of his game.

When I returned, T.L. was waiting for me with two of his crab traps sitting on my dock.

"You got any crab bait?" he asked.

"Wait a minute; let's see if I got this straight. You want *me* to furnish the bait for *your* traps, use my boat and gas to put your traps out, and then you'll expect me to cook and clean the damn things, and then, and then, you'll want me to make crab cakes for you and Lizzie. Is that about the way you see it?"

"Ah, shit Matt, don't bust my chops. I haven't crabbed in years."

"I know. Yeah. I've got some fish heads in the garage freezer, go grab a bag."

On the way out, I filled T.L. in on Collinson's accident and the chat I'd had with Chief Everhart about the Poseidon situation.

T.L. grinned. "I never would've believed it–a wetback in the Poseidon. Now that is indeed royal Matthew, just royal. Man, I can promise you it never would've happened back when I was there."

We were in the middle of the waterway. I cut the motor off.

"What did you just say?"

"I said I can't believe there's a wetback in the Poseidon."

"No, no, after that."

T.L. looked at me, probing his brain. "Oh, you mean about me having belonged to the Poseidon?"

"Yeah, that part."

"What, you don't believe it?" he laughed. "Well, I guess I've never mentioned anything about it, but yeah, I was a member about six years ago now, before Lizzie and I moved here to the island. My Dad was a member, as was my grandfather, so I more or less grew up there at the club. Swim team, junior golf team, all that country club bullshit. My Dad died a few years back and they offered me the membership. I did it for a couple of years and quit. Too damn expensive to keep up, and they weren't my kind of people anyway. Never did feel comfortable there, even as a kid. The only reason most of 'em belong is because they're members of the L.S.C."

"What's the L.S.C?"

T. L. grinned and replied, "The Lucky Sperm Club."

I laughed, sat silently in the boat for a moment then restarted the motor. We dropped my three traps and T. L's two, about a hundred yards apart. I still hadn't said anything.

"You're awfully quiet Matt, in shock over what I just told you?"

"Well, yes and no, but I've been thinking, can you still get in the club as a guest or something?"

"I don't see why not. I still know a bunch of those assholes and there are a couple of the guys I've stayed in touch with off and on. Why?"

"Tell you what, I'll perform all the tedious tasks required to get this batch of crabs to your gluttonous palate if you buy me a drink at the Poseidon sometime soon. Actually, the sooner the better. How's that for a deal?"

"No problem, you're on, but why a drink at the club?"

"Curiosity, Tommy Lee. Aren't you just a bit surprised that a 'wetback' has broken the snob barrier and become one of those 'pretentious bastards' you're so fond of at your former club?"

"Well, yeah, come to think of it, I guess so." He threw his head back and laughed.

"Shit, I'll tell you one thing Matthew," he said, "There's got to be one hell of a story behind this guy. Really, one hell of a story! You've got my curiosity peaked. Hell yes, let's do it!"

He was enjoying this idea so much I didn't have the heart to tell him of my ulterior motive.

There's no way we could have known that this somewhat whimsical, off-the-cuff decision, made while sitting in a small fishing boat in the middle of the Atlantic Intracoastal Waterway, would have a traumatic impact on several lives, particularly mine and Lindy's.

Chapter 22

La tienda was a short walk from The Sand Dunes Harbor Park. The store sold everything from basic staples and prepared Mexican and American food stuffs to clothes, toys, cosmetics, medicine, and even under the counter lottery tickets smuggled in from South Carolina. North Carolina had not yet implemented a lottery system and the illegals had habitually purchased *billetes* in Mexico. No matter how poor, no matter how desperate the situation, the weekly purchase of a *billete* was to buy hope, the hope of escaping poverty. To not buy a *un billete de loteria* was to lose that hope, to give up, to abandon the dream of one day being rich and happy.

La tienda sold on credit, made cash loans, and charged exorbitant interest. It was the Latino version of the old Carolina mill town company store. Many illegals were in debt to *La tienda*, however none of them was remotely aware that *La tienda* was one of dozens of such stores owned and operated by *la Eme* throughout the southeast. Nor did any of them have the slightest clue that each store manager was a key member of the Mexican mafia organization.

In addition to being a lucrative investment, this network of general stores was *la Eme's* primary means of keeping tabs on each local Hispanic community; store managers reported regularly to el *numero uno*, Señor Miguel Delgado. They were the important, grass roots eyes and ears of his organization.

It was María's habit to walk the dirt path to *La tienda* each day. After being cooped up in the trailer listening to crying children, a blaring TV, Gina sobbing, and unbearable odors, she needed to get out. The store offered an enjoyable diversion. She would spend time admiring the pretty new dresses on display. She could imagine herself applying the exotic cosmetics kept under the glass case, particularly the lipsticks; and, she would linger by the perfumes, deeply inhaling their enchanting fragances.

Ernesto Santiago, the store manager, had no problem with this. Although he discouraged loitering, particularly when he knew the loiterer was unable to purchase anything, even on credit, María was the exception. She was too attractive to chase off. In fact, he enjoyed engaging her in conversation during which time he enjoyed even more visualizing her naked body and himself in bed with her.

Today he had a specific reason to chat with María. He'd told Delgado what time María usually came to the store, and Delgado had told him to make sure he kept her there until his arrival.

As usual, María first looked at the dresses. She didn't linger long as they were the same dresses she had seen for the last several days. She moved on to the cosmetic area and was admiring the various shades of lipstick, when Ernesto approached.

"I've told you before, *Señora*, you have no need of cosmetics. If all women were as pretty as you, there would be no cosmetics industry."

María was not used to compliments, and although she remembered the man telling her this previously, she nevertheless, blushed.

"One day, I will come here and buy lipstick from you," she replied, then added, "and also a new dress. That red one over there is one like I will buy."

Ernesto turned to look at the red dress on the mannequin.

"*Sí*, it is very pretty, but expensive María. I could put lipstick on your account, but I'm sorry, not the dress."

"*No, gracias*, I will buy both when we have money."

103

"That is best. Your husband, he has not found work yet?" Ernesto, of course, knew the answer to his question. He was getting anxious, and had to stall for time.

"No, but he is trying very hard," she replied.

They both heard the bells on the door jangle and turned to look as a tall, handsome Latino man, wearing dark aviator glasses, came through the doorway. He had jet black hair, a large, neatly trimmed black mustache and was wearing a black *guayabera* shirt and crisply pressed tan slacks. He walked with an air of authority.

María realized instantly he was not one of them; he was a man of importance.

"*Hola Ernesto, como estás?*" he said cheerfully with a wave, walking towards them.

"*Bien Miguel, bien,*" replied Ernesto. "We are good."

As he approached the two, Miguel smiled and said, "And is this one of your customers Ernesto? And are they all so pretty? If so, you are a very fortunate man. ¡*Qué suerte*! How lucky you are!"

María was again embarrassed. Standing before her was an impeccably dressed, clean man. An important man, certainly, and there she stood before him in one of Rosa's faded, oversized dresses and a scuffed pair of old loafers on her feet that had a hole in the right shoe. They were the ones she had worn since before fleeing Mexico, and she hadn't showered since the previous morning. She felt every inch the filthy peasant she knew she was.

"*Sí*, she is a customer Miguel, and believe me, they are not all so *bonita*. As a matter of fact Miguel, this is María Martinez, the Señora you said you wanted to see."

María was not sure she had heard correctly.

"*Ah, sí*," replied Miguel, with a feigned look of surprise. "Ernesto, is there a place Señora Martinez and I can chat for a couple of minutes?"

María had no comprehension of what was happening. "I do not understand . . ."

"*Es okay* María," Ernesto answered, nervously. "Miguel needs to talk to you. Here, *aqui*, follow me to the office."

María did not move. While at first she had felt a sense of respect for this man she had just met, that admiration swiftly turned to a sense of caution, even fear.

"*Por favor, Señora,*" Delgado said softly, "Please, this will only take a minute. It is very important that I speak privately with you." He took María gently by the arm and steered her towards the rear of the store.

The room he led her to was a combination office and mini warehouse. Several boxes of canned red beans, large burlap bags of rice, cardboard boxes of toilet paper and several containers of canned fruits and vegetables were stacked against the walls. There were several old, avocado-colored filing cabinets. The desk had a PC on top, and a leather chair behind it. One white, plastic, outdoor chair had been placed in front of the desk.

Ernesto held the door open for María and Delgado. He then closed the door behind them and returned to the front of the store.

"*Por favor*, please, sit down *Señora.*"

María remained standing. Her knees trembled. This was every bit as frightening as when she had been swept downstream, if not more so. There was something evil about this man, María sensed it.

"What do you want?" she asked, her voice quivering.

"*Señora, síentese*, please, sit down," he said, an edge to his voice.

María braced herself with one hand on the back of the chair, and unwillingly sat.

Delgado stood behind the desk looking down at María.

He said nothing.

The reports had been right; she was not only attractive, but indeed, beautiful. Her face had classic features with high cheekbones, perfectly arched eyebrows, a thin nose, large, soft, jet black eyes under long, black eyelashes. Despite the ridiculously large dress she was wearing, he could envision the perfectly shaped body that went with the face. Cleaned up and properly dressed, she would be absolutely stunning.

For a moment, much like Ernesto, he imagined himself in bed

with her. It was a pleasant visual. So pleasant that he momentarily considered changing his plans and saving her for himself. But he knew that wouldn't work. He didn't need those kinds of complications. Best he stick with the Vegas imports, and, when in need, Carmen.

He pulled the leather chair out from behind the desk and sat down. "May I call you María?"

María did not, could not speak. At this point, she was terrified, her throat had gone dry, and her knees continued to tremble.

"I'll assume it's permissible. We have a very serious problem, María. I imagine you know what it is?"

María, staring at the floor, managed to slowly shake her head.

"Well, *el problema* is very serious and it's necessary that something be done. Something *pronto*. You and your husband, Carlos, owe Señor Don Orencio a great deal of money, a very large sum. He has received practically nothing for having helped you and your husband out of Cárdenas and getting you all the way here. Now, as you know María, Señor Nuñez is a good man, a decent man, but he is upset María, very upset, and he wants his money."

María still didn't understand and thought, *Why is he talking to me? He should be speaking with Carlos about the money, not me.*

She lifted her head slowly, and, barely able to speak, said "My husband, he will get the money when he finds a job. He will get the money as soon as he has work and we will give it all to Señor Nuñez."

"I'm afraid it's been too long already, María. Something must be done now. Don Orencio has lost patience with you and Carlos."

"Carlos is trying Señor; he has been trying hard to get work."

"I know; it has been very difficult. But work is very limited now and unfortunately Señor Nuñez will wait no longer. He paused and looked directly into María's eyes. "But there is a way to do this. There is a way to get the money to pay what you and Carlos owe."

Staring into Delgado's eyes, at that instant, María realized what was about to happen. She understood why this man was talking to her and not Carlos.

Her entire body trembled and her stomach began to cramp and churn violently.

"María, you must be aware that you are a very attractive woman. Many men would find you to be beautiful. I don't know quite how to say this María, but since Carlos is not working, it will be necessary for you to work to pay what you owe. There is no other way. We have many men here who are alone. They left their wives and families in Mexico. They are lonely and need . . . companionship."

Light headed and barely able to speak, she managed to keep her gaze on Delgado. Leaning forward, and bracing herself with one hand on the edge of the desk, she said, her voice trembling, "You want me to become a *puta*, a whore? Is that what you are asking?"

"No, that is not the right word María. You will be a 'companion,' a brief companion, for some of the lonely men."

María's head was spinning. She could not believe the ugly words she was hearing.

"No. I will do no such a thing. I am not a *puta*!" María, nauseated, felt herself becoming sick.

Delgado paused. This had become more unpleasant than he had anticipated, but it was necessary. Yes, he wanted the money he had paid Nuñez, but more importantly, he couldn't let these peasants slide on their payments, not even this attractive creature.

"María, listen to me. This is very serious. You do not want harm to come to Carlos, do you?"

There was a pause. Delgado waited for the impact of what he had said to sink in. It only took a moment.

María stared at Delgado, eyes blazing with a combination of hatred and fear. "You, you are the one responsible for Pablo! You murdered Pablo!"

"Pablo?" he feigned innocence, leaning back in the chair and raising his hands in protest, "I know no Pablo. Who is Pablo?"

María, eyes now downcast, murmured something that Delgado

could not understand.

"I'm sorry, I couldn't hear you."

She looked up directly at him and hissed, "*Estoy embarazada.* I am pregnant."

"No! I don't believe it!" Delgado exclaimed. "Stand up! Let me see you!"

María remained seated.

"Well, even if you are, it changes nothing. I cannot tell, no one can tell. Listen María, it will not be so bad. It is all worked out. Carlos spends each day looking for work. You will be picked up here after he leaves and taken to where you are needed. You will be back by early afternoon. Carlos will never know. Most of your work will be at lunch time. Here they call it noon time. In fact," chuckled Delgado, "they refer to these short romantic activities as "nooners." .

María sat silently, having no comprehension of what Delgado had just said.

"If what you say is true, the sooner you begin the better. See Ernesto when you leave, he will tell you of the arrangements. *Buena suerte, María*, good luck. It is the only answer. This way, *por seguro*, for sure, Carlos will be here when your beautiful baby is born . . .*Sí?* I'm certain that is what you want."

He rose and walked around to María. With the front of his forefinger he lightly stroked María's cheek.

"*Quien sabe*, who knows?" he said with a sadistic smirk, "You may even get so you look forward to these little 'nooners,' no?" He chuckled at his own little joke, and with that, left the room.

For several minutes, María remained in the white, plastic chair, her face buried in her hands, softly sobbing.

Everything is my fault, all my fault, and now this. They will kill Carlos. I wanted to have my baby here, that is all, nothing more. They killed Pablo. Now I am to become a puta! A dirty, filthy whore! No! No! Why can't they leave us alone! No, no, no, no!

She stood to leave. Turning towards the door, María took one faltering step, felt her knees weaken, and clutched her stomach as she collapsed to the floor.

Chapter 23

The recent incidents that had created such havoc for Chief Curt Everhart, not so coincidently, were the very ones that Delgado now felt were safely behind him; everything had fallen nicely into place.

Friday evening, after having spoken with that half-assed officer who had the balls to try and blackmail him over the phone, he realized the need to move swiftly. The call to Las Vegas was returned within the hour. Early the following morning, he made the three and a half hour trek to Charlotte's Douglas International Airport. They had determined that location would suit their purpose better than Wilmington or Myrtle Beach. While seated in two of the dozens of large, white rockers overlooking the runways, Delgado and the recently arrived passenger from Las Vegas, known to Miguel for years simply as "Che," quietly discussed the details of the contract while each sipped a Starbuck's coffee.

It was a brief meeting.

After finalizing the deal and acquiring the paperwork for Che's Hertz rental, the two men left the terminal and walked to Delgado's car. There, a small package was removed from the trunk and handed to Che. The two men shook hands. Delgado climbed into his Town Car and headed back to the coast. Che claimed his rental, a black Lincoln Town Car with Sirius Satellite Radio, so he could listen to Howard Stern, got in, and also headed east on US 74.

Early Monday morning Delgado received a call informing him that the contract had been fulfilled, having gone off without a hitch.

"Unless there's something else . . ."

"*Gracias,*" Delgado said.

"*Por nada.* If, in the future, you need me . . ."

"Everything is under control now," he replied.

In the afternoon he'd had his chat with María at *La tienda,* which had gone about as well as could be expected. Let's face it; he knew she had no choice.

He watched the local NBC news out of Wilmington Monday evening. There was a report with film footage and an on-scene reporter covering Officer Dean Collinson's tragic death. No indication was given that it was anything other than an accident. Perfect. Che, as always, had done his professional best.

After the news, Miguel was in excellent spirits. All was well. It was definitely time for a *Recuerdo.* He poured a double shot, lit a Cuban cigar and walked out to the patio overlooking the Atlantic. The night was beautiful, with a full, orange moon glistening off a placid ocean and stars that looked like they could almost be touched.

Delgado, looking out over the ocean, took stock of his situation. *When the police finish the investigation of Collinson's accident, that situation will be behind me. I'm pushing the cockroaches hard and will get my money back. María will be very popular with the piss ants. Collinson needs to be replaced, I could promote Ernesto, he's a good man. No, I should bring in someone no one here knows.*

He felt a presence behind him. Turning, he saw his housemaid, Carmen.

"*Sí?*" he asked.

"I'm going to bed Señor Delgado, is there anything else you need?"

"*Sí,* It's a beautiful night and I feel like celebrating."

He extended his arm, handing her the empty glass. "*Otro*

Recuerdo."

She left and returned shortly with the refill.

"*Buenas noches, Señor,*" she said, turning to leave.

"Carmen, I think, *sí,* take a shower and go to my bedroom. I'll finish this drink and join you shortly."

She started to reply to Delgado, thought better of it, then turned and left. He could not see the look of repulsion on her face.

Delgado took another sip, and another drag on the delicious Cuban cigar. He looked out to the ocean and smiled. "This is the life," he whispered into the nighttime expanse.

Chapter 24

When she agreed to the part-time job, Lindy had been advised she wouldn't have to concern herself with Tuesdays; "Tuesdays are always slow, so you won't be needed," she'd been told.

Driving to the clinic on Tuesday morning, she couldn't recall when she had last had a Tuesday off; there was now a constant stream of new arrivals. One of the nurses had mentioned just yesterday that she had heard that aside from California, North Carolina had the largest influx of illegals of any state, including Texas and New Mexico. Lindy didn't know if that was true, but certainly the number of mothers with kids, and the large number of expectant mothers showing up each week at the clinic, was proof enough for her. She remained sympathetic and concerned for each and every one of them, but even Lindy, "The Bleeding Heart of North Carolina," as Tommy Lee had once called her, was beginning to wonder when and how it would ever end. Certainly there would come a point when there simply wasn't enough money to support all the free care and services now being provided to the illegals. It already must be an astronomical amount. The day also would arrive when there weren't enough jobs for the huge influx. Then, as T.L. had predicted, "Da shit is really gonna hit da fan."

Well, that's all beyond my scope, she thought as she pulled into the clinic's parking lot. Until something happens, this 'bleeding heart' will do her best to help. Matt and T. L. can worry about that other stuff.

Lindy had no sooner entered the clinic, reached her desk and put her purse away, when she heard her name called from the direction of the entrance. Looking up, she saw Rosa rushing towards her, a child in each arm and the eldest trotting behind as fast as his little legs could carry him.

"*Señora Lindy! Señora Lindy, por favor, por favor,* please, come with me! You must come with me!"

"Rosa, slow down! You're going to kill yourself, or one of the children! Come here and sit! Give me Juanito and *sientate!*"

Rosa handed the baby to Lindy, and sat, exhausted. The two year old was on her lap and the three year old sat on the floor, pulling at Rosa's skirt. All three children were crying.

Rosa attempted to catch her breath.

"*Por favor Señora Lindy,* we must go to the hospital! You come with me!"

"Rosa, what are you talking about? *No es posible!*"

"*Sí,* you must Señora Lindy, it is María, she is in the hospital!"

"*¿Porque,* why? What happened?"

"We do not know, she says nothing! She is in bed, she does not talk."

"What do you mean you do not know? Was she in an accident?"

"We do not know, Señora. Please, come to the hospital with me now!"

"I cannot leave, Rosa. We have many people who must see the doctor and I am the only interpreter here today. Tell me what you know."

"She is not awake."

"Not awake?" Lindy asked.

"Her eyes are not open. She just sleeps *en la cama.*"

"Is she hurt?"

"*El doctor* he said 'no' no injuries.'"

"Is her husband, Carlos...?"

"*Sí,* Carlos he is with her."

"Rosa, take *los niños* home. I will go to the hospital as soon as I can, but it will not be until much later, but I promise I will go."

"*Por favor, Señora*, please."

❧

Lindy did not get away until late afternoon, and then drove directly to the hospital. María was in the observation ward. Carlos and Rosa were by her bed.

¿*Como está*? How is she?"

"No change. She has said a few words in her sleep, but they make no sense." Rosa replied.

Lindy looked at Carlos and then introduced herself.

She hesitated, then asked, looking at them both, "And the baby?"

"The doctor, thank God, says the baby is okay," replied Rosa.

"What did he say about María?"

Carlos and Rosa looked at each other.

"He talked to us, but we don't understand," Rosa responded.

There aren't enough of us to go around, Lindy thought to herself.

"What has María said?"

Again, Carlos and Rosa looked at each other, but this time neither spoke. They both appeared to be embarrassed.

After several awkward moments, Rosa said, "*No puta, no soy puta*."

Lindy was certain she had heard incorrectly.

"I don't understand," she said to Rosa.

"María said," Rosa hesitated, looked over at Carlos, and then continued, "María said she, she is not, '*Una puta*', a whore."

The three looked at each other with puzzled expressions.

Lindy said, "I think I'd better find the doctor."

❧

It was past seven by the time Lindy walked through the front door.

I was in the kitchen preparing one of our favorite dishes, flounder encrusted in panko and fried in butter and olive oil.

"How about a nice select port for the hard working lady?" I asked, looking up from the stove.

"You bet! I'd kill for one right now!"

"I got your message," I said, pouring the wine. "But I didn't understand all that stuff about the hospital and what's her name, María?"

"Well, I don't understand it all either. Let me get settled and I'll fill you in."

A few minutes later she emerged from the bedroom wearing jeans and a Carolina Panther's sweat shirt.

"That's better. Where's that wine?"

I handed her the glass.

"The bottom line is, María's vital signs are good and she should be okay. I think I've told you about her before. She's pregnant, and they determined that the baby is also okay. The doctor says she's in some kind of shock, or experiencing hypertension."

"What happened?"

"No one knows. She just showed up at the hospital entrance, and was unconscious. They ran tests, and found nothing wrong."

"What did she say happened?"

"She hasn't spoken yet. Well, at least nothing that makes any sense."

"Well, whoever took her to the hospital..."

"That's the thing," Lindy interrupted. "Whoever brought her to the emergency entrance disappeared! The hospital learned who she was by checking her purse. They found her WIC folder, and an address scribbled on a piece of scrap paper. "

"Strange."

"Tell me about it."

"They have no idea who brought her in?"

"None."

"Well, it'll get cleared up when she snaps out of it. Let's eat."

"Okay, but I may as well tell you the whole story."

"Do I want to hear this?"

"Yes. She did mutter something. It was something about the fact that she wasn't a whore."

"Well, that's nice to know. Her husband's gotta be pleased."

"Matt! I know this girl...there's no reason for her to say anything like that!"

"Listen Lindy, I know how you feel about these people, but you're beginning to bring too much of this stuff home with you. It'll all get straightened out, now, let's eat."

"There's just one other thing that doesn't make sense."

"Okay, let's hear it, but make it quick please, everything's getting cold."

"I was getting ready to leave the hospital and María said something else, one word–"del.""

"Del?"

"Yes, d-e-l."

"What's that mean?"

"A literal translation to English means 'of the', like say, the steering wheel 'del', meaning "of the" car, or the bottom 'del', 'of the' lake."

"So all she's said at this point is that she's not a whore and 'of the.'"

"Right."

"Sounds like something that should be on *Jeopardy*, or what's the one I can't stand, *Wheel of Fortune*?"

"This is serious Matt . . . she was trying to tell us something important."

"Well, when she comes around, the riddle should be solved."

"You're probably right," Lindy replied, "But Matt; I have a strange feeling about this. We may not want to know the answer to this riddle."

'Lindy, I really don't care at this point what the answer is, and if you keep getting more deeply involved, and bringing it home, we're going to have to seriously rethink this whole working thing of yours."

You really don't care, do you?"

"Nope, let's eat."

Chapter 25

It was Tuesday morning before Ernesto had gathered sufficient nerve to call Delgado.

"What in the hell do you mean, 'she was on the floor?'" Delgado asked.

Ernesto was nervous, fearing he would upset Delgado, and made every effort to speak as calmly as possible. "After you left, I expected to see María come out of the office. I was helping one of my clerks with a customer, but several minutes passed and she had not appeared, so I went back to the office. She was lying on the floor.

"Go on."

"I didn't know what to think. I checked her breathing and pulse. Then I went to the front and told the clerks I had to leave for a while. I drove my car to the back entrance, placed the girl in the back seat and drove to the hospital. I didn't know what else to do."

"You should have called me."

"I know, but time was of the essence, and I didn't want to concern you."

"Go on."

"When I got to the emergency entrance, I left the car running, went in and told them there was a seriously ill girl in the car that needed immediate help. Two attendants hurried out with a wheel chair and removed her. I told them I would park the car and be right back. Of course I left and returned directly to *La tienda*."

"You gave them no names?"

"None."

"No one else saw you?"

"No, I am certain of it."

"You still should have called me," Delgado said. "Have you heard anything about the girl this morning?"

"Nothing."

"Find out what the situation is. She most likely became upset and fainted. But, I doubt that there is anything seriously wrong with her. This changes nothing. They are not off the hook. I expect her to start working very soon–this week for sure. Do you understand? We cannot let this kind of thing slide."

"*Sí.*"

"Call me the moment you hear something."

"*Sí.*"

"One other thing, our former associate who handled this kind of thing is no longer with us. You may have heard of the unfortunate car accident this morning?"

Ernesto had heard about Collinson, but had been hesitant to bring the subject up.

"Just something briefly," he lied.

"Well, until he is replaced, I must count on you to handle this situation with the girl yourself. You understand?"

"*Sí.*"

After they'd hung up, Ernesto was even more curious about Collinson's "accident," and wondered what Collinson had done to cause Delgado's wrath. One thing was certain; as he had seen before, pissing Delgado off could be detrimental to one's health.

❦

Tuesday afternoon, looking confused, María opened her eyes and saw Carlos.

"You are in the hospital *mi amor*," he told her.

The frown remained on María's face, but she said nothing.

"*No sé*, I do not know what happened to you. We do not know

118

how you got here. But the doctor says you are okay. Nothing is wrong with you *mi amor, nada.*"

María looked down and placed her hands over her stomach.

"The baby is well, María, there is nothing wrong," Carlos assured her. "The doctor says everything is okay . . . both you and our baby are okay. We have been waiting for you to wake up."

María still had not spoken. She closed her eyes, and slowly the nightmare of *La tienda* returned to her.

Por seguro, I must not tell Carlos. I cannot tell him what happened. He will go crazy and he will be killed. Dios mio. My baby will not have a puta for a mother. I will not let that happen. I will kill myself! No, no es possible. I want my baby, I want my baby. Why won't they leave us alone? What can I do? Who will help us? Dios mio, please tell me what to do!

⁊⪜⪜⪜

We were finishing dinner Tuesday evening when Tommy Lee appeared at the front door, and I waved him in.

"Damn, looks like I'm a few minutes late–story of my life."

"Sorry, but all is not lost, you're in time for coffee," Lindy told him.

"Thanks, but I can't stay, I just wanted to tell Matt that we're on for Thursday."

"On for what?" I asked.

"That drink at the Poseidon. You still want to go, right?"

"Absolutely!"

"Okay. We're going to meet an ol' buddy of mine in the clubhouse bar for lunch. He should be able to tell us something about that south-of-the-border guy."

"Sounds good T.L., thanks."

As he headed back out the door, he turned and said, "Oh, and Matthew, lunch will be on you."

"What happened to southern hospitality?" I asked too late. The door closed before I'd finished.

"What was that all about?" Lindy asked.

"Probably nothing. The chief mentioned something about the

119

Poseidon having a Mexican member. He was out there looking into the murder of that caddy."

"So?"

I explained my curiosity to Lindy.

"Matt, I thought you didn't want to get involved and now you're playing amateur sleuth."

"Well, since you ask, it's this Collinson thing, I'm not sure Curt has his act totally together yet . . . Hon, I'm going to step outside for a few minutes."

"Hey wait, I have an idea," she said.

"I don't think I want to hear this," I responded.

"Oh, but you do. While you're out there polluting our atmosphere with your filthy cigar, you should wear a trench coat and fantasize that you're Colombo! The answers to whatever is bugging you should come in no time flat!"

"I knew I didn't want to hear it."

"You'll solve your little mystery, but you have to remember Matt, squint one eye like this or it won't work."

Lindy hunched forward, squinted one eye and raised her hand, holding an imaginary cigar.

In spite of myself, I had to laugh.

"Okay, that was sorta cute Hon, but this is something I want to do. At worst I have lunch at the Poseidon, where I've never had the pleasure of dining before, and it should be a fun afternoon with T.L."

Lindy became serious. "I'm just pulling your chain, Matt, except for the cigar part. I'm surprised, but impressed, that you want to look into it. I guess no harm can come of it, unless you run up a humongous tab; I hear it costs an arm and a leg to eat there.

"I know," I answered. "But how much can a peanut butter and jelly sandwich run?

"Oh," she said, "I think we can afford something nicer, why not go nuts and have a pimento cheese on whole wheat?"

"Wow, you think we can handle that?"

Chapter 26

The Poseidon was even swankier than I'd envisioned. Over the years I'd been in some pretty impressive, even opulent settings, but never had I been so overwhelmed by polished wood, brass, marble, original oils, fresh cut flowers, statuary, antiques, and the sheer unadulterated odor of money that permeated the air as when T.L. and I walked through the front door and into the lobby of his old club. It reeked of luxury and extreme wealth, and beat anything I'd ever seen.

I paused a few feet in. "So this is indeed how the other half lives," I whispered to T.L.

The other half?" he glanced back at me with raised eyebrows, "How about the friggin' one tenth of one percent?"

"Shhh, you'll get us thrown out before we even make it the clubhouse."

We strolled through the lobby walking on the plush, maroon carpet, just as though we were members in good standing. A marble stairway led us back outside, and onto an antique, red-brick path towards, I assumed, the clubhouse.

Impressed by the lushness of the vegetation, the gardens with their profusion of color and the symmetrical perfection of the landscaping, I looked over at T.L.

"And you just decided one day to give this all up, huh?"

"Matt, you would've done the same thing if you were me. It's all make-believe you know, no different than Disney World.

It only exists so the phony bastards can impress one another, and anyone else they care to invite into their smug little universe."

"Well, they convinced me. I'm impressed."

T.L. shook his head and kept walking.

"Listen," he said, "we're early. Let's mosey over to the caddy shack, I want to see if that old fart Charlie's still working. He was one of the few good guys around this Taj Mahal I actually liked."

Approaching the shack, it became obvious that "shack" was a misnomer. Lindy and I would have no problem making this "shack" our permanent address. Lush vegetation and a radiance of colors from the abundant flowers surrounded a white stucco building, and, a few paces beyond, a practice putting green that would easily rival the greens of Augusta and Pebble Beach, sat meticulously landscaped.

As we entered the shack, an elderly, skinny guy with cropped white hair, a fading, white mustache and a deep tan looked up from a golf club he was in the process of repairing. There was no one else in the shack.

"Oh my God, I can't believe these sorry, old eyes," he exclaimed. "T. L., how in the hell are ya!" He appeared to be genuinely pleased to see Tommy Lee.

"I'm fine, you old bastard, but I can't believe you're still kicking! What are you now, a hundred and fifty?"

"Hey, for your information, I still shoot my age, which happens to be in the low 80's!"

"Good for you Charlie, that's really terrific," T.L. replied with a laugh. He walked over and embraced Charlie, then introduced us.

As the two of them chatted, I remembered that the chief mentioned Charlie as one of the people he had spoken with. I also noticed the sound of Louis Armstrong singing *Basin Street Blues*. I looked around and spotted the small audio system sitting on a shelf beside a bucket of used golf balls.

At first chance, I butted in and told Charlie that Armstrong was a hero of mine and asked if he was a jazz buff.

"Jazz buff? Yeah, I guess that's what you'd call me. Been one all my life, and I seen 'em all too: Armstrong, Ellington, Basie,

Goodman, Ella, you name 'em, I seen 'em. But Louie, ah man, Satchmo," he said shaking his head, "he was the greatest, seen him several times. Seen him once with Earl Hines up in Chicago, place called The Blue Note. Had Teagarden on trombone, brings tears to my eyes just thinkin' about it. I was right up front, first table next to the stage, I coulda touched 'em. Why you ask Matt, you into it?"

"Is he into it?" exclaimed T.L. "He plays that shit all the time, along with some highbrow crap. He cranks it up so loud I can hear it next door, I'm thinking about suing for noise pollution. Now just give me some good ol' Johnny Cash or Willie Nelson, *then* you're talking *real* music y'all! "

"Charlie, I'll bet he hasn't changed one bit since you knew him," I laughed. "He still ain't got any class."

"Listen," said T.L., "we gotta get up to the clubhouse in a couple minutes. Looks like things are pretty much the same around here, eh Charlie?"

"Well, since ya asked, no, not really. It's different now Tommy Lee. The old members are dying off, or the ones who ain't, are too damn old to play much. They come out here and sit around and drink and bitch and talk about how different it was in *their* day. But ya know, to be honest, they ain't too far off with that. The young ones, ah hell, they just ain't the same. They gotta have the most expensive equipment and they keep changing it out so as to have the latest and the greatest. And they play with a meanness– take it way too serious. They don't have no fun any more. And they play for big bucks too, so the pressure's always there. On top of that, good God, there are more damn women playing. But don't even talk to me about that!" He rolled his eyes to imply that with this one fact he had proven that things had really gone to hell. But there was more. "And listen to this," he lowered his voice and said, "They've even let foreigners in."

T.L. caught the quick glance I shot him.

"What?" T.L. asked, as if startled by the news.

"You heard me right."

"You gotta be pulling my leg Charlie."

"Nope, it's a fact."

Charlie squinted his eyes, took a look around making certain no one else was within earshot, got next to T.L.'s ear and whispered, "And a wetback at that."

"No!" responded Tommy Lee, pulling back in mock horror.

"Yup," said Charlie.

"How in the hell did *that* happen Charlie?" asked Tommy Lee.

"No one knows for sure. Caught most of the members off guard, I can tell you that, some even talked about quittin' the club, but they was just blowin' smoke. Word was, the board approved it for reasons they had to, and he shows up one afternoon like some kinda hot shot. Wants to play right away. Real slick lookin' dude, know what I mean?"

"I'll be damned. Did you let him right on?" T.L. asked.

"Hell yes–had to! Lusch, excuse me, Mr. Lusch, called the whole staff together the day before to give us our marching orders. Told us to treat him like a regular member, which of course, I guess he is.

"He went off by himself that first time," said Charlie smiling. "I gave him the worst caddy I got, and still do every time! He knows what I'm pullin', but he can't do nothin' about it. I ain't really got that much against Mexicans to tell ya the truth, but there's just somethin' about this character . . . ya know, creepy like. "

Since Louis Armstrong had made Charlie and me fast friends, I saw no harm in jumping into the conversation.

"Charlie, the way things are going these days, you've probably even got some Mexican caddies now, right?"

Charlie tightened up and gave me a look. I thought I had screwed up, but fortunately, and possibly thanks to 'ol Satchmo, he relaxed and asked, "You talkin' about that kid that got murdered?"

"I saw something about a caddy being killed the other day, but I forgot he worked here," I lied.

"Only Mexican caddy I ever hired. Did that 'cause I was in a pinch. Tell you the truth, little time I spent with him, he seemed like a decent enough kid. Called himself Pipo. I hooked him up with the hot shot from south of the border."

"As I recall, he had just gotten here or something?" I asked.

"Yeah, it was his first time workin' the club, come in from California a few days before."

"I heard something about that," T.L. said. "So he caddied for your favorite wetback?"

"Sure did. Made sense to me; they both being Mexican and all."

"Did I read where he finished working and no one saw him again?" I asked.

"Exactly–I closed the shack up and left as no one else was going off, so I didn't see him. But I did sorta tell that cop somethin' wrong though."

"What was that?" I asked, containing my excitement.

"Well, the cop, he was a police chief or somethin', asked me if I *spoke* to the caddy after they had finished up, and I told him 'no,' which was true enough. But I forgot to tell him I *seen* him again. I been thinkin' maybe I oughta call that cop."

"Where'd you see him?"

"Right here. The golfers finished up the front nine, went into the clubhouse to grab a bite and two of the caddies come in here and got stuff from the fridge. That's what most of 'em do. I was busy and didn't say nothin to 'em. They come in and went back out to eat."

"I don't think you need to call the cop back for that Charlie," T.L. said, "doesn't sound important to me."

Charlie looked uneasy and started fidgeting with the club he'd been working on.

T.L. looked over at me. "Come on Matt, we're gonna be late."

It was a hunch, but I had to find out before we left.

"Charlie, did you *hear* something when the two caddies came in to get their stuff from the fridge?"

"It's my age, damn it! I just plum forgot. When the cop asked if I seen the caddie when they'd finished, I told him 'no.' He lost interest in talkin' to me, and I just forgot about that lunch thing. Damn, it's hell getting old, fellas!"

"Charlie, what happened?" I asked.

"Well, like I said, I was busy and those two come in, Jamie, he's the other caddy, and Pipo, and they head for the fridge. I couldn't help but notice that this Pipo's all smiles and I think to myself that he's a happy kind of kid; he's laughin' and smilin' the whole time. The two of 'em are jabbering away, but I ain't payin' no attention. Then, just as they're leavin', I heard that Pipo say somethin', at least I think I hear somethin', but with his accent, I ain't so sure now."

"What do you think you heard?" I asked.

"Well, I ain't certain mind you, but I *think* he said somethin' about knowin' that Mexican member to Jamie, somethin' about him and his cousin knowin' him. But I swear I ain't certain!"

Before leaving, we assured Charlie that we were friends of the chief's and that we'd report to him what he had told us.

Hurrying to the clubhouse, T.L. asked me what I thought about what we'd just learned.

"I don't know T.L., I really don't. I think it's important, but nothing's jelling at the moment."

I made a mental note to burn a few CDs for Charlie. We jazz junkies had to hang together, and he'd given us some new information that could prove helpful.

We had no sooner entered the clubhouse when a tall, thin, distinguished looking guy with perfectly groomed white hair swept pass us. He was wearing a blue blazer, grey slacks, a dark blue and white stripped shirt, and a bright red tie. Gold cuff links were peeking out from below the sleeves of his blazer. He had only walked a few feet beyond us when the foot steps stopped. He turned, and a discreet, but noticeable, clearing of the throat followed.

T.L. stopped and murmured a quiet "Aw shit," under his breath.

"I wasn't aware, Thomas, that you had rejoined the club," said the distinguished looking guy in the blue blazer. His head was held so far back I thought his neck might snap. I'd swear he was looking at us through his nostrils.

"I haven't, nor do I ever intend to Lusch. One of your more hospitable members invited my friend and me for lunch."

"And who would that member be?" asked Lusch.

"Why, you want to blackball him?"

"Not at all, just curious." He paused, and apparently decided not to take it any further. "Well anyway Thomas, enjoy your *brief* visit."

He turned and continued on.

"I think I now understand what you've been saying about this place," I told T.L. "Who was *that*?"

"That my friend, was Louis Lusch the fourth, who happens to be the head, pompous ass-hole around this joint and the principle example of what I've been telling you. Let's get to the bar."

As it turned out, we didn't learn anything new from T. L.'s buddy that we hadn't already heard from Charlie. How the Mexican gained membership, aside from the "bullshit" that the members had been given, was open to speculation; the strongest rumor being that the Mexican had dug up some pretty nasty dirt on one of the board members.

The lunch itself was decent enough if you don't mind paying twenty five bucks for a fish sandwich with potato chips. I figured the chips ran about a buck each.

Driving back to the beach, T.L. turned to me and asked, "So what are you thinking?"

"Well, Thomas . . ."

"Cut the shit!"

"Sorry, couldn't resist. Okay, here's what this feeble Yankee brain is trying to process: The chief has a hunch there's foul play involved with Collinson's alleged accident, Lindy thinks there's something weird going on with the Mexican illegals she's working with, we have the murdered Mexican I found, and we have a murdered Mexican caddie who had caddied for the only 'outsider' the Poseidon has as a member, and *he* happens to be Mexican. And if what Charlie thinks he heard is correct, there's a strong possibility of a connection between the Mexican member and the caddy.

You know, just a couple of weeks ago our topic of conversation was wondering if we had made a clean escape through the hurricane season, and now we're knee deep in all this Mexican stuff. Doesn't it seem strange to you? It does to me, but I'll be damned if I can get a handle on it."

"I have a theory," T.L. announced.

"You do?" I asked, stunned.

"Ya want to hear it?"

"Absolutely."

"Well, it goes something like this: there is a direct correlation between a man's ability to think clearly and his having a hand wrapped around a cold beer."

I was disappointed, but certainly not surprised.

"Indeed, an astute observation my friend, and one we should promptly remedy," I replied.

T.L. looked at his watch, turned towards me with a smile and said, "According to my calculations, we should be deep into our thought process in about fifteen minutes."

T. L.'s estimate was right on the money.

Chapter 27

Within fifteen minutes we were seated on my back deck, each sipping a cool one, and, surprise, a cigar had magically materialized.

"Lindy still gives you hell about those things, doesn't she?"

"Well yeah, but since I cut down to one a day, with some days none, she doesn't give me quite as rough a time."

"Matt, it really is a filthy habit."

I turned to him, astonished. "And just who in the hell was it I saw *chewing*, for God's sake, the other day out on the boat? I know it wasn't Karl!"

He grinned, but ignored me.

It was a pleasant, late afternoon. We noticed several schools of bait fish skipping across the canal water, with an occasional mullet bursting through the surface.

"Is anybody home?" Chief Curt Everhart's voice came from the house.

I turned to see the chief coming through the garage towards the deck.

"I knocked up front, then thought I'd try back down here."

"Glad you did. Hey, it's after five, if you're off duty and care to, grab a beer from fridge in the garage and join us," I said.

He hesitated a moment, checked his watch, turned and reentered the garage.

"Jesus," T.L. whispered to me, "he looks like shit."

"Sure does," I agreed.

The chief came back out popping the tab of the beer can.

He sat in the chair I'd placed across from T. L. and me, and I'd swear his uniform was even more rumpled than last Monday.

"Damn Matt, I left my cigars at the office, you got another one of those things around?"

"Yup." I got up to get a stogie out of the stash I keep in the garage.

"Think I'll move down to the dock if both you guys are going to pollute my air," threatened T.L.

I returned, the chief lit up and we sat sipping our beers and looking out at the canal. No one spoke.

T. L. and I had information for Curt, but I felt certain this impromptu visit of his was not purely a social call and decided to wait.

The chief eventually broke the silence, "You fill Tommy Lee in on our conversation about Collinson earlier in the week?" he asked, looking at me.

I wasn't sure how to answer, but figured that the truth should prevail.

"Yeah, I did Chief; I thought maybe, you know, another…"

"It's okay Matt, believe me, at this point I can use all the help I can get. This is turning into a first class rat's nest." He paused and looked around, checking that no one was in ear shot.

He took a long tug of his beer.

"A couple of hours ago, an S.B.I. officer came by with the results of their investigation into Dean's crash."

T. L. and I sat, listening.

"You ain't gonna believe it. Suicide," he said in disgust, shaking his head.

"What!" Tommy Lee and I bellowed in unison.

"That's right, suicide, and that's not the half of it, it gets worse, a hell-of-a lot worse."

"My God, chief," I said.

He took another long swallow. I thought about getting him another, but was glued to my seat.

"Here's the deal, and you ain't gonna believe it; seems that things have been a bit slow lately in the county on the murder front. The only two murders in months have been the one you found Matt, that and the kid, the Mexican caddy they pulled out of the Cape Fear. Anyway, you remember I asked for a detailed look into Dean's accident?"

"Yeah, sure," I replied.

"Well, with things being so slow, they had plenty of time to check everything out, just as I told 'em to. I don't know if you guys are aware of this, but an officer, in addition to the service weapon he's issued, is also permitted to carry one personal weapon of his choice as a back-up. Not all officers elect to do it, but most choose something small, like a .38 caliber revolver. That's what Dean had as his back-up."

He took another swig and finished the beer, then crushed the can with one hand.

"Hold it Chief, I'll be right back."

I returned, handed him a fresh beer, and he continued.

"Thanks, Matt, and this will do it for me. I just needed a couple of quick relaxers. So anyways, the forensics guy decides he'll run a test on Dean's back-up weapon."

"Why?" I asked.

"Because he didn't have squat to do and because he's the same genius who worked the slug taken out of your "gator," Matthew. He was shot with a .38, and guess what in the hell they discovered? The slug from that body you found in the waterway matched a slug fired from Dean's back-up. The bullet in your "gator" was fired from Dean's personal revolver."

"You're shitting us!" T.L. gasped.

"Nope." He took a swig of the new beer. "There's no arguing with the test results, they're conclusive. But hang on fellas," he took another swig and several quick, irritated puffs on the cigar, "it gets even better. Guess what else they found?"

"I'm afraid to," I said.

"In the trunk," the chief said, looking down and slowly shaking his head in disbelief as he spoke, "tucked away behind the spare, wrapped in a towel, was a second revolver. Now, are you two ready for this?" he asked, looking back up. "It turns out it was the one used to kill that Poseidon kid, the caddy"

"Ah shit," groaned T.L. in disbelief, "no friggin' way."

"Afraid so, it's another absolute, positive match. Matt, I think this can had a hole in it, if you don't mind."

I made a quick round trip to the fridge.

The chief gave a strained chuckle as he accepted the beer. "Now wouldn't it be funnier than hell if the Chief of Police needs a designated driver."

I started to say "I'd be happy to . . . ," but he waved me off with his cigar hand.

"Anyways, the county boys are saying that in both cases, Dean was the shooter. They got the guns, and they got his prints on each gun, and only his prints.

"This is crazier than hell," said T. L.

"Tell me about it; they're saying my guy was not only a crooked cop, but sweet Jesus, a hit man? That's pure, unadulterated bullshit."

"You said the county guys are calling his death a suicide?" I asked.

"Yeah, would you believe it? Their theory goes something along the lines of Collinson, realizing he was gonna get caught sooner or latter, made it appear as though he was drunk and checked himself out by deliberately smashing into that tree, fits in with why no skid marks."

"So, he wasn't under the influence?" I asked.

"Nope, the toxicologist's report indicated no booze in the blood stream, which confirms what I told you earlier, Dean didn't drink. They're saying he faked it to cover up the suicide. Since there's proof he pulled the trigger in both shootings, the county boys are closing both cases. Neat. No real motive as far as anyone can determine, but both murders are solved. Ain't that convenient as all hell?"

There was an awkward silence.

"Chief," I said, "don't get teed off with me, but is there some outside chance they might be right? How well did you really know Collinson?"

"He was a good cop Matt! Been with me for three years. Came

132

with the highest recommendations from the L.A. P. D., and you know that couldn't have been any picnic out there. He was a bit of a loner, and stayed his distance, even with the other officers. We weren't friends if that's what you mean, but I try not to get tight with anyone who works for me–found over the years it's the best policy."

He was quiet for several moments.

"Okay, maybe there's some ego kicking in here. As long as I've been in the business, to have one of my own . . . I just can't accept it." He looked at his watch. "Shit, I better get going. There's gonna be all kinds of hell once this gets out." He got up to go.

"You okay?" I asked.

"You mean to drive? Yeah, I'm fine. Thanks, fellas."

He gave a weary wave of the hand and walked out through the garage.

"I really feel sorry for the guy," I told T. L.

"Yeah, is that why you didn't mention that stuff Charlie told us?"

"Right, I thought it would've been too much for now. He's got his hands full. Maybe tomorrow, after things settle down."

"The case is being closed Matt; whether the chief wants to believe it or not, Collinson had to be the killer. They've got all the proof they need. What difference does it make at this point if those two wetbacks out at the Poseidon knew each other or not?"

"I don't know. Somehow it's all too neat T. L., and you can tell Curt thinks so too. What could have been Collinson's motive for killing those people? Was he more than just a cop? Was he a loan shark and these guys hadn't paid him? Hell, he wouldn't have had *time* to loan the caddy money, the kid has just gotten here! It just doesn't make sense. And we never did find out exactly how that guy wormed his way into the club. Aren't you still curious about that?"

"Well, yeah, kinda."

We heard Lindy's car pull into the garage.

I flipped the remaining stub of my stogie into the canal.

"Chicken," T. L. said through a huge grin.

"You got that right," I replied as he made a couple of low

clucking sounds.

"Hi Hon," I called as she came through the garage door.

"Hi, yourself, I can smell the smoke."

"Lady," said T. L., "you ought to quit whatever it is you're doing and hire yourself out to airports as an illegal substance detector. You could make a fortune with that nose of yours.

"And stay high all day? Come to think of it, I guess some folks would consider that a fringe benefit!" she laughed. "Well now, how was 'boys' day out' at the club?"

T. L. and I looked at each other.

"You tell her," I said to T. L.

"Nah, I gotta run, I'll let you have that pleasure."

I thought about the ninety bucks I'd dropped at the Poseidon for three fish and chips and three beers, and realized that lunch wasn't the smartest place for me to begin my recap of the day's events.

T.L. got up to leave as I started with "Well Hon, it's like this, and you're probably aren't going to believe it, but . . ."

"Don't tell me; you had to take out a second mortgage to cover lunch, right?" she laughed.

Chapter 28

Chief Everhart's remark could not have proven more prophetic. By the early edition of each local TV channel's news broadcast, it was apparent that "all kinds of hell" had indeed broken loose. The story of the beach cop turned killer, and his subsequent suicide, took up the major portion of each program. There were even the inevitable instant editorials requesting immediate investigations into police corruption and brutality.

No one in the viewing area was enjoying the coverage more than Delgado. He was ecstatic. He channel surfed frequently in an effort to learn every detail being reported. It was obvious that the county law enforcement officials were holding nothing back, even though the killer was one of their own. And, even though Officer Collinson's victims were *illegal, itinerant outsiders*, it seemed the murders had been conclusively solved.

The plan Delgado and Che had devised at the Charlotte airport had been executed with even greater perfection than they could have thought possible. The pistol Collinson had used to take out that piss ant from Cárdenas turned out to have been Collinson's personal weapon. What an incredible break. Delgado assumed the jerk would have been smart enough to use an untraceable gun, then ditch it.

The scheme he and Che had devised and followed was to plant the pistol Delgado had used to snuff the kid, the one he had given Che in the parking lot at the airport, in the trunk of Collinson's car after Che had pressed Collinson's prints on it. He would then arrange the crash with Collinson's already unconscious, if not dead, body in the car. Delgado would be rid of Collinson, and the kid's murder would be solved. That Collinson used his personal weapon in the other situation was an incredible bonus and Delgado knew now that he was completely off the hook in both situations.

He sat transfixed before the TV, bothering only to surf the news channels and sip his drink. He had polished off three or four *Recuerdos* by this time, but a celebratory drink, along with a cigar, was most certainly in order.

"Carmen!" he shouted.

Carmen was in the kitchen preparing Delgado's dinner when she heard him call. From the tone of it, she was certain something was wrong and ran to the entertainment room, only to find him staring, with a broad smile, at the TV.

"In the refrigerator there are several bottles of Dom Perignon. Open one, put it in an ice bucket and bring it to me." Still with his eyes glued to the TV, he ordered, "Then go to my office and get me a Cubano from the humidor and my lighter–hurry woman!"

Carmen ran out. She had never seen Señor Delgado so excited. She could not find the champagne in the refrigerator. She was afraid to tell Delgado this, but had no choice.

"Damn it Carmen, it's in the one in the basement! You should know that, *mierda*!"

She hustled down the basement steps, located the bottle, hurried back upstairs, popped the cork, put the bottle in the bucket, poured ice around it, and took it into Delgado along with a champagne glass.

"Where's the damn cigar, Carmen?"

She rushed to his office, retrieved a cigar from the humidor, grabbed the lighter and took them to Delgado.

She stood by, apprehensively, as he lit up. Apparently, thank God, the son-of-a-bitch was finished with her as there were no further orders. He remained transfixed by what he was watching. She scurried back to the kitchen and turned on the kitchen TV to the same channel Delgado had on.

As she stood there staring at the screen, she couldn't help but wonder why this news was so interesting, so important to that *hijo de puta*, that son of a whore, in the other room. Of what importance was this policeman and his killings to Señor Delgado? The longer she watched, the more interested she became. There was something there, something she couldn't quite put her finger on, something intriguing . . .

The local news was over. He flipped through the networks, but there was no mention of the law officer turned killer. If this had happened in New York City, or back in L.A., you could bet your ass it would have been the lead story on each of the national networks, plus Fox and CNN. But this was sleepy 'ol North Carolina and the elite, big city media really didn't give a shit what happened here. *Which is just as well*, Delgado smiled to himself.

He turned the TV off after the national news, deciding he'd catch the eleven o'clock local broadcasts for any further developments.

He considered calling Che, to fill him in on how perfectly things had worked out, but decided against it; no sense in giving him the opportunity to request a bonus, as he'd paid the hit man quite handsomely to begin with. Besides, Che was a professional and would most likely consider the compliment an embarrassment.

There was one lingering item to handle, one loose end; the girl...what had happened with the girl? He'd forgotten to check with Ernesto at *La tienda* to see if she had started "working" yet.

He reached the store manager at his home.

"I haven't seen her. She hasn't left the trailer since returning from the hospital yesterday. I've asked several people. No one has seen her. A neighbor of hers told me she heard that the girl hasn't spoken one word since returning."

"Do you remember what I told you?"

"*Sí*. You said she must start by tomorrow, Friday."

"That is correct. But from what you say, it appears we may have a small delay. Go the trailer and speak with her. You cannot discuss this if anyone else is there, but tell her she must come to *La tienda*. Tell her you will take no excuses. When she comes, you tell her she must start Monday without fail. Understand?"

"*Sí*."

"Monday, and I mean without fail."

"*Sí.*"

"Call me after you have spoken with her and made the arrangements for her first 'jobs.' Don't push her too hard the first day; two or three customers should be sufficient. I don't remember if I told you, she's pregnant. She doesn't look it, but she says she is. We'll have to get as much work out of her as quickly as is possible. She and her husband owe me a lot of money. After Monday, make certain she has a full schedule for two hours each day. Do you understand?"

"*Sí.*"

After finishing with Ernesto, Delgado went to the basement for another bottle of Dom Perignon, came back up and headed outside to the back deck. He felt relaxed and quite pleased with the way things were shaping up. He also found himself wishing, once again, that he had arranged for some Vegas companionship for the weekend.

Halfway into the second bottle, and on his second cigar, he had a sudden thought, actually, an inspired one. Why send that girl, what was her name? María, yes, María. *Why send that girl out on Monday? Ernesto can bring her here. I'll be the first to sample the new merchandise. I sure as hell won't want anything to do with her once the dirty little piss ants get their hands on her.*

Grabbing the champagne bottle by its neck, Delgado took a large swig, started back inside, bumped into the door frame, grunted "*Mierda,*" swaggered through the doorway, located his phone, and placed a call to his store manager for the second time that evening.

Chapter 29

Her silence continued. On Friday morning, the others in the trailer discussed taking her to a doctor or back to the hospital.

Carlos was beside himself. If there were some way, *any* way, to get money, he would leave immediately for Cárdenas with María and get the hell out of this terrible place. In his despair, he seriously considered breaking into *La tienda* at night to steal whatever cash was there, or, if finding no money, seizing things of value he could sell. He had seen the jewelry case at the back of the store. He imagined robbing the gas station close to the trailer park. He thought about robbing *la farmacia* of both its drugs and money. It made no difference. In the end, he knew he'd get caught, causing an even worse situation for María. God would not forgive him for what would happen to his wife and baby if they were left alone. From the beginning, he was certain there would be trouble; he remembered his premonition in the truck as they bumped along the dirt roads toward the border, and hopefully a new life. They should have gotten off the truck back then and returned home.

Now his pregnant wife was sick, and no one had a clue as to what was wrong with her. Pablo, his closest friend since they were boys, had been murdered–murdered for God's sake! On the worst day, on the bleakest day back in Cárdenas, nothing had ever come close to being as *horrible* as this.

He pestered José constantly.

"I've told you a thousand times Carlos, no one will give you any money–you owe too much already. And if you should return to Cárdenas, how do you expect to pay what you will owe? There is nothing for you there! *Nada . . . mierda!* You know that *hombre, nada!* Don't you remember; that's why we left? You must stay here. It will get better."

"How can that be?" moaned Carlos. "Tell me José, how can that be? It gets worse here each day, not better! María and I must leave. Look at her! My wife will die if we stay! I am certain of it . . . she will die!"

"There is nothing more I can tell you *mi amigo*, I have no other answers."

⚜

She was, in fact, able to speak. On Thursday morning, unexpectedly left alone in the trailer for a few moments, she whispered a passionate prayer for her baby, for Carlos and for herself. She prayed that God, in His mercy, would look over them, protect them and somehow save them from harm. She could talk to God, but she could say nothing to her husband.

How can I tell him? she agonized. *If I speak of this to Carlos, he will go crazy. He will try to find that monster, Delgado, and try to kill him. Then there will be terrible trouble! But if I don't tell him, there is no way to stop this thing! It is impossible, but I cannot let this thing happen!*

Not knowing how to explain the problem without putting their lives in greater peril, she decided not to speak until she had devised a plan. That was her second prayer of the morning, before anyone returned to the trailer; she prayed earnestly that God give her an idea that would save them–their fate was now in His hands.

⚜

Saturday morning arrived with no change in María.

At mid morning, with only Rosa and María in the trailer, there was a knock at the door.

Rosa wondered who it could possibly be as there were seldom

140

visitors to the trailer. Opening the door she was surprised to find Ernesto, *La tienda's* manager, standing before her, holding a small package. Ernesto was no stranger of course, everyone in the trailer park knew him, but for Ernesto to come to a trailer, well, that was unheard of.

"*Buenos dias,*" he said to Rosa, flashing a broad smile.

Recovering from her initial surprise, Rosa returned the smile, "*Buenos dias,*" she replied, still a bit confused.

They stood at the door for a few awkward moments.

"*Señora,*" Ernesto said, "I understand that María remains sick since returning from the hospital. I have come to see if there is anything I can do. Also, I brought some *dulces*, some candy that might cheer her up. It is excellent *chocolate* from Mexico."

"*Gracias Señor, por favor,* please, come in for a coffee.

"*Gracias Señora,*" he replied.

Stepping through the doorway, the first thing to hit him was the repugnant odor of the place. His brain couldn't process it all so quickly, but his immediate impressions were of sweat, cooking grease, musty furniture and soiled diapers. *Miguel is right, these people live like cockroaches.* The second thing to hit him was the sight of María, huddled on the couch at the far end of the small trailer. He could tell from the short distance that she looked pale, and tense, but nonetheless, still quite pretty. *She doesn't belong with these cockroaches,* he thought, *she deserves much better.*

María, lying on the couch, had overheard the exchange between the two at the door. Her reaction upon hearing Ernesto's voice was of intense apprehension. She gave an inaudible gasp as a chill shot through her body. She sat up, slid to the far corner of the couch, drew her legs under her and tucked her hands under her legs. She then quickly withdrew her hands and placed them across her stomach as though to protect her baby from some evil force.

Rosa, immediately after offering the coffee, realized she had made a terrible mistake. They had run out two days before. She would have to go borrow some, and quickly.

Ernesto and Rosa both looked over at María, as though observing a patient.

"Still, she does not say anything *Señor*; we do not know what is wrong. Perhaps if you speak with her. I must run next door, but for only a moment. *Por favor*, please sit down and visit with María. Try to have her say something."

Realizing she would be left alone with this man, this creepy colleague of that monster, María became increasingly distressed.

Rosa left to locate some coffee and Ernesto picked up a yellow, plastic chair, with broken slats off the small, worn kitchen floor and placed it directly in front of María. With Rosa gone this would be, perhaps, his only opportunity before Monday to speak with her alone. Looking at her closely, Ernesto was startled to see just how frail she had become since he had last seen her. But God, he'd swear that her fragility, her very vulnerability, made her even more desirable.

"María," he said, "relax, please don't be afraid." As he spoke he could not resist raising his right hand to gently touch her pale face.

María's head flinched back.

"Don't be frightened, it isn't necessary," he told her.

As he spoke, his hand slid down to her neck. "I brought you some *chocolate*."

He stroked her neck lightly with the back of his hand.

"It's from Mexico; it is the very best. Would you like some now? It will help you to feel better."

María gazed blankly at Ernesto, her eyes wide with fright, her body further repulsed by his touch. Softly whimpering, she pushed herself back as far as she could into the corner of the couch.

"I have some very good news for you María. You will not have to start doing that, ah, 'thing' on Monday, that 'thing' with all those different men. You will not have to become a *puta*. Do you understand what I just said? That is good news, *si*?"

Ernesto could no longer constrain himself. He had daydreamed—no, he had lusted, too often about being alone with this beautiful creature. The back of his hand was now sliding up and down her dress over the top of her breast, rubbing with a little more pressure with each pass

She continued her soft whimpering; her hands remained clasped firmly on her stomach, her entire body in a frozen state.

"Instead, I am going to take you to see Señor Delgado on Monday. He would like to, ah, spend some time with you. So would I María, believe me, so would I. But it will have to be later for me. *Sí? Es posible? Sí, es posible.* After Miguel. This is much better than that other thing you spoke with Miguel about, don't you think? Yes, of course you do. It will work better for each of us. Possibly, you and I, we could make a little arrangement, and you would not have to do that other thing at all. Wouldn't that be nice? "

He turned his hand, and with mounting excitement was now cupping her full breast with his palm and eager fingers.

"You must not say anything to anyone. You are doing the right thing by not speaking. It is very smart of you, María. I knew when you first came into my store that you were *muy inteligente* as well as *muy bonita.*" He continued, now sliding his other hand along María's thigh. "Come to *La tienda* on Monday, I will take you to Miguel myself." Ernesto's eyes, which were on fire, were met in return by eyes of ice.

"Everything will be fine. You will see. You will not have to worry about anything any more."

Through it all, María's hands protected her baby from the sinister force scorching her body.

Ernesto was in the process of losing control, when the sound of the trailer door opening brought his advances to a sudden halt. He quickly jerked both hands back.

"Ah," said Rosa, entering the trailer, "did you have some success with her?"

The irony of the question was not lost on Ernesto.

"I'm afraid not Rosa, she will not talk to me either. But I told her to come to *La tienda* on Monday. We have a new shipment of dresses she will like. They are the prettiest we have yet received."

"*Sí*, that's a wonderful idea!" replied Rosa. "A walk to *La tienda* is just what you need María! I will see that she does it *Señor*. Now, let me prepare us coffee. It will take only a moment."

Ernesto, rising from the chair, looked at Rosa apologetically. "*Señora*, I am sorry,but I just remembered something and must return to my store.. It is *muy importante*, or I would stay and enjoy some of your fine coffee. I am certain it is *delicioso*."

He turned to María and said, "María, we have also received new lipsticks, some are samples. You *must* come to the store and I will give you one. You may have your choice from all of them!"

"*Sí* María!" exclaimed Rosa, "How nice of Señor Ernesto. Now there is no question about it, you must go to *La tienda* on Monday!"

Ernesto left the trailer. Although only a short distance between the store and the trailer, he had driven his car. Driving slowly along the gravel road, he could still feel his touch upon the girl. Oh, how he envied Delgado!

He was convinced that nothing more could be done between now and Monday. He was also convinced of one other thing, if his efforts proved unsuccessful and neither he nor Rosa were able to persuade María to come to his store on Monday, he, Ernesto Santiago, was in very deep, no, make that *extremely* deep shit, with one Miguel Delgado.

Chapter 30

The weekend passed quietly, at least for Lindy and me. Without question, Chief Everhart would have described it differently. Friday evening Lindy and I watched the extensive news coverage regarding the alleged crimes and ultimate fate of Officer Dean Collinson, and through it all, couldn't help but feel sorry for our friend. Unfortunately, there was nothing we could do to help.

At one point, Lindy remarked, "The poor guy must be going through hell."

"I'm sure of it," I replied. "But we can't call him. If he wants to hide from the press, or just wants to chat, or have a drink, he'll call and we'll invite him over. It's going to be difficult for a while, but this is something he'll have to work his way through. He knows we're here if he needs us."

With the local and national news over, I switched off the TV and told Lindy I was going to my room to burn some Louis Armstrong CDs for Charlie, the caddie master.

I was headed upstairs when I thought to ask, "You haven't mentioned anything about that Mexican girl, the one that was in the hospital."

"No, I haven't heard anything since I saw her Tuesday. I thought about going out to the trailer, but since they haven't called or come by the clinic, I'm assuming she's fine."

"Well, you're probably right," I said, heading for the stairs.

"No news is most often, good news."

"So they say."

In the Poseidon's caddy shack yesterday, I'd taken note of Charlie's Armstrong CDs, and he had indicated to me that they were the extent of his Satchmo collection. It was apparent that he was missing a few essential Armstrong recordings. I spent the balance of Friday night burning Armstrong's *Town Hall Concert* with Jack Teagarden, his *Armstrong Plays W.C. Handy*, the one in which the great blues composer, upon hearing the tapes of this record, had tears streaming down his face as he listened to how beautifully Louis played his music, the two incredible sets with Ella Fitzgerald that Norman Granz produced, and a reissue of the early, classic *Hot Five* sessions on Columbia. These would round out Charlie's collection and his essential Armstrong music would be complete.

My plan was to run out to the Poseidon early Monday morning and surprise Charlie with my musical C.A.R.E. package. I was certain he'd appreciate it, and, selfishly, I got a kick out of doing this kind of stuff for fellow jazz buffs.

Saturday and Sunday passed quickly, with the weekend's highlights being food related.

For lunch on Saturday we dropped by Archibald's Delicatessen, located on the other side of the bridge. Archibald's is a favorite local eatery and prepares the finest Muffuletta sandwich outside of New Orleans. Lindy and I split one and then could not escape without Lindy, ordering for takeout, a couple of their fabulous Bran Muffins. We munched down on those while walking across the street to L. Bookworm to pick up the latest copy *Cook's Illustrated*, which we both considered the premier cooking magazine of the zillion out there.

Then on Sunday, we made our umpteenth stab at yet another shrimp and grits recipe. Over the years, we'd taken several shots at this southern classic, and it had become something of an obsession; our personal search for the southern seafood holy grail. Much to our delight, this one turned out excellent and clearly surpassed anything we had previously attempted, and even those we had been served in several of the southeast's finer restaurants.

This we considered a major triumph and the recipe was placed in our permanent file, next to the ultra secret shrimp and crab bisque recipe.

By Sunday evening all seemed well with the world and tomorrow would begin the fun and frolic of a new week. I felt that things would settle down now that both murder cases were closed, the situation with the Mexican girl that Lindy was fond of appeared to be okay, and I was looking forward to seeing Charlie in the morning and having a little jazz chit chat. Indeed, things were just fine on our little island paradise.

Chapter 31

"Good God, they must be bringing them in by the bus load today!" exclaimed Sandy, another of the nurses, as she slid into the chair across from Lindy in the break room.

"Mondays are usually busy, but this is crazy," Lindy agreed. "It's been hectic alright, and have you noticed all the new ones? I've only seen a couple of regulars all morning; most of them have just gotten here."

"Same with me. And those new ones, God they drive me nuts. Each one's got ten thousand questions, and most of them unrelated to what they're here at the clinic for. I'm not a nurse anymore–I'm a social worker, baby sitter and information booth!"

Lindy laughed. "I know what you mean. I'm supposed to be interpreting, but I find myself giving advice on everything from how to use condoms to where to catch a bus. It's crazy. They get here and don't know anything about anything. But you have to give them credit Sandy, they've got guts."

"Oh, they've got guts alright, along with a few other things," Sandy replied with a laugh.

"Okay, I'll bite, why the laugh?" asked Lindy.

"I had a guy this morning . . . I looked for you but you were busy so Leslie interpreted for me, anyway, I had this young guy, illegal of course, who arrived here a couple of weeks ago and he's got syphilis *and* gonorrhea. I asked him where he got them and he looked at me with a straight face, just as serious as he could be, and said, 'Out of the air.' I told him that was impossible, so again he looked at me just as serious as he could be, and said, 'It must have been from the toilet seat. There are fourteen of us in the trailer I stay in, and one of the others must have the diseases and left them on the toilet seat.' I told him it couldn't happen that way either. So then he said, and this is good Lindy, I've never heard this one before, he told me he had been given a pair of old pants from a friend and the friend must have these things so he got the diseases from his friend's old pants. I couldn't help but laugh, and during this whole time, while she was interpreting, I thought Leslie would fall out of her chair. But it's actually an extremely serious situation. He could be, and probably is, spreading this stuff. I called in social services to talk with him. So now we've got to get him cleaned up and find out where he got it and who he's been with and get *them* cleaned up or we could have a damn epidemic. I don't dare mention this story to Curtis, or he'll have another fit over what it's costing us, or rather, what it's costing *him* in taxes to take care of these people. I think I told you before; he gets royally pissed every time I bring up something about this. I really try hard not to talk about my work at home."

"Well, I hate to say it, but your husband has every right to get upset, particularly in a case like this where it's costing a ton because of this guy's raunchy, not to mention promiscuous, sex life. You know Sandy, I think we do a lot good and I can justify it in my own mind, but to pay for someone screwing around like this idiot . . . I don't think so."

"Oh, you're right, Lindy, and so's Curtis. It's just that he really blows when he hears about this kind of stuff."

"Then you won't be able to tell him about Anita either," Lindy said, smiling.

"What about Anita? Oh no, don't tell me, she's pregnant again!"

"Yup. She was in today. Number four is on the way."

"I don't believe it!" exclaimed Sandy.

"*And* number five."

"What? Twins? Jesus, this is getting to be too much!"

"I don't think I'll even mention this one to Matt. You know, she goes back to Mexico after she's had each baby. She goes back, but leaves her kids here with her sister. When she gets pregnant again, she returns here to have the baby. That way each kid is a United State's citizen. We pay for each birth and for each kid's basic needs, along with Anita's health care 'til she's well enough to return to Mexico."

"Lindy, why in the hell can't we do something about this kind of stuff? I'm a nurse. I want to help those who really need it, but damn if I want to work for, and have to *pay* for, all those damn cheaters."

"I don't know; I feel the same way about the abusers, it makes me sick. But with the border the way it is, most of these people have found ways to come and go as they please. I even know a couple that crosses back and forth five and six times a year; it's amazing how easy it's become."

Sandy looked up at the clock and said she had to run.

Lindy sat at the table for a few more minutes finishing her coffee and thinking about some of the other situations she had run into that were nothing short of incomprehensible. The one she didn't tell anyone about was the Cuban family she had helped a few years ago when she and Matt were still living in Raleigh. The Catholic Church had sponsored the family, which consisted of the grandparents, the parents and four kids. The Church had gotten the family out of Cuba through Mexico. Although the family received the usual services and benefits, the thing that blew Lindy's mind was that the grandfather, who was sixty-five, and who had never worked a day in the US, immediately started receiving Social Security payments. It was some kind of a special deal for Cuban exiles and some other kinds of political refugees.

Lindy shook her head and grinned thinking about what Tommy Lee's reaction would be if he knew such a thing was going on. He'd go totally ballistic! For that matter, so would Matt!

She was just finishing her coffee when she heard the P.A announcement: *"Lindy, you have a call on line nine. Lindy, line nine."*

150

Chapter 32

Driving out to see Charlie Monday morning, I thought back to the original reasons T. L. and I had first gone to the club and realized that the information we'd been seeking on that trip was no longer of any consequence. The fact that the club had a Mexican member no longer held any interest. With Collinson having murdered the caddy, if there was any connection between the Mexican member and the caddy, as indicated by what Charlie had overheard, that was now irrelevant.

There were several kids hanging around outside the caddy shack when I walked in. Charlie was busy inside giving a couple of caddies their assignments.

It was a gorgeous day and many golfers would try to take advantage of it. I thought I'd just hand Charlie the CDs then leave as it was obvious he was going to be a very busy guy.

He looked up, gave me something of a puzzled look, then in apparent recognition, smiled, waved and said he'd only be a minute.

The two kids left and Charlie came out from behind the counter.

"Matt, isn't it?"

"You got it Charlie, good memory."

"Nah, just lucky, I remember 'cause of the jazz."

"Speaking of which," I handed him the Armstrong CDs.

He looked through the small pile.

"Jeeze, this is awfully nice of ya. There's some great stuff here. I used ta have a couple of these on LP, but I'll be damn if I know what I done with 'em."

"Well, I hope you enjoy these Charlie; 'ol Satch was the main man and I never get tired of hearing this stuff. Looks like you're pretty busy here, so I had better run along."

"Where's your buddy, Tommy Lee?" he asked.

"I think he's on the links somewhere today, the man's a golfing and fishing fool."

"He's that alright, shame he can't play here no more."

I started to nod my head in agreement, but the way Charlie had said 'can't play here no more,' aroused my curiosity.

"Yeah, well you know how it is," I said, trying to push the conversation along.

"They still together?" he asked.

"They . . . ah . . . they?"

"Yeah, him and, oh, what the heck's her name? Funny sort of thing . . ."

"Lizzie?" I said.

"Yeah, that's it, Lizzie. Tommy Lee and Lizzie! Matt, ya shoulda been around here back then! Boy, those two sure caused some sort of a ruckus I'll tell ya!" he said shaking his head and grinning.

"I'll bet," I said, continuing to fake my way through the conversation. "And yes, they're very happy together."

"Good for them. But still, just 'cause they was both married don't mean Tommy Lee shoulda been throwed out."

Aha!

"I know, and you're right," I replied, giving Charlie a serious nod of agreement while desperately trying to hold back a smile.

"The thing is," Charlie continued, "after they was found out, they didn't do nothin' as far as Lizzie was concerned, and then her and her husband dropped out of the club and go and get divorced anyways. Then Tommy and Lizzie go and get hooked up."

"Yeah, that's what I heard," I lied. "But really they're doing great and are terrific neighbors. Listen, you're a busy man and I gotta run. You take care Charlie, and enjoy the Armstrong."

"I will Matt, can't thank ya enough. You're a swell guy. Listenin' to a couple of 'em will be like visiting an old friend. Be sure and tell Tommy Lee 'hey' for me."

I barely made it to the car before howling!

T.L. had been caught shacking up with Lizzie, a fellow member's wife! He hadn't left the Poseidon because of the snobbery–they'd booted him out! Oh my, my, my. I had learned something I wasn't sure I even wanted to know, but even so, driving home, the broad smile on my face never faded.

I'd keep this to myself . . . well really, I'd try my damnest.

Chapter 33

As luck would have it, he *was* in deep shit, and it *was* of the extreme variety.

By mid morning Monday, while Matt was out at the Poseidon chatting with Charlie (and picking up some unexpected dirt on Tommy Lee), and Lindy was swamped at the clinic with new arrivals, and while Delgado was eagerly anticipating his afternoon tryst with beautiful María, Ernesto Santiago was pacing the aisles of *La tienda*, straightening the displays, rearranging the same ones several times over and in the process, shouting orders and making life miserable for his two store clerks.

He knew. He had known the moment he laid eyes on her in the trailer on Saturday that María would never make it to *La tienda*. She was too frightened. It wasn't going to work. The sooner he called Delgado, the better. But damn, he really didn't want to make that call. He needed to go back to the trailer one last time in an effort to persuade the girl it was her only hope, that she had no choice. That much he should do before facing the wrath of his boss and possibly losing his job . . . or worse.

As he slowly made his way back along the dirt road to the trailer, he noticed several people gathered in front of Rosa's. He recognized Rosa, her husband José, their kids, Gina and several other residents of the trailer park. Rosa was waving her arms excitedly as she spoke to the group, and was in an obvious agitated state.

He'd barely gotten out of his car before Rosa was by his side, screaming.

"They are gone!" she cried into his face.

"Who is gone, what are you talking about woman?"

"María and Carlos, *Señor Santiago*, they are not here, they are gone!"

Ernesto tried to hide the panic that swept throughout his body.

"Rosa, get in the trailer," he commanded, grabbing her firmly by the arm and steering her hurriedly towards the door. José, the children, and Gina, followed, but Ernesto turned and ordered them to wait outside.

Once inside, he grabbed both of Rosa's arms, swung her towards him and stared straight into her panicked eyes.

"Now *Señora,* don't lie to me, tell me exactly what has happened," he commanded.

"I don't know, I don't know!" she exclaimed. "I get up to cook breakfast. Every day I do this. I try always not to disturb María or Carlos or Gina. This morning I go to the kitchen and it is very quiet to me, too much quiet. I look at the couch and there was nobody. I look all over and see only Gina. No María. No Carlos. Gina, she was asleep. I go outside to look. No one is there. I think maybe they go to the hospital or something. But that was many hours ago. I ask Ariel, my neighbor, to call. He goes to the phone outside *La tienda* and comes back and says they are not at the hospital. I tell you they have disappeared *Señor Santiago!*"

Oh shit, I'm as good as dead, thought Ernesto.

He hurried over to the door; "José, get in here!"

José walked quickly into the trailer.

"José, do not lie to me, where have they gone?"

José gave Rosa a quick nervous glance.

Now standing behind Santiago, Rosa gave a nearly imperceptible shake of her head.

"I do not know *Señor Santiago.* They have no car. They have no money. They have nothing."

Ernesto went back outside, walked over to Gina and stared fiercely into the shaken woman's face. "And you tell me, where have they gone?"

Gina slowly shook her bent head as tears welled in her eyes.

"Since Pablo was killed," said José, "she does not talk much, she mostly cries."

"Think, think hard, all of you! Where would they go?" he commanded of the group.

Everyone, including the children, shook their heads.

"We are all they have," Rosa said softly. "They know only us."

Driving slowly back to *La tienda*, which in all probability wouldn't be his much longer, Ernesto ran through the options. Actually, there weren't any. He had to call Delgado. Once harboring thoughts of rising within the ranks, he knew that possibility was now shot to hell. It could be worse, but he'd rather not think about that.

☙❦❧

"Gone! Gone? What do you mean, '*Gone!*'" Delgado screamed into the phone.

"No one knows where they are," replied Ernesto, with all the calm he could muster. "They disappeared early in the morning, before any one else in the trailer was awake."

"Gone! I give you one thing, one simple goddamn job and you screw it up. I thought maybe you were ready to advance, that you were smart, that maybe you could be more than a store clerk for us, and what do you do? You fuck up the first special assignment I give you! You are hopeless! Listen to me! You are a hopeless shit! *Mierda!*"

Ernesto was holding his cell phone several inches from his ear. He had been witness to many of Miguel's tirades in the past, but never one directed at him, and never one as vehement.

"*Sí,*" was all he could think to say.

"Ah, you stupid shit, so you agree with me!"

Ernesto was at a loss for words. He knew it best not to respond.

There was a pause. He could hear Delgado's irritated, heavy

breathing on the other end.

"What about the other cockroaches in the trailer, what did they tell you?"

Ernesto reiterated, as best he could under the circumstances, the entirety of his experience at the trailer.

"They are lying; those cockroaches know exactly where the two piss ants of Cárdenas are hiding."

"With your permission, I think they speak the truth. They were confused and upset. They were asking their neighbors if they knew, or had seen anything. I even spoke with the children. They know nothing."

"Bullshit, someone must know something!"

"*Con su permiso,* these two have no money, no car, they know no one, and the girl is sick. I saw her Saturday. She is very ill. Whatever they are doing, they cannot go far. I will find them. I commit to you, I will find them."

"*Find them*? You couldn't even keep them where they were! I am disappointed with you, very disappointed. You do nothing. Do you understand me? You do nothing until you hear back from me. Just stay where you are and run your goddamn store, which is apparently all you are good for. Do you understand you simple shit?"

"*Sí,*" Ernesto said, relieved that he apparently still had his job, not to mention his life.

❧

After hanging up on Ernesto, Delgado needed to cool down–literally He went to the bedroom, slipped on a pair of trunks, grabbed his robe and headed out to the pool.

Emerging after a few furious laps, he felt the slight chill of the autumn air and slipped on his white terry cloth robe. He then stuck his head in the door off the pool and called for Carmen to bring him a cigar. He thought about having a drink, but knew, regretfully, it was too early in the day.

"*Un tabaco y un Café Cubano,*" he ordered. Then, giving it a second thought, "*y un Kahlua!*"

Sitting in the lounge chair, now somewhat relaxed and warm in his robe, cigar in one hand, the small cup of strong Cuban coffee, laced with a shot of *Kahlua*, in the other, he had settled down and began working through the situation.

The fact that he wouldn't get laid today irritated him but was the least of his concerns. The fact that the two peasants from Cárdenas had skipped out; now that was major. The fact that all the other cockroaches would think they could get by with doing something similar, well, that just couldn't happen. He would have to find those two. He would find them and demonstrate the price to be paid for trying such a half-assed stunt.

He had to figure out how they'd pulled this off. He shook his head–something didn't add up. He was certain someone in the trailer was lying; someone in the trailer knew exactly what was going on.

Delgado looked at his watch. It was early morning in Las Vegas, especially for the night people, of which he knew Che was one. Still, time was of the essence; the two cockroaches must be found . . . and squashed.

Chapter 34

It was mid afternoon. I was on my way home and still grinning over what I'd learned from Charlie concerning T. L. and Lizzie's little indiscretion. I congratulated myself on the wisdom of burning the CDs for Charlie. As someone once said, *you have to give to receive.*

Making the turn into the driveway, the grin vanished. The garage door was up and Lindy's red Miata convertible was sitting inside. Mondays were the clinic's busiest day and she was never home until well past five. Something was up.

Uneasy at the sight of her car, I left mine in the gravel drive and sprinted up the steps.

Fumbling for the key, I opened the front door, took a few steps in, and froze.

Seated on the couch directly in front of me were two strangers, a man and woman, and there was absolutely no doubt in my mind that they were a couple of Latino illegals.

Huddling tight as I entered, they both gave me an uneasy stare. I couldn't help but think of two stunned deer caught in the headlights of a car. I looked for Lindy, didn't see her . . . and returned their gaze.

I was about to ask them what in the hell they were doing in my house, when Lindy appeared from our bedroom doorway.

She looked at me, surprised, and said, "Oh, Matt. I didn't hear you come in."

"Who are these two? I walk in my own home and . . ."

Before I could finish, Lindy continued with, "Matt, I've got a lot to tell you, but just settle down, everything's fine . . . sorta. But now I want you to meet María and Carlos Martinez."

The names registered.

"Lindy, aren't they the ones you told me about?"

"Yes, but as you can see, María is out of the hospital . . . Matt, please come over and say 'hello' to them, they're frightened and upset."

So am I, I thought.

Lindy rushed her words, running them together quickly so there would be no possibility of the Mexicans understanding her. I couldn't understand why in the hell she was getting us this deeply involved with illegals. It made no sense to me. I couldn't think of a single reason for them to be sitting on my couch in my home.

Lindy was on edge; more on edge than I'd ever seen her.

I walked over and, giving a nod, shook hands with the man. He stood and I noticed he was taller than I'd anticipated. I then offered my hand to the girl, who remained seated.

"*Con mucho gusto*, nice to meet you," I said.

She looked up at me with beautiful, but weary, dark eyes. I detected the slightest of nods. She offered her frail hand to mine. It wasn't until that moment that I realized, even with her apparent sadness, the simplicity of the natural beauty Lindy had mentioned to me previously, shone through.

Both of them were dressed in well-worn clothes, the girl's dress frayed and much too large for her, the man's shirt and pants, dirty, and with several paint splotches. It was also obvious that they both needed a shower.

Gently releasing her hand, I turned and gave Lindy an, *okay, what's-next* look.

She shrugged her shoulders.

"Listen Lindy, I want to know what in the hell's going on, we need to talk, and we need to talk now!" I didn't know or care if the intruders understood me or not.

"Yup, we sure do," she said with a shaky voice. "Why don't you fix us a drink and we'll go out to the front porch?"

She turned to ask María and Carlos something, then turned back to me.

"They don't want anything. I'll have a screwdriver, a touch towards the heavy side please. "

"Fine with me," I replied, "but isn't it just a 'tad' early?"

"Sure is. But I really could use one now, and trust me, so will you." She walked over and took my hands. Her's were ice cold. "You'll also want a cigar."

Oh dear God, I thought, *a bomb's about to be dropped.* Lindy suggest a cigar? My heart be still!

I made Lindy's screwdriver, but having been forewarned, figured a Bombay Sapphire Martini was definitely in order for me. I grabbed a cigar, and headed for the porch.

"Okay," I said, as Lindy came out, "let's not mess around with this, now what in the hell's going on?" Unable to settle into the comfort of a rocker, I remained standing, leaning against the porch railing.

"Matt, please don't swear at me, this isn't the easiest thing for me to explain"

"Okay."

"Don't get upset."

"Right, I won't get upset."

"Promise?"

"Damn it, Lindy!

"Okay, okay," she said.

She took a long sip of her drink and began.

"María and Carlos are in serious trouble Matt–actually their lives are in danger. It all started with Pablo, the body you found. He was their best friend. Pablo and his wife came here illegally with María and Carlos. The four of them have known each other since they were kids and decided to leave Mexico together. Pablo was killed because he couldn't pay what he owed the people who got them here. Carlos is in the same jam. Since Carlos hasn't been able to come up with the money, they wanted María, you see how pretty she is, they wanted her to begin prostituting herself, in other words, to become a whore, starting today, as a means of working off what they owe. Not only is that disgusting Matt, but damn it, she's pregnant, and the bastards know it"

"Hold on a minute Lindy, who are we talking about here? Who are *they*?"

"I don't know. There's some kind of gang, an organization. It's big. They bring the illegals here and charge them an outrageous fee. They control who works where, who lives where, where they buy food; that kind of stuff."

I didn't interrupt her story, but I knew that *they* had to be the Mexican Mafia that the chief had filled me in on.

"Okay," I said, "Sooo . . ."

"Sooo, María and Carlos had to get away. They would have forced her to start working, *whoring*–today!"

I walked to the end of the porch, sipped the martini and took a couple of puffs on the cigar.

"Lindy, I've a pretty good hunch where you're headed with this. As of now, we're hiding these people, right?" She nodded. "I understand that. I understand it, but I don't like it. Let me say something else before we go any further; if these two stay with us, we're harboring two illegal aliens from the U.S. government, which isn't any big deal, but also, we're hiding them from what I'm certain is the Mexican Mafia. Now that's a big deal. They're the *they* you were referring to."

"My God, is that who that is, the Mexican Mafia? Is there really such a thing? Are you sure?"

"Yeah, I'm sure. This is serious stuff Lindy–as serious as it gets. I don't mean to frighten you, but as long as those two are in our house, you and I are in as much danger as they are. You can bet the mafia guys are out looking for them this very moment. If they find out they're here with us . . ."

"Oh, my God, Matt, I didn't know what else to do. I . . ."

"How did you wind up with them in the first place, and why are they here in our home?"

"I got a call from Rosa this morning, she and her husband rent the trailer María and Carlos were staying in. She said María came to her bedroom in the middle of the night and told her that she and Carlos had to leave immediately; but she wouldn't say why. She only said they couldn't be seen by any one, and that they wanted

José, that's Rosa's husband, to drive them someplace safe. When they got to a safe place, Rosa was to call me and let me know where they were. María told her I would know what to do and that I would help them. She told Rosa it was their only chance."

Rosa said the family put on a good act this morning of convincing everyone that María and Carlos had simply disappeared during the night. But Rosa still doesn't know why María was so insistent that she and Carlos had to leave so quickly."

"So where did . . ."

"José."

"Where did José take them?" I said.

"He drove them, would you believe, to the library. Actually, that was pretty clever. The chances of any one they know seeing them there were pretty slim. As often as I'm there, I've never seen a Mexican near the library. I guess it was the safest place he could think of."

"So Rosa called you and told you where they were. You left the clinic, drove to the library, brought them here and got us into the thick of it."

"Well, yes and no. I didn't bring them here immediately. We sat and talked in the car in the back of the library parking lot. It was only after María told me why they had to get away, the stuff about her being forced into becoming a prostitute, that I just didn't know any other place they'd be safe for now. I didn't know what else to do, Matt. Like you said, they can't be seen or those thugs will get them. They can't go to the police, that's for sure. It's just a mess."

"Yeah, and now it's *our* mess. One thing's certain Lindy–they absolutely can't be seen here. They can't be seen in or outside this house. If some Mexican worker comes by and recognizes either of them, it'll be just as dangerous for us as for those two. As of this moment, they don't set foot outside the door, not for a single second. You have to make that very clear to them."

"I will, but what're we going to do Matt?"

"I don't have the slightest idea, but it looks like we have *house guests* until we do get it figured out."

"Please don't be upset with me," Lindy said, with a helpless look on her face.

"I'm not Hon, really, not now that I understand. You feel deeply for these people and want to help them. I haven't gotten to know their situation like you have, at least not until now. There's no way I could have cared as much as you do, but now . . ."

I touched her arm lightly and smiled. "Which one of our friends said they were so bored with retirement they didn't know what to do with themselves? They oughta come stay with us for awhile."

"For sure," she agreed, with a grin.

It felt good seeing her lighten up after what she'd been through.

"I'll go in and check on our *guests*, emphasize the importance of staying in the house, and fix us another drink. After that, I'll think about getting dinner for all *four* of us. And Matt, thanks. I love you."

"I love you too. And Hon, don't worry, we'll work something out. I think I'll switch to port," I told her as she reentered the house.

While Lindy was inside, my mind raced: *Do I tell Chief Everhart about this? If what this girl told Lindy is true, and Pablo was killed because he owed money to the Mexican Mafia, and Collinson was the one who killed Pablo, does that mean Collinson worked for the Mafia? My God, of course it does! Then why did he kill the caddy? That had to be mob-related also. And just what are we going to do with those two inside?*

I once heard a legendary corporate titan say that 'sometimes the best decision to make is to make no decision at all.' I didn't buy into it back then, but maybe the old fart was right after all.

Lindy returned to the porch with our drinks.

"Okay," she said, "I went over the ground rules; they are not, under any circumstances, to step outside this house. I also gave María some clothes. They'll be a little big for her, and I gave Carlos the sweat suit I gave you for your birthday last year, the one you've never worn. I showed them where they'd be sleeping upstairs, and told them they could use the shower. They were very appreciative."

"Good, now listen, no decisions yet," I said. "We need to digest all this. Tonight, if they're up to it, I'd like those two to fill us in on everything that's happened. Everything from the time they left Mexico. Once we know the whole story, then maybe we'll get a handle on what to do next."

"Okay, sounds like a plan," she said.

"In the meantime, *vivo el porto vino*," I said raising my glass.

"Your Spanish is truly horrendous Matt."

"I know, but something tells me it's gonna get better real fast."

Lindy laughed, got up from her rocker, came over to me and threw her arms around my waist.

"Thanks Matt, I love you Hon," she said, pulling me tight against her.

Chapter 35

We didn't see them again that evening. Figuring our guests could use a substantial meal, Lindy asked me to grill four large T-Bones, while she prepared a salad and baked potatoes.

When everything was ready, it occurred to us that the last sounds we'd heard from upstairs were that of the shower running quite a bit earlier. Lindy called up the stairway and received no response. We climbed the steps, looked into the guest room, and saw María, enclosed in Carlos's arms, both fast asleep atop the bed spread, both freshly showered and wearing the new, clean clothes Lindy had given them.

We decided to save the big meal for breakfast, put everything in the fridge and pulled a couple of crab cakes out of the freezer.

"They've gotta be exhausted," Lindy said. "We should have thought of that."

"I guess," I replied, "but I was really hoping to talk to them tonight. We need to get the details of what's going on, but it looks like it's *hasta mañana* for now."

"Wow, that *hasta mañana* was really quite good."

"I knew you'd be impressed. Actually, the day hasn't been a total loss, I did learn a little something." It was on the tip of my tongue to tell Lindy about T. L. and Lizzie, but I changed my mind. I'd save it for a more appropriate time.

"What's that?"

"Ah, the next time you suggest I have a cigar I'm heading

south in *Ol'Crab*, far, far south, all the way to Sloppy Joe's, where several cold brews will be served to me by one of Key West's finest looking wenches."

"I guess my little cigar ploy was pretty obvious, huh? Sorry."

The momentary lightness felt good. We both realized difficult decisions were staring us smack in the face, not to mention the very real possibility of danger hovering as the result of the two illegals now in residence.

∂∞∫

The following morning our two timid guests appeared downstairs earlier than anticipated. Lindy's dress, much too large for María, actually looked cute on her. My unused warm up suit fit Carlos perfectly.

The first several minutes were awkward, with no one knowing quite what to say. Lindy tried to put them at ease, chatting away in Spanish, while my major contributions were to smile and nod frequently, having no idea of what was being said.

We ate dinner as breakfast in the dining room, with some scrambled eggs thrown in.

In all likelihood María and Carlos had never laid eyes on a spread of such proportions. Lindy and I had determined that getting them relaxed and gaining their confidence would be our initial objectives, and that we'd hold off on the important questions until after we had eaten. I realized last night, and now accepted the fact, that I was involved.

Lindy explained that María and Carlos had apologized for having fallen asleep so early last night, and I said something along the lines of *"Yo comprende"* and they both grinned at my butchered Spanish.

As we ate, I sensed the atmosphere becoming more comfortable, with some things being said that must have been pleasant enough, as occasional smiles appeared on the faces of the other three.

Uninvolved in the conversation, I became the silent observer. The night's sleep had done them both some good. Yesterday, María appeared pale and on the sickly side. This morning it was obvious that with a few days of continued rest and good meals, she would be completely restored to the attractive young lady Lindy had initially described to me. The clothes she had arrived in, and those Lindy had given her, were much too large for her delicate frame, making her pregnancy indiscernible. Carlos was taller than any Mexican I had ever seen, and, as with María, the night's rest had brought about a change in appearance. With tossed, jet black hair matching María's, along with a full, black mustache, dark eyebrows above intelligent jet black eyes, and a strong square chin, Carlos was indeed a handsome young man.

I don't know why I notice such things, but during the course of the meal it was clear to me that both María and Carlos were adept with each dining utensil and their table manners were impeccable. Having seen on TV the squalid living conditions of the uneducated poor in Mexico, and having seen for myself the less than desirable situations under which the illegals were living in our area, I'd been expected something far less from these two. I was surprised by their behavior, and felt guilty about my conditioned prejudice.

After breakfast I cleaned up the kitchen while Lindy sat with María and Carlos and had coffee. I overheard enough, and understood enough, to determine that Lindy was telling them a little something about us, our family and basically continued her effort of making them more at ease.

I was beginning to get antsy, and felt the time had arrived to move the conversation forward along a more constructive course.

After finishing in the kitchen, I joined the threesome in the living room. It was time to get down to the nitty gritty. But I had to wait a few minutes before asking any questions as Carlos continued with what was, noticeably, a lengthy story.

"Matt," Lindy said turning to me, "Carlos was just telling me a bit of their background, it's really fascinating."

I couldn't help myself. That initial annoyance was returning. "Good, has he filled you in on who wants him dead and if it's the same guy who wants his wife to start getting laid by strangers?"

"We haven't gotten there yet Matt, just hang on, okay?"

"Sure, but the clock is ticking and at some point very soon, like right now, we have to cut the chit chat and find out what's going on."

"I'm doing my best, maybe you should have another cup of coffee," she said smiling through her teeth.

"I'm okay, where are we?"

She explained something to Carlos then turned back to me.

"Okay, the first thing is that I was surprised at how beautifully they speak their language."

"Yeah, well I noticed how they handled themselves at the table."

"I caught that also. Now I know why. You're getting fidgety Matt, so I'll give you *The Reader's Digest* version."

"The super, ultra condensed, please."

"Well, to start with, they're not your average illegal immigrants," she began. "It seems that some time back, both of their families were worth a great deal of money. In fact, their grandfathers were business partners, and the two families have remained close through the years. At one time, the partnership owned thousands of acres of land consisting of several farms. They raised cattle, fruit, corn . . .lots of different stuff. The farms were so large there were even small villages on them with their own stores."

"The old company store's been around a long time," I said.

"Many of the workers," Lindy continued, "were born and raised on these farms. Anyway, with the revolution, somewhere in the early 1900s, the partnership lost a great deal of its holdings and most of the land was divided up among the peasants. The two families were permitted to keep enough to stay in business, but just barely. With continued reform over the years, and some other problems, they wound up losing everything. By the time Carlos and María came along, both families had been pretty much reduced to peasant status."

"That's the same kind of thing that happened in Cuba," I said, "but Castro made it happen a hell of a lot quicker."

"Exactly," Lindy continued. "Both sets of parents remembered something of the good old days, and while there was no longer any money, the parents instilled in their kids, Carlos and María and the others, a sense of pride and of values. That isn't the case with many of illegals we run across."

"Is that pretty much it?" I asked.

"I guess. As you heard, Carlos did most of the talking. María said there's no way they're going back, absolutely none. She wants her baby born a United State's citizen. They want to work hard and become good citizens of this country."

I looked over at our two house guests and nodded my head.

"Tell them we'll do everything we can to help, and I mean it."

"I already have," she said.

"Okay, now tell them that in order for us to help, there are certain things we have to know."

Lindy explained this to them, and they nodded their heads.

"Explain that the key to their safety, and now ours, and the key to their being able to remain in this country and have their baby born here, is to let us know who it is they are running from."

Lindy hesitated, gathering her thoughts on how best to present this important question. She took longer than I thought necessary to explain what I wanted, and when she was finished, there was no immediate response from Carlos or María. They moved closer to each other and then, in unison, shook their heads.

"I explained it as best I could, but you saw what happened. They're scared to death to say anything."

I looked out the front window. It was still early enough for the sunrise to be casting an orange hue across the sky and the waterway. It was going to be a beautiful day, but not like the many beautiful days we'd shared with each other in the past. We'd become involved in the most serious situation of our long marriage.

I turned and looked at both of them, crossly. Why couldn't they understand they had to help us help them?

"*Es necessaries* that you tell *mi* who *quires* to hurt *tu*!" I said, hoping my botched language might loosen them up.

It didn't work.

Now I was becoming royally pissed. "Damn it, do you know that whoever it is is out there looking for you two right now!" I looked straight at Carlos. "Do you know what will happen if they find you *here*! Do you know what will happen to Lindy and me if they find you in my *casa*!"

"Matt, you don't have to shout at them."

"The hell I don't. If scaring the be-Jesus out of them is what it takes . . ."

"You can't frighten them any more than they already are!"

The four of us sat in tense silence.

Carlos and María had locked arms, clinging to one another.

Lindy's face was flushed.

I got up and stomped towards the front door.

"Matt, where are you going?"

"Out. I think I have the answer. Tell them to stay put. I'll be back."

Chapter 36

It was two days before Che returned the call.

"I was unavailable," was his only explanation.

"Listen, I need you to get back here to finish up some stuff," Delgado said.

"You told me I wouldn't be needed any more."

"Things have changed–get here as quickly as you can."

❦

They met late the following afternoon at the Holiday Inn Express on Hwy. 17, not far from where Che had previously arranged for Collinson's fatal date with a tree.

Delgado filled Che in on the disappearance of María and Carlos Martinez, and then contracted with Che to find them. That was one part of the contract, and to terminate them–that was the second part.

"I don't care how you do it, but make it ugly. I want this to be a lesson the other pissants won't forget. When I say ugly, I mean terrifying."

"They could be anywhere by now," said Che.

"I know," said Delgado, "but start with the trailer where they were staying with the girl's cousin. They lied to Santiago. Someone in that trailer knows where those two *cucarachas* are."

When Che walked through the door of *La tienda*, Ernesto

Santiago knew he was a dead man. Delgado was taking him out. *Mierda*, he thought.

He had never seen Che, but had been around the organization long enough to recognize a pro when he saw one.

Che walked directly to Ernesto, who, now having broken out in a fast sweat, was standing behind the cosmetics counter.

"Ernesto Santiago?" he said.

"Yes," said Ernesto.

Che reached into the inside pocket of his sports jacket . . .

I'm screwed, thought Ernesto.

. . . and pulled out his silver cigarette case.

He's playing games with me! thought Ernesto.

"Miguel said you would fill me in on the disappearance of a couple of your customers," said Che, as he lit his Marlboro.

"Let's go back to my office, please," said Ernesto, breathing a sigh of relief.

✿

Within a matter of minutes, Che was knocking on Rosa and José's trailer door.

Rosa was home with the three kids and Gina.

As Rosa opened the door, Che threw his arm against it. He swiftly entered the trailer and in the process, knocked Rosa to the floor.

"Get up woman," he said to the panicked Rosa.

She grabbed the armrest of the old, blue plastic recliner and pulled herself up.

"Wh . . . wh . . . who are you," she stammered.

Gina, seeing this, sat frozen on the couch. The three children began screaming.

Che didn't answer Rosa. He looked around the trailer.

The odor of fried tortillas, combined with that of soiled diapers, musty furniture and sweat hung in the hot air. "It stinks in here. How can you people live like this?" he said, brushing off the arm of his coat, a look of disgust on his face.

"Who are you? What do you want?" Rosa again stammered,

rubbing her sore elbow, her panic increasing. She needed to get her children out of the trailer.

"Get those kids to shut up," he said.

Rosa ran over and lifted the baby from the crib and handed it to Gina.

She walked quickly to the other two, took one in each arm, and held them. They continued to whimper, but the loud crying stopped.

"That's better, now I'll tell you who I am," said Che, stepping directly in front of Rosa.

"I'm the man you are going to tell the truth to," said Che. "I'm the man you will tell where those two *cucarachas* have run off to."

Rosa hesitated.

"I . . . I don't understand what you mean *Señor*," she said, tightening her grip on the children.

Che slid his hand inside his sports jacket for the second time within the last half an hour, but this time, he retrieved a gun.

With his arm outstretched, never taking his eyes off of Rosa, he pointed the gun directly at the baby on Gina's lap.

Gina put both her arms around the baby and twisted her back to Che.

"I will count to three, *Señora*, if I do not hear the truth, I will shoot the baby."

"*Uno . . . dos . . .*"

"Stop! Stop! I will tell you," screamed Rosa, desperately reaching for the gun while holding the babies.

Che swatted her arm away. "I'm sorry *Señora*, but that was not quick enough."

He lowered the gun while reaching into the other side of his jacket. He removed a silencer and attached it to the pistol.

Again he raised his arm and stared directly into Rosa's eyes . . .

"*No, Dios mio! No!*" screamed Rosa.

. . . and pulled the trigger.

The bullet tore into the couch, an inch above the baby's head.

Rosa let out an agonizing scream and slumped to her knees. The two children fell from her arms.

Che looked over to the couch.

"*Mierda*" he said, "How in the hell did I miss?"

He then leaned down, grabbed Rosa under an arm and pulled her to her feet.

Propping her up against the wall, he again raised his arm and pointed the gun at the baby.

"*Uno* . . ."

"Stop! *No más, no más*! I will tell you! I will tell you everything," she cried.

He let her loose, and she again fell to the floor.

Rosa crawled back to the recliner and pulled herself up.

She sat in the chair, her head in her hands, and her sobs more like wails.

The two children she had been holding were again screaming, each clinging to one of Rosa's legs.

Che walked over to Rosa, grabbed a handful of hair, and jerked her head up.

"*Dime*! Tell me," he said.

"They went to the library," Rosa sobbed.

Che gave her an incredulous look, not believing what he had just heard.

"What in the hell does *that* mean?" said Che, giving her hair a fierce jerk, snapping Rosa's head back even further. *They went to the library*? What kind of shit is that?"

He started to raise his gun.

"No, no, *es verdad*, it is true!" screamed Rosa, "they went there to meet someone!"

"Who? Who did they meet?" demanded Che.

"Lindy," said Rosa, "they went to meet Señora Lindy."

"Who's Lindy?"

"She is at the clinic. She speaks Spanish there. She helps us."

"What's her last name?"

"I don't know, I don't know" sobbed Rosa.

Che gave her head another quick jerk and raised his gun toward the baby.

"*Dios mio*, I swear I do not know! She works at the clinic. She is a good person. She helps us!" Her tears were now running in torrents, her throat congested, she gasped for air.

"Why did they meet this woman?" asked Che, giving her hair another brutal tug.

"She was the only one they thought could help" she managed to utter through her sobs. "I swear on my babies that is all I know!"

Che threw her hair out of his hand and Rosa's head fell to her chest.

He again looked with disdain around the room and sneered.

"You pigs, you people are worse than cockroaches. Now listen to me, if you mention my being here to anyone, to *anyone*," he stared at Rosa, "I will kill each of your children and you will watch while I do it, do you understand?"

"*Sí, sí Señor*, yes, I understand."

He raised his gun one last time and pointed it at the baby in Gina's arms.

"The baby will be the first you watch die."

❧

He drove back to *La tienda*.

"What's the clinic?" he asked Ernesto.

Ernesto explained about it being a government agency that helped poor people who couldn't pay for their medical needs.

"Most of my customers use it, it costs them nothing."

"Anyone can go? Even the illegals?"

"Right, anyone who can't pay for such services,"

"Amazing, really amazing; only in the good 'ol U.S., right?

"Right," said Ernesto, happy to agree.

"Have you ever heard any of the cockroaches mention a woman named Lindy who works there?"

"No, I've never heard the name," said Ernesto.

"Tell me how to get to this fucking clinic," said Che.

Chapter 37

Always the fastidious dresser, Che drove to the clinic the following morning wearing clothes purchased the previous afternoon from The Good Will Store. After buying a pair of oversized, worn jeans, a brown, plastic belt several inches too long, a much-too-large, faded, red and white checkered, long sleeved cotton shirt, and a pair of work boots, he had returned to the Holiday Inn. There, he took his newly-acquired wardrobe to the rear of the motel and, out of sight, rubbed the cloths in dirt and grass and severely scuffed the boots.

Che hadn't showered, combed his hair, shaved or brushed his teeth. He'd executed one hundred and fifty push ups in the motel room to work up a decent sweat.

Seated in the rented green Taurus in the clinic's parking lot, Che observed the flow of people. He was astonished at the number of what were obviously illegals, entering and leaving the place. If he hadn't seen it with his own eyes, he wouldn't have believed it. Che had no idea there were would be so many, or that such a place was available to them.

It's gotta cost a fortune to run this operation. If I paid taxes, I'd be royally pissed . . . if I paid taxes.

Scattered among the illegals he spotted a few nurses, a couple of doctors with their stethoscopes hanging from their necks, and several administrative looking types. One of those must be Lindy, the lady the pissants held in such high regard.

Comfortable with the situation, Che left his rental and walked over to the clinic. He timed his entrance perfectly, blending in with several mothers and their children.

Once inside, he held back, leaned against the wall, and watched. The mothers went directly to the receptionist, who asked them to sign in, and then, with their children, they took seats in the waiting area.

Hands in his jean's pockets, head bowed, shoulders hunched, Che ambled towards Pam, the receptionist.

She heard his approach and looked up.

"Yes?" she said.

Che hesitated.

"Yes?" she repeated.

"*Señora Lindy, por favor,*" he said.

"Señora Lindy?"

"*Sí.*"

"Why do you want to see her?"

"No speak English," Che said.

"Why . . .see . . . Lindy?" Pam said slowly, speaking louder.

"No speak English."

Oh, terrific, another new one; just what in the hell we need, thought Pam.

"Sign here," she said, pointing to a line on the sign-in form.

"No Speak English."

Pam then spoke the one word she knew, other than *sí.* and *no* and *gracias.*

"*Nombre,* your name," she said, pointing to a line on the form.

Che looked at the form, took the pencil the receptionist held out to him, awkwardly positioned it in his left hand and with intense concentration, drew a scraggily "X" on the line the receptionist had indicated.

Pam looked at the "X," shook her head, sighed in exasperation, and pointed to an empty chair.

A half hour passed. Che became impatient. He didn't know how much more he could take of the crying, runny-nosed little monsters, some even tripping over his feet, the mothers screaming at the sniveling brats and the pregnant women holding their stomachs with expressions of extreme discomfort.

He was considering going back out to the car when an attractive, middle-aged lady, wearing tailored black slacks and a white, long-sleeved blouse appeared in the reception area. She had an elegant, professional look about her.

The lady walked over to the receptionist and picked up the sign-in chart. Looking over the names, she said something to the receptionist, who in turn lifted her arm and pointed to Che.

The lady walked towards him.

"*En qué lo puedo ayudar*, how can I help you?" the lady said, looking down at Che.

Che stood up, slid his hands into his pockets, lowered his head, stared at the floor, shuffled his feet and said, "*Tengo un dolor Señora*, I have a pain."

The lady asked his name.

"*Ramiro*," said Che.

"*Soy Lindy*, I'm Lindy," said the woman.

Bingo! thought Che.

Che looked into Lindy's face. So this was the little lady who knows where the two pissants were hiding. Well, now they were his. She would lead the way. It would be over very soon.

Of course, when the bell rang, now that she had seen him, she'd also have to go.

There was a pause. The woman tilted her head and gave Che a quizzical look.

"*Síentate*, sit down," she said. She told him she'd return when a nurse became available to check him over, then left the waiting room.

He sat back down and after a minute, reached into his shirt pocket and removed a cigarette. He looked around and saw the sign, in English and Spanish, which he had anticipated: "NO SMOKING," and written below that, "NO FUMAR."

"*Mierda*," he said just loudly enough to be heard by those seated close to him. He shrugged his shoulders, stood up, making a show of the cigarette in his hand, and left the clinic. From all appearances, he was headed out for a smoke.

Che considered calling Delgado from the clinic's parking lot, then thought, what the hell, it'll be over soon. He'd call after he'd fulfilled both contracts.

He moved the Taurus to a less conspicuous spot, but one from which he could still keep an eye on the entrance. After a couple of cigarettes and becoming bored, it occurred to Che that if this Lindy worked a full day, he'd be sitting there in the Taurus for another six hours.

That was dumb. He'd be noticed for sure. He pulled out and drove back to the motel.

Che went for a swim, returned to his room, showered, shaved and decided there was no need to put those stinking clothes back on–they had served their purpose. He'd found the lovely Ms. Lindy; the pissants were not far behind.

Che went to the front desk, and, on a whim, asked the desk clerk where he could find some of that great Carolina barbeque folks were always talking about.

"Pat's Place, on Main got about the best on the coast," said the desk clerk.

Seated at Pat's Place, he ordered the sliced barbeque, slaw, hush puppies and, having heard of them, a side of collard greens.

The waitress brought his food, and, out of curiosity, the collard greens were the first thing he tasted.

That was a mistake. He couldn't believe that people actually ate this crap. He spit the collards back out onto his plate, threw a twenty on the table, and left the restaurant.

He drove back to the clinic. It was an excellent move. He had no sooner backed into a parking space with a good view of the entrance, when Lindy came out. She climbed into a red Miata convertible and drove off. *Lady has a sporty little set of wheels, he thought, and she wasn't working a full day after all.* He'd returned just in time.

❦

There was little traffic on the single lane roads Lindy took, so he tailed her at a respectable distance.

The two cars traveled several miles before approaching the bridge which spanned the Intracoastal Waterway and connected the mainland to the island. Che was taken aback by the imposing, long, high-arched bridge, not expecting to see such an impressive structure in this po-dunk area. He had seen the sign indicating he was headed for Holden Beach.

Holden Beach, he thought. *Who in the hell ever heard of Holden Beach? How in the hell did they get a bridge like this?*

At the crest of the bridge, an expansive view of the ocean, with several trawling shrimp boats was laid out before him. Even Che, who had seen about all there was to see in this world, had to admit it was an extraordinary view.

Lindy made a left onto Ocean Blvd. at the bottom of the bridge, drove two miles and hung another left. The street had a large bend where it approached the water and both cars were now traveling slowly along the road adjacent to the Intracoastal Waterway.

There was a row of homes on the left, and the waterway with its marshland, on the right. She turned left into a driveway. Che was well behind her as the garage door lifted and Lindy drove in under the house. Che continued another half a block before having to stop. The street ended in an empty cul-de-sac. He was looking over an inlet which branched off the waterway. He could see that the short inlet led to a canal which ran behind the row of homes he had just passed.

Shit, she's got water in front and water in back.

Che turned in the cul-de-sac, drove past Lindy's house again and back onto Ocean Boulevard.

He drove the length of the island and learned it was very narrow, no more than a quarter of a mile wide, about ten miles long and the only way in or out was by the bridge he had driven over earlier, or by boat. Ocean Boulevard was the only street that ran the length of the island.

He didn't like the set up. Access to the island, and to and from the house, was very limited. If something went wrong, getting away could be a real bitch.

What he wanted to do was drive back to the house, go in, find out where the two cockroaches were, take care of the little lady and get the hell out. But that was way too risky. If anyone spotted something funny going on and called the cops, all the cops had to do was block the damn bridge and his ass was grass.

This was going to require more planning than he'd thought. There was no way to pull it off today.

Chapter 38

Hopeful that my theatrical departure would rattle them, and by my returning with the chief, María and Carlos, confronted with a uniformed officer of the law, would come to their senses. I headed for the police station. Once the chief got into the act, Lindy and I would be out of danger and out of the picture all together. The police would take the whole mess over.

Unfortunately, upon arriving at the Sheriff's Shack, I was informed by Officer Pete Foster that Chief Everhart was attending a four-day conference in, would you believe, Las Vegas, and wouldn't return until late in the evening.

"Tell me," I asked Officer Foster, "what does a visiting Chief of Police do with himself in Las Vegas for four days? A city, by the way, which is not generally considered by most to be a model all-American community?"

"Well sir," he replied, standing erect and looking me square in the eye, "Chief Everhart's attendance at this extremely critical conference will result in a higher level of professionalism for our entire law enforcement staff, thereby improving the safety and well being of the fine citizens of this community."

Suppressing a smile, I said, "Wow, Officer Foster, that was most impressive. Now where's the cheat sheet the chief left here so you could memorize all that garbage?"

"Sir, we were each required to memorize it before he left. Actually sir, what he said to tell you if you really pressed us was,

'What happens in Las Vegas, stays in Las Vegas.'"

"Aha, now that sounds more like our beloved chief," I said. "But seriously officer, no joke, it's important that I speak with him as soon as he gets back. Please have him call me immediately, I'd appreciate it."

I left the Sheriff's Shack and returned home only to find everyone seated exactly as I'd left them.

"Anything?" I asked, looking at Lindy.

"Nope," she replied.

I filled her in on my busted idea of involving the chief.

"So, what now?" she asked.

"Well, I have an ingenious back-up plan. That paint we bought for the two upstairs bedrooms last week," I said, turning my head towards Carlos, "seems to me, we now got us an expert house painter in residence. Between Carlos and me, we should be able to knock out both rooms in no time. I'll take a shot at working with him on some English while we're painting, and you can do the same with María while you two are doing whatever it is that women do together, other than go to the bathroom."

"Okay wise-guy, that's only in restaurants. María and I can do some cooking and other stuff around the house. But Matt, are you sure we shouldn't mention something about this to the police, they could drive by occasionally to check us out."

"Lindy, the fewer people who know that these two are here, the safer it is, and right now, the only ones who know are us. So relax Hon, we're gonna be just fine."

I hoped I sounded more confident than I felt.

ﬆﬆ

After casing the island, Che drove back across the bridge and was headed for Shallotte and his motel when he spotted a roadside sign for The Provision Co. Restaurant. Remembering that he'd hardly eaten the day before, he followed the dirt road to Provision's. Turning into the parking lot, he noticed that the restaurant had a terrific location overlooking the Intracoastal Waterway.

This lunch menu looked pretty decent; no grits, collard greens or okra. After ordering a beer, steamed shrimp and a grouper sandwich at the counter, he found his way to a waterside table.

Sipping the cold Heineken, and glancing at the activity on the water, he considered his options. There was little question that this job was going to be a bit trickier than he'd anticipated. He had to get to this Lindy either in her house, which he now considered risky after checking the layout, or while she was driving to or from work, which had its own risks. Well, he'd have to figure it out. The lady knew where the two cockroaches were, and one way or another, he had to get that information.

While eating, the activity on the waterway caught his interest. He had asked his eye-catching waitress, Keri, what the several large boats with the huge nets on each side were, and was told they were shrimp boats. As much as he liked shrimp, he never knew how they were actually caught.

There were several young couples jet skiing slowly by in this designated *No Wake Zone*, and there were at least a dozen fishermen in small boats, anchored, and occasionally, reeling in a fish. A large, private yacht made its way past the restaurant. He wondered how many millions a boat like that would run; it'd certainly have a price tag way beyond his means, even though he did rather well in his unique line of work.

As he watched the action on the water, an idea began to take shape. He wouldn't be able to stake out the house on land, the physical layout made that unrealistic, if not impossible. But if he could get his hands on one of those small fishing boats....

Two hours later Che was sitting in a rented, twelve foot johnboat, having received instructions on operating the simple, twenty-five horse power, outboard engine and also getting a quick lesson on the use of his newly-acquired rod and open faced reel. Gus, the old timer at the marina, rigged his gear, and except for actually slipping shrimp bait on the hook, he was set to perform his stakeout under the guise of a fisherman.

After a short ride under the bridge and then a mile's ride up the waterway, Che spotted Lindy's light blue house on the right. He drove the boat past the house and took a right into the inlet at the end of her street. Within a few hundred feet he came to the canal which ran in back of Lindy's house and then hung another right. He held the boat to a slow pace and counted off fourteen houses until he came to the light blue one. Tied to the dock in back, was a boat a few feet longer than his rental. He continued slowly past the house, and then turned his boat around. He saw the name *Ol'Crab* inscribed across the back of the other boat.

He made his way back out to the waterway and dropped anchor a couple of houses down from the blue house. Taking into consideration the lawns, the street, the large marsh area and the water, he estimated he was less than a hundred yards out from the house. Not bad. From all appearances, he was just one of the boys out hoping to catch a few fish.

He sat in the johnboat wearing a ULV baseball cap, sun glasses, a new tee shirt with *Festival By The Sea* written across the back, and a pair of jeans. He had a cooler containing a six pack of Bud Lite, chilling. He didn't intend to drink any of the stuff, but the old geezer at the marina asked, and had made it sound like it was a necessity if he intended to catch any fish. Che picked up the rod, held it upright, and with his other hand grabbed the sinker at the end of the line threw the hook and sinker out over the side and let them drop into the water. He lit a Marlboro. He looked over at the unopened plastic bag of bait shrimp. *No fuckin' way*, he thought.

Che sat holding the rod, with a baitless hook attached to the line, and watched the house.

Ya never know what's gonna happen doing this, but it's never failed me yet, he thought. *It might happen in five minutes, or maybe five hours, but somethin's gonna happen . . .*

And with his customary luck, it did.

Chapter 39

While Carlos and I painted the master bedroom, María and Lindy spent most of their time in the kitchen. Lindy wanted to learn a couple of Mexican recipes, particularly *mole poblano,* the popular poultry dish often referred to as the national dish of Mexico, but decided it was in María's best interest to pick up a few pointers on American style cooking.

Realistically, there wasn't any need for María to learn this as there were now Mexican grocery stores everywhere, on every corner it seemed. The immigrants had no problem finding their native foods. Still, she thought it might eventually prove useful for María to learn how to prepare a traditional American meal.

Lindy decided on a pot roast for dinner and was explaining the simple steps in preparing this basic dish, while at the same time hoping that during their chitchat, María might slip up and divulge a tidbit regarding the source of the trouble she and Carlos were experiencing. But by lunch time, she hadn't any luck in that regard.

❧

Lindy called us for lunch, and while we munched on grilled ham and cheese sandwiches with potato chips, very little was said. Carlos and María exchanged glances a few times, as if to say to one another, *You didn't say anything*, did you? They were continuing to keep some important information from us, information we needed to know.

While painting, I made several efforts at some simple conversational Spanish, but each attempt was countered with a torrent of words from Carlos that I couldn't grasp. I'd smile, vigorously nod my head and continue painting. Forget about the English lessons, they weren't going to happen–so much for good intentions.

I didn't know the actual hour, but instinctively knew it was, without doubt, time for a drink and a cigar.

Lindy and María were in the kitchen when I came down.

"How's it going?" I asked.

"Okay," said Lindy. "Can't say much for the cooking lessons, nor for the English lessons for that matter, but we've been having a nice time"

"Pretty much the same for the men's team," I said. "I gave up the lessons early on. All I earned from trying to chat was a sore neck. I'm headed out to unwind, how about joining me?"

"Be there shortly," she said.

Out on the front porch, I unwrapped my stogie, lit up and surveyed the scene. The late afternoon sun was dazzling and the air was crisp with an invigorating touch of fall. Although I also said this every spring, I really did believe this was my favorite time of year. Scattered about on the waterway were several small fishing boats. Each had two or three guys in them, except for one not too far off to the left, who was fishing solo. You don't see that too often; fishing is a guy-bonding kind of thing, like poker or golf. I wasn't sure what they were all fishing for, but my guess would be flounder, or possibly spots. I never understood why anyone wasted time on spots; they're small, they're skinny, it takes a zillion of them, fried no less, to make a meal, and they absolutely aren't worth the effort. Flounder on the other hand . . .

A few days ago I passed a boat on the water named *THE SPOT REMOVER*. Now that's clever, really clever, and I was envious of the ingenuity of such a name. The owner of that fine craft obviously had a keener imagination than the owner of *Ol' Crab*! But even so, why anyone would concentrate on catching spots was something well beyond me.

Lindy came out the front door, gave the cigar a disgusted look and said, "Do you have to?"

"Yup," I said, "I've earned this moment of pleasure and shall not be denied. Sit to my right and it shouldn't bother you. What's the time?"

Lindy looked at her watch. "Going on five," she said, settling into the rocker.

"Not too early for a drink," I said.

"In a few minutes. So, what do you think at this point?"

"What do I think? I think tomorrow can't arrive quickly enough. We get Curt over here and he sweats the information out of these two. Seeing the chief's uniform should do the trick. Then he does whatever he has to do to get to the bottom of whatever it is that's going on, and the authorities do whatever, if anything, they have to with these two," I said, pointing my thumb back to the house. "And then my lady, we're done with it."

"Just like that?"

"You betcha."

Off to the right I saw a mega yacht barreling down the waterway. This time of year it isn't unusual to see the large pleasure yachts headed south. Most of them were considerate of the fishermen and slowed down as they passed by, but not this one. It wasn't full throttle, but she was going fast. She quickly passed the first few boats while the fishermen shouted obscenities and gave her the finger; one guy even stood up against the large wake, and with both arms raised, rocking perilously back and forth, shot her both index fingers. When she passed the lone fisherman it was an altogether different story; he was hanging on for dear life with arms stretched, gripping both sides of his johnboat.

"Look at that poor guy," said Lindy.

"Well, the captain of that yacht's really an asshole, but I think the guy in the johnboat's a rookie. I've been watching him." I said, "He has no idea what he's doing out there. He hasn't even reeled his line in, not once. The other guys are catching fish, but he hasn't even bothered to check his bait. He's just sitting there smoking and looking around. Strange."

"Some guys will go to any lengths to grab a sneak smoke," she said, giving me a look.

"Okay funny girl, for that, you get to make the drinks. I'll go easy on you, just pop me a brew."

Lindy went in and was back out in a few minutes with our drinks. It looked like a screw driver in her hand, rather than her usual Zinfandel.

"You okay?" I asked.

"Sure. Matt, Carlos would like to come out for a smoke."

"Oh, come on Lindy, you know the ground rules, so does he."

"Matt, it doesn't take any time to smoke a cigarette and I can't handle any smoking in the house, you know that."

"No, absolutely not."

"Matt, he can stand right by the front doorway. We can watch for any cars or trucks coming around the curve, or any coming the other way. If one does come, he can duck back in before anyone even sees him!"

"No."

"Matt, you can't sit here and smoke that cigar and not let him have a cigarette, it just isn't fair, particularly when there's no danger at all of his being seen."

"Damn it Lindy. Okay, but he's gotta make it quick, and I mean really fast!"

A minute later she came back out with Carlos, who stood by the front door and lit up. He took a deep drag, turned towards me and gave me a quick nod of appreciation. I nodded back and pointed to Lindy's watch. He understood.

Carlos inhaled, devoured, is more like it, the cigarette in record time. When he finished, I pointed to the railing and he flipped his butt over the side onto the gravel drive.

"See, no harm done," said Lindy as Carlos headed back in.

"Okay, you're right, 'no harm done,' but we can't make a habit of this, it's still too risky," I said as I looked back out to the waterway. A couple of the boats had left and the others were in the process of heading out; except for the Lone Ranger, who continued to sit out there and smoke.

"Maybe he's going to stay there all night," I said. "But he hasn't caught any fish that I can see, so I don't know why in the hell he's staying out."

"He's probably having one last smoke before going home to that perfectly dreadful wife of his who doesn't understand or appreciate him," she said. "Not everyone has had your kind of luck, kiddo."

"You're right; the poor bastard doesn't know what he's missing."

"Matt!"

"Sorry. The unfortunate chap is obviously dejected and quite miserable at this precise moment, unlucky fellow, he."

We got up and went inside to share a good 'ol American Pot Roast with our two illegal guests. It would all be over tomorrow. We would return to the fine life we were used to prior to all this trouble, and I could hardly wait.

❧

Che couldn't believe his luck. He had sat in the fucking boat all afternoon in the hot fucking sun and been rocked back and forth 'til his guts were killing him from all the fucking boats that charged by and that last big one had made him want to pull out his fucking weapon and blow the fucking brains out of the driver, or mate, or captain, or whatever the fuck they're called.

He occasionally glanced at the other boats to see what they were doing, and decided there was no way he was going to screw around with putting bait on a fucking hook. And what kind of fucking fish were they catching anyway; you could barely see the little fuckers. No, he'd keep his eyes on the house. And finally, after a couple hours of waiting, he saw a guy come out; *must be the broad's husband*, he thought.

He watched as the guy sat in a rocker and lit a cigar. He checked his pack of Marlboros. *Damn, that's what I shouda done . . . cigars. I'm gonna be out soon. Shit.*

A few minutes later *she* came out. *The little lady of the house– actually, for an older broad, she ain't too bad. Who knows, by the*

191

time this thing's over . . .

He was down to two cigarettes. He watched as Lindy went back in house, then returned to the porch with a bottle of beer in one hand and a drink of some kind in the other.

No sense in staying out here, he thought. *Looks like they're dug in for the night.*

He was looking at the engine, trying to remember what the old guy at the marina had told him about starting it. He lit his next to last cigarette. Shit, do I pull the fucking anchor first or start the fucking motor first? Shit, it must be the anchor, no wait, it's the motor. Shit!

He gave the cord a couple of pulls and nothing happened. *Wait, there's a choke, gotta move the choke.*

As he was messing with the choke he looked over his shoulder to check the house one last time.

What the . . .

The sun was beginning to set, and the front of the house was now in full shade, but he could swear there was a third body on the porch, standing by the door.

He saw a match struck, then flame, a cigarette lit, and he clearly saw the face of the third person. A third person with dark skin, dark hair and a mustache. It didn't take a genius to figure it out.

He sat back in the boat and smiled. He reached into the small bag for his pack of cigarettes, removed the last one, crumpled up the empty pack and threw it overboard. He lit up.

He reached into his bag again and, grabbing his cell phone, punched in the numbers he by now knew so well.

"Yes?" came the voice on the other end.

"Bingo," said Che.

Chapter 40

Delgado closed his cell phone. The call had come sooner than anticipated. Che had located the two cockroaches quickly. No doubt about it, the man knew his stuff.

He wasn't quite clear as to why Che mentioned needing assistance on this one, but it has something to do with the layout. They had agreed Che should stay put and that Delgado would take his boat and meet Che on the water. It would take Delgado approximately an hour to get there, and he'd bring along some basic *tools* in the event they made a move tonight.

❧

Che started the engine and pulled anchor. There was no way he was going to sit out there an hour, possibly longer, without cigarettes, and he needed to arrange to keep the boat overnight. He and Delgado would most likely ditch it, but he had to cover his ass for keeping it after dark or the old geezer at the marina might come looking for him.

He returned to the marina. The wind and the outgoing tide were both strong, making the docking of the boat rather ugly, resulting in a crash landing. He saw a couple of old timers on the dock shaking their heads and smiling. He thought for a moment about making the old bastards swallow their smiles, but knew he's have to let it pass. Che managed to secure the boat, and then went into the marina for two packs of Marlboros. He paid the old guy for the overnight boat rental.

"'Bout now, damn Yankees come chargin' down the water as there ain't no tomorra' and they'll blow your ass out of it if you ain't got your lights on. Bastards might do it anyway, so's ya best stay awake and on alert," the old guy said. "Ya need more beer?"

Che told him no, but the old codger did convince him to buy a can of insect repellent as the bugs "was bad at night," particularly after all the damn rain they'd had.

Che returned, anchored in a different spot near Lindy's house, then lit a cigarette. Within minutes he was spraying himself; the old fart hadn't been lying, giant damn mosquitoes were already on the attack.

Gotta get out of here, he thought as he sprayed his entire body, *done tonight and in Vegas tomorrow*. He threw the sinker and empty hook overboard and gripped the rod handle. The sun was setting quickly and he hoped Delgado wouldn't take longer than he said to get there.

Several large yachts cruised by, and shortly before the hour was up, a huge cream-colored boat, with black trim, slowed, passed him, and cut its engines off. He made out the name *TO LIFE* in fancy lettering across the back. Che saw Delgado at the wheel and heard him shout: "Come out here, the tides low; I can't get to you."

The yacht's engines started again, but the boat held position.

Che restarted his engine, pulled anchor and headed towards Delgado, who had *TO LIFE* sitting in the middle of the waterway.

"Bring your boat around to starboard and I'll throw you a rope," shouted Delgado.

"What?" Che yelled back.

"Bring her around to starboard!"

"What the hell's that?" shouted Che.

"Bring your damn boat around to the other side, the right side," shouted Delgado.

Why the fuck didn't he say so in the first place, thought Che.

Che brought his boat along side *TO LIFE*.

Delgado threw him a line, which Che caught and Delgado pulled him in.

Once on board, Delgado told Che they'd keep the johnboat until they had their plan finalized

"Now, before we lose light, tell me the deal on the layout," Delgado said.

Che nodded toward the blue house, and had Delgado take *TO LIFE* to the inlet entrance.

"I'm only drawing three feet, its damn near dead low tide."

"I showed you where the house is from the front. You go down this canal to the right, and that's their back side; like I said, nothing but water front and back."

"Okay, I've gotta turn around before we get stuck. Watch the johnboat."

Back in the middle of the waterway, they cruised slowly past the house again.

"That bridge you came under, it's the only way on and off the island," said Che.

"The marina I passed just by the bridge, is that were you rented your boat?"

"Yeah, but it's closed by now."

"Good, we'll tie up there. We're going to handle this tonight."

"Fine with me," said Che.

⚜

After dinner Carlos wanted another cigarette. I had no objection. It was dark and there was no harm now in his sitting on the porch. Lindy said it would do María some good to get a few minutes of fresh air. If a car came on the street, they could both duck back in. An added benefit was that I could grab a smoke while enjoying an after dinner B & B.

It was a clear night, with the moon casting a long beam down the waterway.

"Looks like he finally gave up," Lindy said.

"Oh, the idiot who had no idea what he was doing out there?"

195

I said, looking to the left. "After the day he had, we won't be seeing him around here again."

⁊⧬ꝫ

Che and Delgado towed the rental boat back to the marina. There was no activity and the building was dark. They sat on the two back deck chairs of *TO LIFE*.

"I see what you mean, the layout stinks. But no matter, we do it tonight," said Delgado, lighting a Cuban cigar.

"You got another one of those?" asked Che. "They help keep the damn mosquitoes off. I got some bug repellent if you want some."

Delgado got Che a cigar and said, "That girl, María, knows who I am. If she hasn't said anything yet, she will. She's probably told those two at the house by now. Che, we gotta do all four."

"I already figured that. The lady, Lindy, she can identify me, we can't screw around with this."

"Using a car is out," said Delgado. "Any mistake, any noise, anything abnormal a neighbor sees or hears and the cops nail us at the bridge. We've got more options with a boat."

"It's tricky no matter which way we go," said Che.

"I think I got it," said Delgado.

Chapter 41

"Hey, turn the light off, Hon," I groaned, swinging my arm up across my eyes.

"I'm not 'Hon'," said a gruff, throaty voice.

I shot up in bed; my heart racing. "What the!"

Lindy sprang up beside me, then screamed and grabbed my arm; her finger nails digging in deep.

"Not a word, not a fucking word," he said. He was standing in the doorway by the light switch, gun in hand.

"Out of bed . . . now . . . hurry!"

We climbed out on Lindy's side, farthest from the doorway, and stood up.

He tossed a roll of silver duct tape to me.

"Tape your mouths shut. Do it good."

"Can we get some clothes on first?" I asked.

He was in front of me in a flash, whacking me across the face with such force it knocked me back onto the bed. Along with the pain, I could feel the flow of blood trickling in my mouth.

"You don't listen good. Get back up."

Woozy from the clout, I stood up and taped both our mouths.

Lindy slid behind me again, sobbing. She was doing her best to conceal herself. I felt the entire length of her trembling body against mine.

"Don't flatter yourself lady; you're way over the hill for me."

I wanted to wipe the dirty grin off the bastard's face and started forward, but the blood in my mouth reminded me it would be a dumb move.

"*Now*, get your fuckin' clothes on. Fast."

I don't know what had taken me so long to make the connection. Slipping on my jeans, it hit me; this was the S.O.B who'd been out front fishing all afternoon–same hat, same shirt. *Well hello, that explains that*! He was short, maybe five feet six, but very muscular and very quick.

We were no sooner dressed than María and Carlos were shoved through the doorway. Their mouths were also taped. A tall Latino looking guy, wearing a black guayabera shirt had a gun on them.

He pushed them towards us.

If anything, María was trembling more than Lindy. I sensed her fear and felt the hatred burning through her panicked, dark eyes. Looking at her, I realized who this Latino looking guy must be; *Numero Uno*, the one María and Carlos had been running from, the one whose name they wouldn't reveal to us, the one who needed to get rid of them, and now, us.

"Your keys on the boat?" the Latino asked me, obviously in charge.

I nodded.

Herding us toward the back door, I saw the circular hole cut in the glass next to the lock bolt and handle. So much for the security of glass doors.

Once outside, incredibly, the beauty of the full moonlit night struck me. There are nights here that are so crystal clear, so perfect, you'd hope the sun would consider waiting a few days before returning. Tonight was one of those, and I realized there was a good possibility that this might be the last such night Lindy and I would ever see.

A johnboat was tethered to *Ol'Crab*. So that's how they'd come in, probably the same damn boat I'd been seeing all afternoon. I could have kicked myself. I should have realized something funny was going on with that guy sitting in the boat doing nothing but smoking.

On the dock, they motioned for us to climb aboard *Ol'Crab*. The Latino set the johnboat adrift while Shorty untied *Ol'Crab* and pushed off. He whispered for Carlos and me to each grab a paddle and head for the waterway.

We paddled while the two creeps kept their guns on María and Lindy. There were no lights on in any of the homes we quietly paddled past, not at this hour. Chances of anyone spotting us were between slim and zilch.

We reached the waterway and I was told to get behind the wheel.

"Start it up, go slow and head for the marina," the Latino said.

I understood the "go slow," less noise, but why the *marina*?

While gradually moving the throttle forward, it fell into place for me; there was a larger boat at the marina. They needed a bigger boat to take us off shore and then dump us at sea. That had to be it.

I half turned and looked back at Lindy. With the light of the full moon bouncing off her beautiful face, I saw tears streaming down her cheeks. She had it figured out too, she knew.

Damn, I gotta do something. God knows how much I love that lady. It's been an incredible life together, with more great stuff ahead. I can't let these two bastards screw it up; not now, not like this.

We slowly passed under the bridge and approached the marina. I'd guessed right; tied to the dock I saw a large yacht with the name *TO LIFE* across the stern.

An idea hit me. It would take some luck, well quite a bit, to pull it off, but there were no alternatives. Once on *TO LIFE*, ironically, it would be over for the four of us.

I turned again to look back at Lindy. Her face was pleading for me to do something. I responded with a wink. Hopefully the wink told her to trust me, and to get ready.

We bumped up along the dock and the short guy jumped off with the bow line in one hand and his gun pointed at me with the other.

This was one of the mistakes I'd hoped for. I needed one or two more.

After hurridly securing the bow line, Shorty hustled towards the stern line and loosely secured it.

The Latino ordered us off the boat. Carlos was the first off and nervously helped the women onto the dock. That left just me and the Latino–*Numero Uno*. This was the second break I'd counted on.

Neither of them had noticed I'd left the engine running. As the Latino waved his pistol at me to get off, I thrust the throttle forward and *Ol'Crab* lurched ahead. I quickly yanked the throttle stick into reverse, and then back into neutral. The rough, jerky boat movements knocked the Latino bastard off balance. I leapt toward his gun hand. But by the time I landed on him, he was swinging the gun back toward me. I heard Shorty, standing on the dock scream, "What the fuck!" as he raised his pistol.

The Latino and I were now upright with arms locked struggling for control of the gun.

Shorty couldn't chance a shot as our two bodies were frantically twisting and turning. The Latino and I continued the death lock for his weapon. The gun was now between us and I could feel the cool iron on my belly. A shot went off and I felt the sharp sting of heat, certain I'd been hit. But it was the Latino who gasped and started to slide down. I struggled to hold him up, keeping him between me and Shorty, my other hand grasping the gun.

I wasn't quick enough. Shorty let off a shot that smacked into my shoulder. Carlos lunged at Shorty who swung around and fired at Carlos. I heard the muffled screams through the duct tape of the two women as Carlos spun sideways from the impact and fell to the dock. Shorty quickly turned back to me getting off a second shot which grazed my head. Falling backward with the Latino still in my clutch, I fired at Shorty and saw his gun drop as he grabbed his shoulder. Losing my balance, I tried to grab the guard rail behind me and missed. *Numero Uno* and I both toppled backward over the rail, plunging into the waterway.

We were sinking. I pushed him off using my good arm and both legs and struggled upwards. Breaking the surface, I reached for my mouth, ripped off the tape and gasped for air.

Surfacing behind *Ol'Crab*, I quickly looked around for the Latino. Not seeing him, I slowly treaded my way towards

Ol'Crab's bow and risked sticking my head out to steal a look at the dock.

Shorty was sitting against a piling, holding his right shoulder where he had taken my shot. Lindy was standing over him, crying, shakily holding a gun with both hands pointed at his chest. She must have grabbed Shorty's gun after I shot him. She kept glancing out to the water through her sobs.

María was on her knees next to Carlos with both hands pressed to his abdomen. The sound of her sobs pierced the night. Even from my perspective, I could see the blood from Carlos's wound oozing between her fingers.

"Keep the gun on him Lindy," I shouted, "I'm okay! Don't take your eyes off him! If he moves, shoot the bastard!"

She gave an uneasy nod.

I did a one arm doggy paddle to the dock, hoisted myself up, rested for a moment, stood, then stumbled, more than walked, towards the group.

"My God Matt!" Lindy gasped when she glanced up and saw the extent of my wounds. In the moonlight, she spotted the blood running from my shoulder and from the graze I had taken to the head. Both wounds hurt like hell.

"Gotta get to the radio, don't take your eyes off him again, Lindy." I said and climbed aboard *Ol'Crab*.

I radioed a *Mayday* call for emergency police and medical assistance, emphasizing we had three men down from gunshot wounds, maybe four. *Numero Uno* was out there in the water somewhere.

I replaced the mike and was climbing out of *Ol'Crab* when Shorty swiftly swung a leg under Lindy, dropping her to the deck. The gun fell from her hand as she hit the boards. I dove for it, but Shorty was closer and faster.

"Hold it," he hollered, grabbing the gun and pointing it at Lindy. "Anybody moves and the broad's dead."

"I'm getting in the boat," he said, struggling to stand while keeping the gun on Lindy. Blood was running down his shirt. Shorty was hurting.

He managed to crawl aboard, backwards, never taking the gun

off Lindy.

We heard sirens in the distance.

"Shit! Untie me! Fast!"

I untied both lines.

Panicked at the sound of the sirens, Shorty pushed the throttle forward. Losing his balance from the quick start, he regained control and steered *Ol'Crab* to the middle of the waterway with his good arm. Once there, he made a quick turn and headed towards the Lockwood Folly inlet.

At full throttle, with a one hundred and twenty-five horse power engine, *Ol'Crab* could run thirty-five miles an hour, which was about what she was doing down the middle of the waterway as she headed straight towards the luxury yacht coming up the waterway from the opposite direction. They must have spotted each other at the same instant. The yacht gave a blast of its horn, tried to maneuver a turn and threw its search light on. The powerful beam made a swift sweep of the water and locked onto the rapidly advancing *Ol'Crab*, headed directly for her.

The brilliant light blinded Shorty as he frantically rotated the wheel with his one good arm.

He managed a turn, narrowly missing the yacht, but was now speeding towards the waterway's edge. At low tide, there wasn't enough room to execute another turn. At full throttle, he crashed into the waterway's shoreline, flipping *Ol'Crab* forward with her stern rising rapidly from the water. Shorty's grip was torn from the wheel and his body hurtled into the air. The yacht's search light remained fixed on him as his body, like that of a circus human cannonball, shot through the night sky. We heard his cry of anguish just prior to his body crashing into the roof of a gazebo at the end of a private pier. We heard the sharp crack of wood splintering as his body smashed through the roof. We saw him jerk to an abrupt stop as his foot became wedged at the top. Shorty hung upside down now, the bright search light locked on him as he slowly swung back and forth. Even from a distance, we could see that Shorty's head was twisted at an unnatural, bizarre angle.

"*Dios mio*," whispered María.

"My God," said Lindy.

Carlos, now sitting up on the dock, eyes transfixed on the scene, shook his head in disbelief.

"Well, as far as I'm concerned, it couldn't have happened to a nicer son-of-a-bitch," I said.

I went over to check Carlos. The blood flow from his wound had slowed and my shoulder and head wounds were bleeding and still hurt like hell.

I lied and told Lindy I thought we were both going to be okay.

The blue flashing lights of a cop car and the red flashing lights of an ambulance appeared simultaneously in the marina's parking lot. We heard doors flung open and saw uniformed men running our way.

María, kneeling next to Carlos with her hands still covering his wound, looked out to the water.

"*Y el otro hombre, Señor Delgado?*" she asked.

"She's wondering about the other one," Lindy said to me.

I looked at María, "*El Hombre, Delgado, Numero Uno?*"

"*Sí,*" she nodded.

I looked at Lindy, "Now we learn his name. If they had . . ."

"This isn't the time Matt."

"I know. Tell her Delgado is now fish bait and won't be heard from again."

Lindy told her I thought Delgado was dead.

María gave us a hopeful look, but we saw it slowly fade as her head turned and she stared apprehensively out over the water.

The paramedics were the first to reach us, followed by a huffing and puffing Chief Everhart and Officer Foster.

"Jesus Matt, you're bleeding all over the place, what the hell's going on?"

"Later," said Lindy, "he's going with the paramedics now."

"There's a gun in the water, right off the dock," I told Curt.

"Matt, damn it, that can wait!" screamed Lindy.

A medic took my good arm and steered me towards a stretcher."

"Okay, but . . ." I didn't get to finish as my legs gave out and blackness engulfed me.

Chapter 42

Lindy was by my hospital bed. I'd been advised a few minutes ago that my condition was excellent, considering I'd been shot twice. The head wound was just a graze, and the hit to the shoulder hadn't inflicted any significant damage. Other than topping off the blood level and getting some rest, I'd soon be good to go.

Carlos hadn't been quite so lucky. His wounds were more severe, but not life threatening. He'd be in the hospital for a while, but, fortunately, there would be no permanent damage.

"Good morning, nice to see you amongst the living," Chief Everhart said, bursting through the doorway.

"Thanks, the pleasure's all ours, and please, don't bother to knock. And gee, how was Vegas?" *Why wasn't this man smiling*?

"Let me get straight to it Matthew, you up to talking? The nurse says it shouldn't be a problem."

I nodded.

"The reason I ask is, we've had some rather uncooperative witnesses," he glanced at Lindy, "to last night's events. I want statements from the two of you, *now*."

"Sorry," Lindy said, looking at me. "But I told him I'd wait for you before saying anything."

"Listen chief, don't get teed off at Lindy. You'll get your statements, you know that, but we need to cover something with you first."

"Cover something?"

"Right, what we'd like to do," I continued, "is give you the straight story, everything exactly as it happened, but ask that you don't write anything down, not 'til we're finished. Then we'll talk about it and *then* give you our official statements."

He held his skeptic stare. "You're asking me to do something highly irregular here Matt. You either have a statement of the facts or you don't."

"This situation's irregular," I said.

He walked over to the door, closed it, grabbed a chair from against the wall, and placed it beside the bed, opposite Lindy.

"You're infringing on our friendship, but I guess you realize that," he said.

"I do."

There was another pause, followed by a deep sigh. "Okay, let's have it."

I recapped everything, beginning from when we first noticed the guy in the johnboat until he and the ambulance arrived at the marina. When I'd finished, there was silence in the small room.

"You're lucky to be alive," he said quietly, "all of you."

"No doubt about it," I said.

"So, what I don't get is, what's the hang-up here? Why can't we run with what you just told me, use it as your statement?"

"Chief, Carlos and María are illegals."

"So?"

"So, they don't need any complications with the law. Can't we just leave them out of it and include only Lindy and me?"

"Matt, that's mighty swell of you, but not necessary. From what you've told me, they can't get into any trouble for this."

"You're positive?" I said.

"Matt, it's self defense all the way around."

Lindy and I looked at each other.

"Okay," I said, "if you feel that certain . . ."

After we'd finished our statements, he said he wanted to obtain María's and Carlos's. As Lindy was approved by the county to interpret and translate, he asked her to go with him to Carlos' room.

They returned as I was falling asleep watching a rerun of *Cheers*.

"They seem like pretty decent people," said the chief, sitting in the same chair as earlier. "Everything's in agreement with what you two told me, and we even have a name to work with as far as wrapping this thing up."

"Delgado," I said.

"Yeah, Delgado. How'd you know?"

"María mentioned his name last night."

"Well, with that name and the other guy's prints, we should be able to put this thing to bed pretty quick."

"Did you find the gun off the dock?"

"Oh yeah, sure did, right where you said. We'll have a ballistics run on it."

"So, you have one of the guns, you have one of the bodies, albeit a bit mangled, you have the name of the other jerk, Delgado, and you have prints from two boats, the johnboat and the yacht. Be nice if Delgado's body showed to sort of tidy things up."

"Chances are we won't find it Matt, not from what you and Carlos told me. That was last night. He musta been bleeding pretty good when he went over," he looked at Lindy.

"I get the picture," she said. "Matt already told me, he's fish bait."

"That'd be my guess," he said.

"Well, let's hope we're right," I said, trying to push myself up with my good arm.

"Now, I'll tell you what I'm gonna do, Mr. Chief Curt Everhart," I said, getting comfortable, "I'm going to make you an offer you can't refuse."

"Stop right there Matthew, I'm an entrusted officer of the law and cannot participate in illegal activities of any nature, no matter how minor."

"Wait a minute, you just got back from Vegas."

"It's legal out there and besides, *what happens in . . .*"

"I know, I know."

"But just out of curiosity, run it by me."

"Okay, here 'tis," I said, "I'll wager you a bottle of *Bombay Sapphire*, which I know is your gin of preference, plus a top quality cigar, hand-rolled with tobacco from Cuban seed, that all this mess is tied together."

"All what's tied together?"

"Everything, Curt, absolutely everything; what happened last night, the body I found, the caddy, and get this, even Collinson's car crash, somehow they're all part of the same deadly package. Too much has happened too fast to be coincidental."

"No way," he said, "impossible, there's just no damn way." He hesitated. He shook his head, thinking.

"Okay, you're on, but just to be clear, it's the large *Bombay Sapphire*, right, not that puny little fifth?"

"Right."

"Gents," Lindy interrupted, "I'm delighted you two can be so sporting about this, but I'm telling you that María and I, and Carlos for that matter, won't feel safe about this until we see proof that that Delgado creep is no longer of this world."

"Hon," I said, "relax, he's gone, I'm sure of it; this thing's over."

ကြွေ

I was propped up in a lounging position on our couch, sipping on orange juice, *sans vodka*, and filling our visitors, T. L. and Lizzie, in on our high adventure of the previous evening. T. L. had drunk a couple of beers, and Lindy and Lizzie were each enjoying a glass of wine. Earnest pleas for an additive to my fruit juice went unheeded by iron nurse Lindy.

"No booze for two days, and then very limited for a week," she said with a smile. "Even heroes have to mend."

"Heroes," I pleaded, "have their every wish granted. That's their reward for performing heroic and death-defying deeds."

"In due course Love, in due course."

"Promises, promises," I said.

"So," said T. L., picking up where we had left off, "what's

next? Seems to me the bad guys have been done in, and your two live-in Mexican slaves are off the hook for any more payments."

"Maybe," I said. "But not until we learn . . ."

There was a knock at the front door and we saw Chief Everhart through the glass.

"Hope I'm not intruding," he said as Lindy let him in.

"Not in the least Chief, hey, how'd you like an O.J. and vodka?" I asked.

"Can't, still on duty," he said.

"He was hoping you'd say 'yes' so he could switch drinks with you," T. L. informed him. "Nice try, hero."

"Rat-fink squealer," I said, giving Tommy Lee a look.

"Did I come at a bad time?" the chief asked.

"Nah, it's okay," chuckled T. L., "our hero's just sulking 'cause he's been forced on the wagon for a couple of days."

"Tell you what, if you got a cold brew handy, I could handle that," he said, looking at me, smirking. Yes, it was definitely a smirk.

Lindy got him a beer, which he made a grand production of popping open, and after the first swig, produced a huge sigh of satisfaction.

I wondered if maiming an officer of the law carried additional penalties beyond the norm.

"Okay," he said, sitting at the far end of the couch, while, with pronounced, theatrical relish, he took another pull of the beer. "I thought you'd all be interested in an update."

In spite of the strong urge to slay the scoundrel, he got my, and everyone else's, attention.

"We've had a good day, starting with your sky diver. From the prints we determined that he was, well, he had several aliases, but it seems he was actually one Che Hite. Now the fascinating thing about Mr. Hite is that he was, ah, ambidextrous, meaning he was employed by both the Italian *and* the Mexican Mafias as a hit man, which is highly unusual. He was considered, in his line of work, world class, and came at a price that could tempt even a dedicated officer of the law to change professions."

"He didn't impress me as being a world class kind of guy,"

said Lindy, "unless there's a world class category for jerks."

"So," said T.L., "are you saying that the mafia hired this guy to knock off Matt, Lindy and the two Mexicans?"

"Appears that way," said the chief.

"Why?" asked T. L.

"I can answer that," I said. "María and Carlos knew who the other guy was, this Delgado. Seems he's the head honcho behind the local mafia. It makes sense that once María and Carlos ran off, he realized it was only a matter of time before they'd talk to someone and he'd be exposed. He had to find them, and get rid of them. Once he'd located them here, with us, that put all four of us in his sights."

"Oh damn!" exclaimed Lindy.

There was a stunned silence in the room.

"My God, the lady swears; what a day this is turning out to be!" said T. L.

"No, it just dawned on me! Remember Matt, I told you when I was in the hospital room with María, and she muttered the word 'del' a couple of times and it didn't make any sense; I thought she was saying 'of the.' If she had just finished with the name then, none of this would have happened! We would have found out about Delgado!"

"What have you learned about this Delgado?" asked T. L., looking at the chief.

"We know he was definitely Mafia, Mexican Mafia, and that he's originally from L.A. Except for an incarceration when he was in his teens, he'd managed to avoid any kind of trouble that could be pinned on him. He's lived here four years and has been, for all we can determine, as clean as the proverbial whistle. We have an address, and are at this very moment seeking a search warrant."

"Where's the house?" I asked.

"Poseidon Marina Estates, on the water adjacent to the club's golf course," said the chief.

I smiled.

"That doesn't prove anything Matt," he said.

"I'd like to go with you when you get the warrant," I said.

"Can't," he replied, with a slight degree of gruffness. "We're going to treat it as a crime scene."

"You could deputize me."

"Matt's right," said T. L. "After what he and Lindy have been through, he ought to go along. And while you're at it, deputize me, I want to go."

The chief stared at T. L. as though he was crazy.

He looked at me.

He turned to Lindy.

"Ma'am," he said, "do you think you could find another cold beer out there?"

Chapter 43

Not surprisingly, Tommy Lee wasn't with us as Chief Everhart, Officer Foster and I passed the guard gate at the entrance to Poseidon Estates the following morning.

"Deputizing you was a stretch," the chief had remarked, "but T. L. Matt, they would've had my badge for that."

We drove along a curved road with lavish vegetation on either side, and beyond, homes that Publisher's Clearing House Sweepstakes winner would've had a tough time purchasing– immense, palatial residences, each one more imposing than the previous.

We eventually turned into the driveway of the number given as Delgado's. At first glance, it didn't appear quite as intimidating as many we had passed, but the closer we drew we realized it was a sprawling Mediterranean-style ranch, with white stucco walls and rich, orange clay roofing tile.

"Between what that Che fellow was pulling down as a hit man, and seeing this, I'm convinced that crime indeed pays, and it pays really big time," said the chief.

"Son-ova-bitch," was the best Officer Foster could muster, mouth agape, looking bug-eyed from side-to-side.

The front door was opened by an attractive lady; my guess would be in her early thirties, with Hispanic features.

Chief Everhart displayed his credentials.

"I'm sorry, but Mr. Delgado is not here," she said, with a slight

Spanish accent.

"I know," said the chief, "if we may come in, I'll explain the situation to you. And you are?"

"I'm Carmen, Mr. Delgado's housekeeper."

The chief explained to Carmen, as compassionately as he could, what had happened to Delgado and why we were there. He presented the search warrant and asked her not to leave the premises as he would most likely have some questions later. He then asked her to show us to Delgado's office, figuring it to be the place to start.

We walked across an interior courtyard, which exhibited a profusion of plants, flowers and even several colorful, exotic birds resting on their perches. There was a large water fountain with a replica of some Greek goddess in the center, water lilies at the base and I could see gold fish of some kind, swimming about.

When Carmen showed us the office, the chief told her she could go back to whatever she had been doing.

Not surprisingly, the office was also imposing. In the center stood a massive desk constructed of dark wood with hand carved trim and paneling. The combination bar and liquor cabinet was also exquisite, with glass shelving housed in a beautiful wood I couldn't identify. One wall was lined with books, my guess being all first editions, and also, I would guess, mostly, if not totally, unread.

I walked over to the immense picture window that over-looked the pool, the view expanding to the marina, which housed several yachts docked in their slips, and beyond that, the Atlantic.

"Nice, Chief, really nice. A man could become accustomed to this," I said.

"Well, you see where it got Delgado."

"There's that," I replied.

"Listen," said the chief, looking at me, "why don't you find that housekeeper, Carmen, and see if you can get anything out of her. You're dressed in civvies and speak a little Spanish, so maybe she'll be more comfortable with you."

"Chief," I said, "did you notice when you told her about Delgado that she demonstrated no emotion, I mean none whatsoever? You'd think she'd show some distress or sadness, or shock or something. If anything, I sensed a feeling of relief on her part."

"Yeah, I did, that's why I want you to talk to her."

After wandering aimlessly into several large rooms, I found Carmen sitting at the kitchen table. Like the other rooms, the kitchen was enormous, with a high beamed ceiling and the entire décor carried out in earth tones. One wall was constructed of rustic orange and brown brick. A large oven was set in that wall, and next to it, a spit with a large rotisserie and separate vent.

"My God," I said more to myself than to Carmen, "you could roast an entire pig on that thing."

"I have," she said.

"Carmen," I said, settling in a chair across the table from her, "my name's Matt. I'm not with the police, but I have some special interest in what's going on. I'm sorry about Mr. Delgado, I know you worked for him, and this must be difficult for you, but he was…"

"He was a son-of-a-bitch," she said, matter-of-factly.

"I wasn't quite expecting that reaction."

"He was that and more. He was a bastard; an evil man, a very evil man."

"I don't understand, then why are you here? Why do you, did you, work for him?"

She leaned back in her chair, and between tears and sobs, began to unload her story. She had fled Mexico on her own, several years ago. She left behind her parents and a younger sister. Initially she found work in San Diego, then later, in L.A. She kept in contact with her parents. Four years ago they said they needed to leave Mexico; life had become increasingly difficult for them. They were too old to try it on their own, so they contracted with smugglers, coyotes, to get them out, along with their other daughter. The cost was two thousand dollars each, American.

By then Carmen said she had left California for North Carolina, and had worked as a resort maid, a motel maid, and off-and-on as a farm laborer. Once her parents arrived, they were told to make their payments to an Officer Collinson. It wasn't long before they realized how difficult, if not impossible, it would be to keep up with the steep payments, and they fell behind. Collinson took Carmen to see Delgado. He offered her a job as a live-in housekeeper to help pay back the money her family owed. Initially, seeing no reason to refuse, she gratefully accepted his offer. She quickly learned that her new boss was involved in several illegal activities, but more importantly to her, she soon discovered that the services she was to provide went beyond those of a normal housemaid. She had made the worst mistake of her life.

"I take it the other services were of a sexual nature," I interjected.

"He was a pig, an animal, but I had no choice. Once I knew he was a gangster, and that he wanted to screw me when he didn't have those *putas*, those whores from Las Vegas flown here, it was too late. One night he became very drunk and raped and beat me. He said if I left, or told anyone, he would have my family killed. And he would, I know it! I had to stay. I had to do every vulgar thing the bastard demanded."

"I'm sorry Carmen," I said. "but hopefully this ordeal's over for you. He's gone. Now, please wait here, I'd like you to talk to the chief. Don't worry, he's a good guy. You can probably help us, and maybe we can help you. Okay?"

"Okay, you don't think I'll get in any trouble?"

"No, help us out and I'm certain everything will be fine."

"Will you help me out with the police?"

"I will," I told her. "You've been through enough. Wait here, and I'll come back for you."

I walked back to the former Señor Delgado's office only to find it empty. My fuzz friends must be snooping around elsewhere. I started to leave to catch up with them, and then thought, *what the hell, may as well have a look-see myself.*

Several desk drawers were open, and papers that had been lying neatly on top of the desk were now scattered about. There was one item that had caught my attention when we'd first entered the office earlier; it sat on the far corner of the desk. I walked over and stood before it for a moment, then lifted the lid.

Inside the humidor were two rows of *Cohiba Esplendidos*,

one of the finest brands of cigars made in Cuba, and, of course, quite illegal in the U.S. I looked around, started humming *Bésame Mucho*, one of my favorite Spanish songs, and . . .

I continued nosing around, pulling open and closing drawers, shuffling through papers and was about to go look for the chief when in the process of closing one of the desk drawers, the papers in it slid forward to reveal a video disc in a clear plastic jewel case. The name "Lusch" had been hand written across the DVD.

I was still staring at the disc when the fuzz returned to the office along with Carmen.

"She says she's nervous about all this and wants you to be with her when she talks to us," said the Chief.

"I told her I'd help her." I looked at Carmen, nodded my head and she walked over by my side.

"Okay," I said. "you find anything?"

"Nothing of an incriminating nature," said the Chief.

"Well, I saw this in a desk drawer," I said handing him the disc.

"So?"

"So, the only Lusch I know is one Mr. Louis Lusch the third or fourth or whatever, manager of The Poseidon."

"So?"

"So why would Delgado have a video disc having something to do with Lusch? Chief, don't you remember, Charlie, the caddie master over there, told you, and then me, that the caddy who was murdered worked the foursome with the Mexican club member in it; it had to be Delgado. Charlie told me he was the only 'foreign' member. And if you recall, the caddy was never seen again after the foursome finished that day."

I looked over at the housekeeper. "Carmen, where's the DVD player?"

"He kept a portable in his bedroom, you want me to get it?"

"Please," I said.

She returned shortly, placed the player on the desk and we slipped the disc in.

"Oh my," said the chief, eyes riveted to the screen, "is that Lusch?"

"Well, it's sort of hard to tell from that angle Chief, I've never seen his . . . but yes, I'm certain it's him in all his, ah, glory. What's more, I believe we've just discovered how Delgado was granted membership in the most prestigious PYC. Hey, you want to join? I could have a little chat with 'ol Louie there and swing it for you."

He turned, giving me a look indicating he failed to see the humor of my offer.

"Cut the shit Matt, this ain't cute. Listen, the only thing this *might* prove is that Delgado blackmailed his way into the Poseidon, nothing more. If he was mixed up in all that other stuff, we sure as hell haven't found anything here that's incriminating."

The office was silent as we pondered the next move.

"There's the safe," said Carmen, very softly.

All three of us turned and stared at her.

"The safe?" asked the Chief.

"Yes, behind that painting of his boat over there," she said, pointing to the far wall.

The oil painting of *TO LIFE* was at least four feet long and three feet high. Officer Foster walked over, peeked behind it, then stretched his arms and removed the painting from the wall. And there it was.

"I'm gonna have to get somebody out here," said the chief.

"I know the combination," said Carmen. "I've been in here many times at night when he was too drunk to open it. Sometimes he got so bombed he'd ask me for the combination."

Within the hour, the full picture had pretty much unfurled, much to the dismay of Chief Everhart. The link between his former Officer, Collinson, and Delgado was now evident. Recorded in a hand-written ledger were monthly cash payments to Collinson, and on the day after I had found Pablo's body, there was an additional ten thousand dollar cash payment to Collinson. Between these records and the ballistics report, Collinson's guilt in the murder of Pablo was absolute, and his position with Delgado, and therefore the mafia, was beyond question.

It was all there, including a fifty-thousand dollar cash payment to Che for what had to be Collinson's "accident."

"Well, I said at the time that it wasn't suicide, but I sure as hell didn't expect this," said the Chief, slowly shaking his head.

In a second hand-posted ledger was an extensive list of illegals, how much they had contracted for to flee Mexico, and the balance remaining. Most had been paid in full, but some like Carlos and María, and the now-departed Pablo, and even Carmen's family, showed substantial balances.

"Chief, Delgado's dead," I said. "These records, be nice if they never saw the light of day, particularly if some other hood slides into Delgado's spot in the organization."

"They probably belong locked in our evidence room," he said with an understanding look. "I'll see that they get there."

"Thanks," I said. "be nice if these people could at least have this problem off their backs."

"Well, it looks like I'm gonna lose that bet on everything being tied together, but we still don't have hard evidence that Delgado did the caddy in," said the Chief. "But I guess it doesn't make a hell of a lot of difference at this point; you win."

"Chief, it was a lucky guess on my part and I'll let you off the hook, that is, if you'll do me one small favor."

I took him aside and I told him what I wanted.

"Highly irregular, Matthew, highly irregular."

⳥⳥⳥

After two weeks, even María was convinced that Delgado was dead.

Carlos was on crutches and María was, mercifully, in spite of the entire trauma, still pregnant.

Lindy and I had made some major decisions, decisions that required a few sacrifices on our part, including a monetary outlay, but we felt we were doing the right thing.

First and foremost, we determined that Carlos and María would stay with us until their baby was born. After our harrowing, but bonding experience with them, and with María's absolute determination to have their baby born a United State's citizen, we felt it was the least we could do. Their situation after the baby's arrival wasn't quite so clear. I had made a few calls to the Department of Immigration and Naturalization, which was now part of Homeland Security, and was told, as best as I could understand it, that each case was handled on an individual basis. There was the possibility that Carlos and María might have to return to Mexico, to initiate their application for residency. It's a protracted and complex procedure. But Lindy and I could petition on their behalf, and that might help. We'd see what we could get done over the next four months. In any event, they'd be with us until the new little citizen's arrival.

The other commitment we made was to see that Gina, Pablo's widow, was returned safely to Cárdenas. She couldn't survive here on her own, and she had family in Mexico. We learned that getting an illegal back, legally, is not the simplest of tasks, but were determined to see it through.

❧❧❧

"So, you're really going to keep those two here," he said, nodding his head toward the inside of the house.

It was early evening and Tommy Lee and I were sitting on the front porch enjoying a beer.

"Yup," I replied.

"Well, things will be a little different for you for a while, but I guess it's no worse than having a damn Yankee living next door," he said.

"'Bout the only thing *worse* I can think of is having a foul mouthed red neck for a neighbor," I said.

We both chuckled, looked at each other, and clicked our beer bottles.

I hadn't yet mentioned the little present I'd tucked away just in case he and Lizzie fancied rejoining the Poseidon. A copy of the "favor" the chief had let me "borrow" from Delgado's desk was in my top dresser drawer–I'd returned the original to Chief Everhart.

"Now that you've been back out there, do you think you'd ever want to belong to the Poseidon again?"

"Hell no Matt, like I've told you before, I've left that pompous-ass lifestyle far behind me, don't like it, don't want it, don't need it."

I decided at that moment I'd destroy the CD.

We were staring out at the waterway when the Chief's patrol car made the turn.

"Careful," I said, "here be da fuzz."

"That was a pretty rotten deal, finding out about that officer of his," said T.L.

"It was, but Curt's a good guy, and smart, and he'll put it behind him."

Chief Curt came bounding up the steps with a brown paper bag cradled in his arm.

"I didn't want to be beholden," he said, handing me the bag.

I looked in. It was a large bottle of *Bombay Sapphire*, which I knew had set him back a fistful of bucks.

"That wasn't the deal, remember? You did me a favor. Call it square," I said with a slight nod towards T.L.

"I know, but the results came back today, the DNA from the blood stains we found in Delgado's Town Car were a match with the caddie's; you batted 100 percent Matt, and I couldn't let it slide. I had to get you this, or offer you a job on the force. This seemed like the more prudent thing to do. Oh, I couldn't find a cigar from Cuban seed, so here's a Swisher Sweet," he said handing me a small, thin cigar, wrapped in plastic.

"Yuck," I said, grimacing, "you think you can buy me off with *that*! Hold on a minute," I said getting up from the rocker. "You want me to grab you a beer while I'm in?"

"Well, I was sort of hoping . . ." he said, staring at the bag in my hand.

"Of course, how stupid of me, be right back."

When I returned, I handed him his martini. He took a sip and sighed a deep sigh of satisfaction. 'Tis indeed the nectar of the gods, Matthew, the nectar of the gods."

"It is Chief, and if I'd known you were going to be so generous to me, I wouldn't have opened this beer. But really, thanks."

"You're more than welcome. Ya know," he continued, "Its

sorta poetic justice, or rather, the illegal's justice, would be a better way of putting it."

"I think I know what you mean," I said. "The illegals were in the sights of the bad guys, but it's the bad guys that got their comeuppance."

"Exactly, funny how it turned out. Not always, but most of the time, things work out the way they should. Hey Matt, you got another one of those," he asked, looking at my cigar.

"I thought you could smoke that magnificent Swisher Sweet you brought me."

"You can save it for later, you know, a special occasion or something," he said, with all the phony seriousness he could muster.

I shook my head, reached in my shirt pocket, removed a *Cohiba* and handed it to him.

He looked at the label. "You didn't," he said, turning towards me with a look of astonishment.

"Didn't what?"

"Matt, I checked that humidor on Delgado's desk; this is the kind that was in there. They're Cuban."

"Really? Cuban? I'll be damned. Hey, wait a minute; let's see if I got this straight. Are you accusing me, your valued friend and fellow crime solver, of pilfering these cigars from Delgado's office? And if so, and their being Cuban and all, you had better give it back. I certainly don't want our chief law enforcement officer smoking contraband, not to mention stolen goods."

"I'm not saying you stole them, I'm saying it's the same kind he had in his humidor, and they're illegal in this country, but you just said that."

Tommy Lee rocked in his rocker, smiling, watching this entire scene play out and knowing full well how it would end.

"Seems to me we have both a moral and a legal dilemma," I said.

"Indeed we do," said the Chief, sipping his *Bombay Sapphire* martini. "I suggest we turn to our learned friend here, the honorable Tommy Lee, to render a judgment on exactly how we attend to this delicate predicament."

"Well, y'all, I've been listenin' and watchin' and I've given this matter the serious consideration it deserves."

"And?" I asked.

"And what you both gotta do is burn the evidence."

"You mean all of it, all at once?" I asked.

"No, over a reasonable period of time and at your leisure will do just fine."

"See," said the chief, "I told you he was a learned man."

Satisfied with T. L.'s solution, our chief law enforcement officer then sat back in his rocker and lit up.

❦

I was getting to the short end of my *Cohiba* when Lindy came out.

"Your two playmates go home?"

"Yup, but we pretty much resolved our, not to mention most of the world's more thorny issues, before they left."

"Uh huh," she said.

I then filled her in on Delgado's also having been responsible for the caddy's death.

"He was a real piece of work," she said. "Now I guess some other creep will take his place."

"More than likely, but whoever it is will have to start pretty much from scratch as all of Delgado's records were removed from his house."

"Good. That'll help a lot of them, at least for awhile."

I flipped the cigar stub over the railing.

"Are they really that much better?" she asked, referring to the *Cohiba*.

"Hon, you can't imagine, they are truly magnificent . . . I'll be right back."

I returned in a couple of minutes with a chilled bottle of a very nice Chardonnay I'd been saving and poured us each a glass.

"What's the occasion?"

"Nothing special," I said, "it's just that we've sorta come to the end of one road, and are about to make a turn onto another."

"That's what makes the journey exciting, not knowing where the next road leads."

"I guess. You want to continue interpreting?"

"Oh my yes, more than ever."

"Hon, no one knows where this situation's headed, but for sure, there will be changes. If they put the brakes on this illegal immigration thing, your work load could lessen. The sheer volume of illegals is overwhelming and can't continue, then there's the security issue, the financial issues, the health care issues; it just goes on and on. If our government ever gets it act together on this, and granted, that's a big if, your job could change."

"I know, but I want to do what I can while I can. What were María and Carlos doing when you went in?"

"Carlos was upstairs. María's in the kitchen cooking up something that smells absolutely wonderful. You know, that smile of hers is really infectious."

"So, you like having a young, good-looking cook with a great smile around the house?"

"I've had a good-looking lady with a great smile doing my cooking for several years now."

"Right answer, my love. Matt, thanks."

"For what?"

"For being you, for understanding, for your kindness to María, Carlos and that poor Gina. I don't know anyone else who'd do this. I've known for a long time that you're something special, and . . ."

"And lucky to be alive and with you," I said, turning to her.

We raised our glasses to each other.

"I really owe you big time," she said.

I paused, found her hand and gave it a squeeze.

"Promises, promises."

Epilogue

The classic, old shrimp boat, *Naughty Nina*, had been out for three days. Water temperatures were dropping fast, signifying the end of the season. Like other bug chasers, Captain Mike Conrad wanted a large catch to wrap up the year. He'd already decided not to work his way south over the winter months. Age, along with forty years of riding the waves off the southeastern coastline, had taken their toll. No way was he trawling down to Florida–not this year.

A second generation shrimper, Mike had helped his Dad build *Naughty Nina* back in the mid 60's. Finishing high school, he mated full time for his Dad until 1985, when his father passed away. Since then Mike, and Willy, his high school buddy turned First Mate, had shrimped together on *Naughty Nina* for over twenty years. Though close friends, Willy always, respectfully, addressed Mike as "Captain," even when they went out for a few beers together; that was just the way it should be.

Naughty was now forty years old, but Mike had lost none of the pride he took in the fine vessel he had helped his Dad build. His father would be pleased with the way he'd kept her up. A fresh coat of white paint each year, and trimming her out in Kelly Green, including green outriggers, she was pretty as a post card. It wasn't unusual to see vacationers taking pictures of her when she was in dock, or when she was trawling the coastline with hundreds of sea gulls following off her stern. Without doubt, *Naughty's* picture

223

was in countless vacation photo albums throughout the country, if not the world.

It had been a good year for Mike, but he was smart enough to see that his days of trawling the waters for shrimp aboard *Naughty* were numbered. Maintenance costs on the old engine had risen dramatically, fuel costs were sky rocketing, and there was a huge increase, world wide, in pond-raised shrimp. If that weren't enough, there were those huge commercial operations with ships so large they were virtual floating shrimp factories, processing shrimp on board; from catching to freezing and even packaging. Each of these situations was a harbinger of the beginning of the end. Mike's generational way of life, and that of the other independent shrimpers, would soon vanish. It was simply a matter of time, and a short time at that.

He and Willie were trawling along the coastline with the Lockwood Folly Inlet in sight off the port side. Mike had planned it this way so they could head back in at a reasonable hour if the catch was good.

He watched as Willie pulled in the try net. This small net, used to test the conditions for shrimp in the area, was checked by Willie at regular intervals.

Willie brought the net in and looked over at Mike, who was standing in the doorway of the pilot house. Willie shook his head.

"Leave 'er there and take the wheel," Mike shouted above the engine's roar.

Mike ambled back to the steps that lead to the hold, where their catch was iced down. Checking each compartment, he roughly figured they had somewhere in the neighborhood of fifteen to seventeen hundred pounds on board; not great, but not too bad for this time of year.

He climbed back to the deck and entered the pilot house.

"We're gonna bring 'em in Willie; there's a fair catch below. With what's out there," nodding towards both outriggers, "that should do 'er. We'll finish up and head for the hill."

Willie went deck side, wondering once again who in the hell had been the first crazy ass seaman to call that flatter-than-apancake coastline "the hill." Whoever it was had a bizarre sense of humor, that's for damn certain.

A short time later, after they'd swung the outriggers in, Willie opened the first net and its contents splattered onto the deck. This was Willie's favorite part of the entire process. Since the nets dragged bottom, you just never knew what in the hell, in addition to the shrimp, they'd bring up.

As it turned out, this haul produced nothing special. There were shrimp, lots of 'em, along with a couple of small sharks, a mess of crabs, a pompano, dozens of trash fish, conch shells and several good-sized flounder. Since this might be the last run, Willie kept everything except the sharks, the trash fish and the conch shells, which he threw over board.

He then shoveled the shrimp from the deck into the hold, and opened the second net.

It was pretty much the same story, except there were several additional large flounder and pompano, which meant that they now had some to sell to the fish house. The pompano, particularly, would bring a good price.

Finished with the sorting, Willie shoveled the second load of shrimp into the hold, went below, iced the last catch down, went back topside, closed the hatch door and walked to the port side railing.

He hated for the season to be over. He wouldn't be seeing as much of Captain Mike, who had a wife and two kids, and there wasn't much for him to do except sit around in his trailer and watch TV.

He lit a cigarette and stood staring out to sea. Towards the end of winter, he'd help get *Naughty* fixed up and ready for the new season, but 'til then . . .

What the hell's that!

They were entering the channel to the inlet. Willie turned and yelled at Captain Mike to stop the boat, then ran towards the pilot house frantically waving his arms.

"What's the trouble, Willie?" Mike shouted as he turned and saw Willie hurrying towards him.

"Shut 'er down Captain, shut 'er down!"

Mike had no idea what was happening; he'd never seen such erratic behavior from Willie. Reluctantly, he idled *Naughty* and followed Willie to the railing along the port side. Willie pointed to a spot about ten yards off.

It took Mike a second or two. "Aw shit, is that what I think it is?"

"'Fraid so, Captain."

"Aw shit," Mike repeated, walking back to the pilot house for his binoculars. Returning, he lifted the binoculars and adjusted the focus.

It was definitely a body, a human body, or, more precisely, the remains of a human body. "Jesus," whispered Mike, "In forty years on the water I never seen nothin' such as this." He handed the binoculars to Willie.

"He's been ate on pretty good," agreed Willy, handing the binoculars back to Captain Mike after a minute of staring in fascination.

Again, Mike focused in. There was hardly any clothing left. What remained of a black shirt clung to one arm by a few threads. Both eyes were missing. The sockets went deep into the skull. Most of the flesh from the face, one leg and one arm had been eaten away. Several fingers were missing. He could see small fish nibbling at the floating carcass.

Mike stood transfixed, staring through the binoculars.

"There's some kinda marks on the shoulder." He adjusted the binoculars. "I can't make em out, looks like maybe a number, maybe a three, no, there's two of 'em, maybe a one and a, ah shit, I can't tell. Willie, damn it, I hate doing this, but we gotta retrieve it. Get the throw net. I'll bring *Naughty* around."

He had turned his back from the rail and started for the pilot house when he heard Willie say, "'Fraid there's no time, Captain."

"What do you mean, there's no . . ." Mike was by the rail again and looked out. He saw why Willie had stopped him. Two large dorsal fins were streaking towards Naughty, headed directly on a course towards what remained of the body.

"Good God," said Mike.

They turned their backs to the water as the first shark struck, locked onto the carcass, gave it a violent shake and ripped off an arm. The second shark quickly tore off a leg. Within seconds there was no trace of the ravaged body, except for what little remained of the black shirt floating on the surface.

When they heard the thrashing subside, both men turned back to the ocean and looked out. The sharks had left, the carcass was gone.

"Jesus," said Willie, "ain't nobody deserve to go like that, not the sorriest bastard I know."

Mike stood staring at the water. After a couple of minutes, he told Willie to get the throw net again. "Let's get what's left of that shirt. I don't know if it'll do any good, but we oughta get it and turn it in. Then Willie, we're heading for the hill."

꿏

Willie was stowing away some gear when Captain Mike emerged from the pilot house with two cans of beer.

"Hell of a way to finish up the year, eh?" he said, handing one to Willie.

"Sure as hell is, Captain, sure as hell is," agreed Willy. "But, 'cept for what's just happened, it was decent enough," he said, raising his beer can. "Here's to next season Captain."

"To next season, Willie," Mike said, tipping his can. Then he thought, *Here's hoping we have one.*

By the time Willie had finished a few odd jobs deck side, *Naughty* was heading up the waterway towards her berth at the fish house.

"We'll be passing by that couple's place in a minute Willie, you know, the ones who are usually out having drinks about now."

"Right, the cocktail hour pair, must be nice," said Willie.

"I guess," said Mike. "But don't ya think it's gotta get pretty boring? I mean, what in the hell do they do with themselves all day, just pass time waiting for the cocktail hour?"

As they passed by, they saw the husband and wife stand and

wave to them as they usually did, each holding a glass. Mike and Willie waved back, as they usually did. Mike raised his beer can to them.

"Ya know, I think someday I'd like to stop by and meet those people Willie, just to see what kind of folks they are."

"I don't know Captain, what would ya talk about? Probably ain't got nothin' in common."

"Yeah, you're probably right, probably nothin' in common at all." Mike waved again to the couple and headed back into the pilot house, Willie followed behind.

Mike reached for his cell phone. "May as well call the law now and let 'em know what we seen and what we got," he said, nodding towards the ragged shirt.

"Good idea, Captain, gives me the heebie-jeebies just looking at the damn thing."

꧁꧂

"Promises, promises, huh?" said Lindy, "Would you mind explaining that a bit further?"

"No, just use your wildest imagination my dear," I replied with a devilish grin.

I looked out to the waterway and saw a shrimp boat coming in. "It's the *Naughty Nina*, you can always tell her by those green outriggers."

We knew most of the shrimp boats' names, and always waved when they passed. The crew invariably returned the wave, and if we weren't on the porch, several of them would sound their horn to let us know they were passing by.

"She's the prettiest of the lot," said Lindy

"She really is. You know, I keep saying that one of these days I'm going to be at the dock when a shrimp boat comes in just to see what goes on and meet the shrimpers. Judging by the way they keep her in shape, the guys on the Naughty Nina might be good ones to meet.

"You think so?" asked Lindy. "I don't know, what would you talk about, your favorite shrimp recipes?"

"Yeah, right . . . looks like they're having a beer. I could grab a six pack and take it along as an ice breaker."

"Okay, so get off your duff and be there when they get in. If nothing else, maybe they'll sell you some shrimp. We can't get it any fresher!"

"I'm gonna do it," I said standing up.

"Your shoulder okay to drive?"

"Sure, you want to go?"

"No, that's okay Hon; you enjoy yourself, just be sure to say 'hi' to the boys for me."

"Watch it, or I won't fill you in on all the cool stuff I learn about the secret lives of shrimpers."

"Well, I don't think I have to worry much, somehow or other I can't imagine anything happening on a shrimp boat that would interest me . . . can you?"

Printed in the United States
67929LVS00002BA/82-135